PERFECT STORM

ALSO BY PAIGE SHELTON

PERFECT STORM

A MYSTERY

PAIGE SHELTON

MINOTAUR BOOKS
NEW YORK

First published in the United States by Minotaur Books,
an imprint of St. Martin's Publishing Group

www.minotaurbooks.com

The Library of Congress Cataloging-in-Publication Data
is available upon request.

ISBN 978-1-250-91046-2 (hardcover)
ISBN 978-1-250-91047-9 (ebook)

First Edition: 2024

10   9   8   7   6   5   4   3   2   1

For my readers. You are the absolute best—thank you!

PERFECT STORM

One

"Beth Rivers, you are under arrest for the murder of Travis Walker. Walker. Walker." Gril's voice trailed off into echoes.

I tried to protest, but my throat wouldn't let me. The truth was the truth, after all. My denial died with a dry croak.

And then I awoke, sitting straight up and gasping for air before realizing I didn't need to work to breathe. I wasn't being choked by either the truth or lies. I was surrounded by more fresh and clean air than I'd ever been before. My fist loosened as I held it at the bottom of my throat. I was fine. I hadn't been arrested.

I hadn't killed Travis Walker. Yet.

The tent door flung open.

Tex looked at me, the almost ever-present glow of the low-hanging August sun glimmering off a few threads of gray in his beard. "You okay?"

"Did I scream?"

Tex squinted. "More like gasped loudly."

"Bad dream. I was being arrested for killing Travis."

Tex nodded. There were no new words to add to the ones he'd already used to attempt to assuage my fears, no matter how they presented themselves. I hadn't been having many nightmares, but I'd had plenty of moments of debilitating anxiety.

He was there. He'd make sure nothing happened to me. I was going to be fine. Travis wasn't going to get to me before my friends and family—Tex, Gril, Viola, Orin, Donner, my parents, maybe even Ruke—got to him first. And that list didn't even take into consideration all the lower forty-eight people who were losing sleep to catch him before he caught me.

We were all on the lookout for the man who'd kidnapped me and kept me in his van for three days just over a year earlier. He'd already been caught once, arrested, and put behind bars, and we'd all been sure he'd never see freedom again. We'd been wrong.

Until that initial arrest, I'd escaped to Benedict, Alaska, where I didn't think I could ever be found—and where I'd surprisingly discovered more of a home than any place I'd known before.

However, apparently, I hadn't hidden nearly as well as I'd thought. Though she was now missing, my mother had found me. My father, who'd left us when I was seven, also found me. When Travis had first been caught, my story became top news in the country—for a few minutes, at least. Everyone knew I was in Benedict, Alaska. Most of the world couldn't have cared less, but according to a note Travis left behind in his recent escape, finding and killing me was all he wanted to do.

I could have run again. I could have found another place to hide. But, along with the fact that running hadn't done much to keep me hidden in this big world, I didn't want to go anywhere else.

I loved Benedict, Alaska. As my time in this place had gone on, I'd vacillated between wanting to return to St. Louis one day or staying in Benedict, until it became clear that I probably should go somewhere else for my safety. It took that moment, that provoking threat of "it's time to hide again," for me to know I didn't want to.

But I also knew I couldn't stay put, wait in my room at the Benedict House, for Travis to come get me. Well, I supposed I could, but there were other options.

It was over a meeting with the most important people in my life, only one of whom I'd met before moving to Benedict, that options had been discussed, decisions had been made. They'd all become my family, in ways I'd never experienced before—better, more caring ways.

My father had been at the meeting, too, but he would be the first to admit that his departure from my life when I was seven might have knocked him out of any sort of blood-family-being-the-best-family distinction.

I'd been with him on his boat, along with Tex, when I'd received the call that Travis had escaped custody in Missouri. We'd been looking at the glaciers in the bay, and, boy, what a sight they'd been. We'd just watched one calve, break off a piece into the water—a stunning sight and rife with noisy groans. It was a good moment. It had been a beautiful day.

The primitive world of Benedict did not allow for widespread cell phone or internet coverage. Pockets of service could be found at the library and the airport, or at Orin the librarian's house, but that day on my father's boat, I learned a new quirk about Benedict: National Geographic ships were often scattered around the surrounding waters and apparently had their own cell towers.

You might think you're getting away from it all on the water, but if your phone picks up on one of those towers, it could disturb your peaceful journey. That day it had been a call from Detective Majors in St. Louis to tell me that Travis had escaped and wanted me dead. The message couldn't have been any more disturbing to that wonderful boating experience.

Though I didn't have the whole story yet, it seemed like Travis had picked up on a brief instant of opportunity, a moment when the officer who'd been guiding him toward a prison transport van set for the Missouri State Penitentiary was somehow distracted. What that distraction had been was still a mystery. I'd spent plenty of paranoid moments wondering if the officer had been in on the escape or if someone else had been there to somehow intervene. I had enough to worry about, though, so I'd tried to put those questions on a back burner.

According to what Detective Majors told me, the officer claimed he had turned away from Travis to relieve his sick stomach—for no more than "maybe fifteen seconds"—when Travis, his ankles and wrists chained, somehow disappeared into the nearby woods.

A subsequent search of the area turned up nothing, but inside Travis's cell was his threatening note to me. The circumstances led most people to think that Travis's escape hadn't truly been chance. Maybe he'd had some help in those woods. The officer was sticking by his story, though, and there was no evidence to contradict him, so it was all just uncertain speculation.

In yet another strange twist to an already bizarre situation, for at least a few minutes, both my father and mother had been considered potential accomplices to the escape.

My father, who'd once been associated with Walker, had been in Alaska during the escape, so he was ruled out quickly. My mother, on the other hand, had been and still was MIA. As strange as it might sound to most everyone else, her helping Travis escape wasn't completely ridiculous. Those of us who knew her could see her doing as much just so she might hurt or kill him herself.

Though no evidence had been found to corroborate that she'd been involved, I still wondered. Travis was out there, his threat to find me most likely real, and anyone who wanted to know where I'd gone was only one small internet search away from finding me and my story. If my mother or someone else hadn't killed him already, he was surely on his way. It's odd to hope for a parent to commit a heinous crime, but I'd had moments of fantasizing that she'd gotten away with killing Travis. That was only a dream, though, because no matter how awful he was, her killing him would put her behind bars, and it wasn't worth it.

The afternoon after I'd received the phone call from Detective Majors, my Alaska family had gathered around a dining table at the Benedict House, the old hotel that was run by Viola and had been turned into a halfway house, as well as the place I'd acquired a room.

The police chief, Gril, had been there, joining us from a fishing vacation he'd been enjoying. Tex and Orin were there as well as Donner, the park ranger who assisted Gril in a legal capacity; my father, Eddy; and Viola, the only one with a gun holstered at her waist.

"I can protect you," Viola had said as she patted the gun.

She could.

"I don't want to put everyone in danger. That's not fair," I said.

At once the rest of them shrugged off my concerns.

They were a tough bunch, forged by the harsh Alaskan climate. They all had large doses of grit, had probably been born with it. I'd been working to acquire my own helping of the same, but I had a ways to go.

"You could just come stay with us in Brayn," Tex had offered. "We wouldn't tell a soul."

I shook my head. "No, Brayn's a small community. I would hate for someone to give me up and then put not only you and your mother in danger's way, but the girls, too."

Tex frowned and nodded. He couldn't argue with that. His two little girls would always come first.

"Stay with me," Orin offered.

"Or us." Gril nodded toward Eddy.

Eddy had been living with Gril, in a spare room that "needed using anyway."

"They all have a point, Beth," Viola said. "This community will keep you hidden. You can trust everyone around here."

They would all protect me to the best of their abilities, but I didn't want to say yes to any of the presented options.

I didn't want to hide.

I didn't want to run.

But I had to do something.

Finally, I looked at Tex. "A while ago, you promised to take me camping."

Tex nodded. "Of course."

"It's still not too cold. Could your mom watch the girls for a couple weeks?" I asked.

"She can watch them as long as is needed," he said.

I'd said, "I don't quite understand why this makes sense, but let's go camping. We can take some time to think about all the other options and try to figure out what I should do next, that is, if Travis isn't caught soon."

Tex had nodded and everyone else had joined in. "Let's do it."

A day and a half later, Tex and I set out, weighed down by backpacks full of supplies, mine made even heavier with the guilt of taking Tex out of his normal routine. I knew he had everything covered, but I sure was asking a lot of the people I cared about most.

However, he knew how to camp, had done so all his life. What was huge preparation for me was routine for him.

I was in good enough shape to keep up with him. Tex had taught me some things about living in this wild world. I'd been working out, but I had never once in my life camped anywhere. I'd quit Girl Scouts when my mother thought the craft projects my troop leader doled out were a "ridiculous waste of time"—she'd aired her opinion one week before my troop was set to camp, and that had been that. No more Girl Scouts for me.

She hadn't cared. Mill, my mother, had wanted to check out a lead on where my father might have gone anyway—another dead end in the long string of them. When I'd only recently found out he'd been in Mexico the whole time, those journeys with Mill had transformed into things of nostalgia.

On that particular trip, we broke a back door window of a small cute house in the woods. No one had been there, thankfully, and as with almost every other lead we explored, there was no sign of my father ever having been inside it.

Before he'd disappeared, he'd sold cleaning products door-to-door. At first it was a legitimate job, but then it turned into a cover as he got deeper and deeper into the local drug trade—which was when Travis Walker became one of his business associates.

Eddy had tried to explain it all to me, how working with Walker had seemed mostly harmless at first. He'd shrugged and said it had been a great way to make money, so he'd found ways to justify his behavior.

He'd also said that Travis Walker had turned out to be such bad news that there came a point when my father knew he had to leave town, or he would be headed for prison. And, as long as he stuck around, he knew my mother and I would also be in the range of Travis's dangerous tentacles. He thought he'd done the right thing, no matter how wrong "up and leaving" might be.

And then he'd just lived in Mexico and, though I still didn't want to hear all the details, seemed to have enjoyed his new stage of life.

No matter what he'd said, I still hadn't bought into any notion that he'd done something noble by running away. However, I was beginning to forgive and enjoy my time with him. And now, just when we were starting to find some common ground, Walker had escaped, disrupting everything.

Tex and I had made our way out of town the day before and were about eight miles into the woods, with the goal of staying at an old cabin about seven miles farther. The cabin was positioned so perfectly that sunsets could be witnessed nightly, even if the sun currently set after nine P.M. It sounded idyllic, though Tex reminded me that modern amenities wouldn't be included.

We hadn't come upon any civilization since we'd left Benedict behind. I'd seen lots of greenery and cold water trickling down streams or moving fast down rivers. We'd discovered small patches of snow that would never melt because they were in the shade. They would be covered up by more snow when it started to fall again in the winter. It was cold out here, but movement kept us warm enough during the day, and thick down-stuffed sleeping bags did the job at night.

Tex had come up with the idea of spending some time at the cabin, a place that Travis Walker couldn't have possibly heard of. Few Alaskans knew of its existence. Tex had said that there was no indication anyone else had discovered it whenever he'd ventured to it over the last few years.

Though the first day had gone fine, the nightmare had rattled me, and I was sore all over, although I'd never admit it. A thin bedroll had been the only thing in between the warm sleeping bag and the cold hard ground. I didn't love camping yet, but I knew I needed to find a way to make it work. I'd always been fairly flexible, but this adventure was certainly packed with more challenges than I'd ever taken on. As Tex reminded me, being trapped in Travis's van for three days was probably worse than a little camping getaway.

"Hungry?" Tex asked after I shook off the remnants of the dream.

The scents of bacon and eggs wafted into the tent. "Starving. You've already cooked? You should have gotten me up."

"You were pretty tired."

"I cannot deny that." I stretched and rolled both shoulders.

"It takes a week or so to get used to all of it. You won't be as sore then, nor as tired." He smiled—I could see crinkles next to his eyes and some movement of his beard. "You might not believe me today, but you'll actually start to crave the hiking as well as sleeping on the ground."

I squinted my eyes. "I do not think I will ever crave sleeping on the ground."

He shrugged his big shoulders. "I guess we'll see."

I got myself out of the sleeping bag and grabbed my toothbrush. Tex waited patiently and then helped me out of the tent.

"You even made biscuits?" I said as I noticed the pan.

"And gravy."

"I really do think we might be soulmates. You are an amazing cook and I love to eat," I said.

Tex laughed. "I could have told you that a long time ago. The soulmates part."

I once read a woman's story that said, *I never really dated. I met my husband and we just stayed together, got married, had kids eventually, but there wasn't much buildup to any of it. It all just kind of happened.*

That was similar to me and Tex. I'd dated some but never seriously. Then Tex and I met and have just been together since. We might get married, we might not, but I do feel a sense of permanence with him. He's told me he feels the same.

And here we were.

We loaded our plates with food and dug in. I ate as if I hadn't had a meal in weeks, but the night before we'd had a dinner of fresh salmon and morel mushrooms. Tex had rounded up both things quickly, the salmon with a fishing line wrapped around a big wooden spool.

I had enjoyed Tex's lessons on which mushrooms were okay to eat and which could kill a person a mere few seconds after ingesting.

I admit it had occurred to me that we should pick some of the poisonous mushrooms and use them on Travis Walker if he appeared. I had murder, or at least self-defense, on my mind.

Tex assured me that the plans for Walker would be swifter than any mushroom's black magic.

I hadn't been included in any sort of meeting where such plans had been discussed, and I felt left out. I'd asked him to tell me the plans, but he'd only shrugged and said he would, eventually. I hadn't argued.

It wasn't that I didn't think I should be included, but something in me was having a hard time accepting everything that had happened, and I didn't mind trusting everyone else's plan and their timing on sharing it with me.

I could only take one moment at a time.

For now, I ate as much as I could, and then a little more. All this fresh air, combined with our hiking through the wild, had taken my appetite to a whole new level.

I didn't mind the size up in my jeans since moving to Benedict at all—at least part of that was muscle. Trudging through the woods, the tundra, required smart clothing choices, good shoes, and sometimes the agility to run from something that wanted to eat you. Muscles helped.

I had gained a physical strength I hadn't ever felt before, and I liked it.

After eating, we cleaned up and broke camp. I was slow and uncoordinated at first, but the tent poles soon became less mysterious, and I picked up the packing pace, though I was still slower than Tex.

He told me I was holding my own just fine.

Once our packs were on our backs and we were ready, I asked, "Seven more miles?"

"We're almost there. Half a day or so."

"Let's do this," I said.

Tex smiled. "Let's."

We started off slowly, but I announced that I could move a little faster, so we did. The weather hadn't been horrible, but it hadn't been perfect. We'd run into rain for about an hour the first day and sought shelter until it passed. But there wasn't a cloud in the sky today. So far. Rain was always on its way in this part of the world.

We hadn't climbed any mountains, but we had conquered a few big hills. Today our hike was a subtle gain in elevation. A couple hours in, we came out of the thick woods and onto a ridge.

The sun shone brightly without the guard of the surrounding trees. I shaded my eyes with my hand as Tex pointed. "We need to walk through there and get to the other side."

Across a shallow valley stood a few structures.

I cocked my head as we glanced at the small old wooden buildings. "Are they all leaning?"

"Most likely."

"Do people live there?"

"A few do, last time I checked. I suppose some are still around."

I looked at him, wondering at his slightly uncertain tone. Tex was rarely uncertain. "Are they friendly?"

"Sure. They are territorial, like most of us. Folks from there hike into Brayn or Benedict for supplies. I haven't seen anyone in Brayn for a while, but Donner said he thought he saw one of the old guys in Benedict last month."

"No way around the place?"

"Nope, not really. Through is the only way."

"Could we run into trouble?"

"Well, there's always a chance of trouble, but I think we'll be okay. Just stick with me."

"I would never consider not."

Tex nodded. "It's a mining community."

"Active?"

"Kind of. Someone found gold out here back in the 1970s, and a mine sprung up, followed by a very tiny community. We call it Blue Mine, but I doubt that's official anywhere. I think they find a little gold every five years or so. Keeps folks sticking around, and I don't know why 'blue' is used."

"So, if we don't threaten their gold, we should be okay."

Tex nodded. "About right." He paused. "I've brought a few things to give them. Spreading goodwill is always smart."

"Food and socks?"

"Yep. Both are mighty valuable out here."

I scanned the area again. One tall skinny structure probably led to the opening of the mine. From our distance, it appeared the other six—maybe seven—were one room, one window, one door shelters, boxy and surely unlivable. I surmised that I would probably much prefer sleeping on the ground than in one of those places.

"When's the last time they found gold?" I asked.

"They don't share that information easily. The rest of us just hear the rumors later. I haven't heard anything in a while."

"And yet people just stay?" It was a question, but I wasn't dismayed by the possibility that people were living out here. Since coming to Alaska, I'd seen a spectrum—from luxurious to more austere than I could have imagined—and I'd been told that, for the most part, people out here lived how they chose.

As well, back when I first got here, I would have asked why someone in authority hadn't closed the mine. It must be dangerous. Authorities up here didn't always have jurisdiction, or they didn't fight all the battles because they had other, maybe larger or more public fights to take on.

"Do we walk through the valley first?" I asked.

"Nope, around this ridge." Tex gestured with his hand, but he stopped about halfway to the other side. "Company."

I looked in that direction, probably about thirty yards away.

A person was leading a horse that carried a large pack over its back. From where we stood, the pack appeared to be the shape of a blanket-wrapped human.

"Oh," I commented. "Is that . . . ?"

Tex sighed. "Dunno. That's the direction we'll be going. Let's hang back here and meet them, but stay behind me until we understand what this is all about."

I'd promised him that I would do whatever he said. Gril had used the words "obey Tex" in his instructions regarding our trip.

As curious as I now was to see what was happening, I nodded and said, "Of course."

Two

We could smell them long before we were in reasonable conversing distance. I knew it would be difficult to keep my nose and the rest of my face from scrunching up from the stink as the distance between us diminished.

Tex spoke backward over his shoulder. "This is suspicious. Be alert."

"Always," I said quietly.

The horse whinnied and showed its yellow teeth when it noticed us. The noise brought the person's eyes up. I could see their surprise and then suspicion, probably equal to what Tex and I felt. No one stopped walking. Everyone kept a brave face, even the horse.

I couldn't immediately tell if the person was a man or a woman. They were dressed in gray woolen pants, seemingly sewn together haphazardly, with a matching jacket over a shirt of indistinguishable color and material. The person's short dark gray hair stuck up from underneath a bucket hat and their face was grimy, but their blue eyes were bright.

Keeping a good distance, we all finally stopped. The person lifted their hand.

"Who goes there?" she asked.

Her voice was deep and gravelly but no doubt female.

"Tex and Beth. I'm from Brayn and she's from Benedict."

"Tex?" the woman asked. "That you?"

"Yes, ma'am."

She squinted even harder. "I'll be damned. I didn't recognize you right off." She reached for a pair of grimy wire-framed glasses on a chain around her neck but didn't put them on. Instead, she said, "I'm—"

"Jin," Tex said, his tone relaxing. "Hello, it's good to see you again."

"It is? Well, I'll be damned again then," she said, though there wasn't a smile to her voice. "What are you doing out here?"

"It's a long story. We brought some things for you . . . and every-one . . . if we might pass through."

"Oh. Pass through?"

"Yes, ma'am."

Jin inspected Tex a long moment. "You in some trouble?"

"A little. I'm happy to explain more." He nodded toward the mine. "Maybe over coffee."

I didn't really want to take time to socialize, and I suspected Tex didn't either, but it felt like the right thing to say.

Jin frowned and nodded. "Sure, I hear you." She paused, bit her bottom lip, and then rubbed her finger under her chin. "Thing is, I've got my own share of trouble here." She patted the horse's neck. "I'm on my way into Benedict, hoping to talk to the police chief, Gril. He's a good man and I'm hoping he can help."

"He can, I'm sure," Tex said. "What's going on, Jin? Maybe I . . . we can help."

"I don't know." Jin rubbed her chin again.

"Is that a body?" Tex asked.

"Yes, sir, it is. My husband, Brick."

"Oh, Jin, I'm so sorry." Tex's tone lost all suspicion now.

She sent the body a sad frown but then turned back to Tex and me. "Thank you kindly."

"What happened?" Tex asked.

Jin's stance changed. Maybe she was uncomfortable or attempting not to be too emotional. I couldn't read her.

She finally spoke. "I don't know, Tex. I think he was murdered."

"What?" Tex and I both exclaimed.

Jin nodded. "Yep, that's what I said, and I'll stick by it until I can get someone to tell me differently."

"How . . . what happened to him?" I asked.

She sent me a suspicious glance, but it was fleeting. "I don't know for sure. Found him dead as a doornail on the floor when I came back from checking traps. His neck, though . . . it looked like maybe he'd been strangled with something."

It probably went without saying, but chances were good that the scene had been compromised by now.

"Jin, let's talk about this and then I'll help you get to town." Tex looked toward the mine. "And let's see if there's anything else we could take to Gril that might help him figure things out. Let's go back together, for now, at least."

"I don't know, Tex." Again, her expression changed. Fear brightened her grime-framed eyes. "I think I should get on out of here. Pass on through. No one will bother you. Tell them I says it was okay."

"Are you scared?" Tex asked her.

"I'm not scart of anything, young man," she lied. "But Brick here is getting pretty ripe."

Tex nodded. "Another hour or so won't change that. I've come to know Gril. He's a wonderful lawman, but I know some of the questions he will have and getting those answers now might help everyone understand what happened to Brick. Otherwise, your mystery might not be solvable, given more time. I know you want justice for him."

She seemed to think about his words a long minute. This was definitely going to throw a monkey wrench in our plans, but if a murder had, indeed, occurred already, it was more important than attempting to run from one that had only been threatened. Tex was right in offering assistance, as well as for wanting to look over the potential crime scene before any more time passed.

She bit her lip again. Finally, she nodded slowly. "All right, all right, but don't say I didn't warn you."

"Warn . . . ," Tex said, but Jin didn't acknowledge it.

Tex and I shared a look. What in the world did that mean? Whatever vigilance we'd been channeling, we ramped it up a little more.

The trail wasn't wide enough for Jin and the horse to make an easy turnaround, but she managed a sort of three-point maneuver. She moved her feet and the horse expertly.

Once she was headed that way, Tex looked at me and spoke quietly so Jin wouldn't hear. "You okay?"

"Yes. You think it's safe?"

"I have no idea. From what I know, these are not violent people, but we need to turn around or get through somehow, and I think Gril would approve of us asking a few questions."

I thought a moment. "They used to be though, right? Violent, I mean. Back in the gold rush days maybe."

"Maybe, but not for a long time. Stick by me," he repeated his earlier command.

"You coming?" Jin had guided the horse a good distance along the ridge before she turned back to check on us.

"Yes, we are," I said.

We set out to catch up.

I looked around, sensing that we were being watched. Since Tex was with me, I wasn't overly concerned about who it might be, and I was close to certain that Travis Walker wasn't out here. Not yet, at least.

As we navigated around another curve, the mine came into full view. I wouldn't call it a town, but it wasn't just a community either. Maybe a small village. It appeared as if some people had stumbled upon the place and decided to stay a bit with whatever supplies they had on them, and then a bit turned into more.

I saw the mine's entryway crisscrossed with rotten planks and frayed pieces of rope.

From this vantage point, I also noticed the smaller square buildings that I'd thought were dwellings, along with what I assumed was a communal gathering place.

A spot for a large fire was surrounded by a rocky border and tree trunk stools. Amid all the natural elements was a green folding chair, dirty but still seemingly a good place to sit—and with a back, which was not available on the tree trunks.

The only people seated around the currently unlit soot were on the ground, their legs extended out in front of them. When I saw that each of them held a mug, I finally smelled the remnants of brewed coffee. It was a pleasant aroma.

I still smelled Jin and the horse, but the open air kept all the scents from settling, and the coffee and some other indistinguishable food smells helped.

The two men stood when they noticed Tex and me. I'd watched closely as they'd spotted Jin first. I wanted to see what their reactions would be to her return. They'd been surprised to see her, if their raised eyebrows were any indication. One of them nodded after he studied her a moment. I tried to see what he was reacting to, but by then the horse blocked me from seeing her, and it all happened quickly. I decided I was probably working too hard to read into nothing.

The one who'd nodded got up easily; the other older one expended a little more effort. Their frowns were tired now, not suspicious, really, just a little unwelcoming.

Folks out here didn't like their privacy disturbed. As I'd already considered, people didn't like to be told what to do or how to live, no matter how impossible, stupid, or ridiculous their life decisions might seem to someone else. That's what I saw in their eyes—they were already defaulting to self-defense mode.

Tex lifted his hand in a friendly and nonthreatening greeting. "Hi there."

The two men grumbled something to each other.

"This is Tex from Brayn. You idiots have seen him once or twice," Jin said.

The men seemed to relax a little.

"This here's Beth," Tex said to them. "I'm sorry I don't remember everyone's names. Could I ask for a refresher?"

"Lonny," one said as he put his hand to his chest.

"Haven." The other one repeated the gesture.

I stepped around Tex, the horse, and Jin and extended my hand. "Nice to meet you."

They both shook my hand in a manner that was more neutral than either friendly or unwelcoming. Haven spoke my name quietly. We were making progress.

"You turned around?" Lonny said to Jin.

"I did, but only temporarily. Tex wanted to know what was going on. I'll get Brick out of here soon." She nodded to the body.

The men seemed to need a moment to think about her words, as if they were trying hard to understand what might really be behind her return.

Finally, Lonny turned to Tex. "Why do you need to know what's going on? None of your business, is it?"

"Tex helps out the police chief, Gril," I offered.

It wasn't a complete lie, though Tex only helped the local authorities officially in the manner of search and rescue. He was good at both, and he'd worked with Gril enough for me to stretch the truth at least a tiny bit.

"Uh-huh." Haven nodded slowly.

"Well, Tex," Lonny said as he hiked up his pants. "Then I guess you need to know that we got us a hell of a problem. We are dropping like flies out here."

"Okay. Care to explain?" Tex squinted.

"I wish I could explain it, but from what we can see, someone out here wants us dead. Somebody's been killing us."

Not one to jump to panic, Tex's expression didn't give away much of anything. After another long moment of looking at the men, he turned to Jin. "I think we need to start from the beginning."

Jin sucked her teeth once and then said, "Can do." She turned to

Lonny and Haven. "Gather the others. Let them know I'm back with Brick and we've got company. No one likes surprises."

They both nodded and then turned to the task they'd been given. Lonny trudged up a hill next to the mine entrance and disappeared into the thick woods. Haven also walked toward the mine. Next to the opening, he reached to the ground and grabbed a rusted metal spatula. He banged it on a pan hanging from one of the planks that crossed in front of the opening.

Jin turned to us. "They'll be here in a minute."

Tex nodded satisfactorily.

"Coffee?" Jin added. "Something to eat?"

It seemed impolite to turn down the coffee, but we declined any food. Jin said something quietly to the horse and then disappeared inside one of the square shelters. For a long moment, Tex and I shared looks with each other, as well as the body over the horse.

"This is weird," I said quietly.

"I don't disagree."

Jin appeared a few moments later with two mugs of coffee—hot enough to make me think it was always ready and waiting for someone to order it.

Tex and I took sips of the strong brew as we waited for "everyone" to get there.

It didn't take long.

Three

took a head count. There were fourteen adults and six children in attendance. But, apparently, there'd been more adults only a couple months earlier. And not everyone was there. Some "had traps to check" or "things to do."

One had died of what everyone thought was natural causes. "Gunter had been almost ninety, after all."

But the other three who'd recently died had experienced what everyone thought were suspicious and untimely demises.

Tex grabbed a notebook and pen from his pack and jotted things down as each death was described.

A woman named Nancy was the first unexplained death three weeks ago. She'd been found behind her house (one of the small buildings was acknowledged) with a "big ol' bump on her head," Jin noted.

Tex peered at Jin. "A bump?"

Jin nodded. "A bloody bump." She paused. "See, even though it didn't make much sense we all thought that maybe she just fell and hit her head."

"It didn't make sense?" I asked.

"Falling and hitting her head might make sense," Tex added.

Jin looked at us and shook her head. "No, you know the placement of the body and everything was off."

"Did anyone take a picture?" I asked.

"No. Didn't even think about it." Jin shrugged.

As Tex continued to scribble, I asked another question. "Did you contact any authorities then?"

Jin huffed a quick laugh. "No, it's not easy to do out here. And I think we were in denial or something. It took for Brubaker to be found with a knife through his heart—"

"Brubaker with a knife through his heart?" Tex interrupted.

Jin rubbed her finger under her chin in what had already become a familiar action. "Well, that, and then"—she paused as she nodded toward the horse—"Brick happened just a day later. By then I knew it was wrong to wait a minute longer. I found Brick just yesterday. Our closest lawman is Gril, and if you two hadn't stopped me, I'd be a lot closer to him."

"Okay, I get that." Tex sounded slightly admonished. "Where are the other bodies?"

"Buried. We have a grave site of sorts. Want to see it?"

"No, we'll let Gril do that." Tex tapped the pen on the notebook.

"I'm sorry for what you've all gone through," I interjected.

"It's scary," a woman said. She was probably in her thirties and sat with two other adults and one little girl.

"I'm sure." I had another question. It felt impertinent to ask it, but I forged on. "Why is everyone still here? Why didn't you all head out together toward Benedict or Brayn after Brubaker or Brick?"

Rumbles spread through the crowd, but I discerned the answer from a few people.

"This is our home."

I also heard a couple versions of "We've been fine until we haven't, I suppose."

I let the answers sink in, but it wasn't easy to understand. How in the world did they manage? How long had they been living this way?

I was doing it again, though—projecting my own life, fears, circumstances on others.

Lonny cleared his throat. "We've set up a watch. Haven and I were on duty when you got here."

"You all trust each other?" Tex's question had probably intended to plant the seeds it obviously spread.

"Of course," Jin said.

"So you think the killer is someone outside the community?" I asked. "Do you have any suspects?"

"Yes, ma'am," Lonny said.

When no one offered up a name, Tex said, "Who?"

Lonny squinted one eye and leaned toward Tex. "Him."

Tex took a moment as he seemed to process whether he should know who that was. Finally, he said, "Who's him?"

"The beast." Lonny slapped a hand on his knee.

"A bear?" I asked.

My question was met with silence and big eyes as the villagers looked at each other with a familiarity that told me they were all thinking something I wasn't. "Or a moose? Wolf or wolverine?"

"No, Beth," Haven said. "The beast."

"What beast, Haven? What sort of animal?" I nodded him on.

"Oh, not all animal. He's part man, part animal. A beast," Haven continued.

Again, I noticed the shared belief rolling throughout the village's population. No one was protesting his words. No one looked like they wanted to.

"Do you mean Bigfoot?" Tex sounded much less judgmental than I would have.

"Some might call him that," Lonny added.

"Sasquatch," someone said.

"Yeti," another voice called.

Jin raised her hand and spoke to her people. "Tex and Beth haven't seen him. We sound foolish."

"He's real," Lonny said. "You'll see him if you stick around."

Tex jumped in. "You think that a beast, maybe like the legend of Bigfoot, has been murdering your neighbors?"

"Yes, sir," Jin said as everyone else made noises of agreement and nodded. "But we aren't fools."

"We don't think you are," Tex said, believably.

"We know what we've seen, and we know you'll see it, too, if you stay here," Jin said.

"I think that's a distinct possibility." Tex glanced at me and then back at Jin. "However, I think getting official help is the answer no matter what or who is responsible."

"I don't disagree." Jin shrugged and slapped her hand on her own thigh. "That's what I was trying to do."

Tex nodded and stood. "All right. Let's look around, just briefly. Show Beth and me the places where the tragedies took place. Then Jin, Beth, and I will go back into Benedict. Okay?"

Though Tex and I hadn't had a moment to discuss that plan privately, he'd probably been thinking the same way I had. We couldn't let Jin go by herself, and I wouldn't stay here without him. I didn't think he'd leave me here, either.

We would both go back with Jin, and maybe turn around and come back, or go someplace other than the cabin next to the fish-filled river. Maybe Travis would have been caught by the time we made it back to town. No matter what, my leg muscles were going to get in great shape whether they wanted to or not.

But first we would look at the potential crime scenes, just so we could offer Gril some information.

Jin patted the horse. "Somebody watch Brick for me. I'll show our guests around."

Lonny and Haven both hurried to attend to the horse and the body on its back.

"This way." Jin gestured. "I'll show you where we found Nancy first."

Jin led us around two of the small structures and toward a third that we'd spotted from a distance but couldn't see close up until we were right upon it, for the slope of the land.

"Nancy lived here." Jin pointed.

Made of the same wood as everything else, the structure's planks seemed to have more space in between them than wood itself. There was no glass in the one window, but an animal hide served as a small curtain flap.

"Can we look inside?" I asked.

Jin shrugged. "Sure. Not much to see."

Nevertheless, she pushed on the old handle and opened the door.

The inside was as small as I expected, maybe twelve feet by twelve feet. A cot took up one back corner, a small potbelly stove the other. Personal items, a comb, and maybe a wallet, had been set on a side table next to one of the front walls.

"We stripped the cot of her bedding, gave it to the Collums up a couple spots. Someone will move in here, but we don't know who or when yet."

"Do you think her bedding might have had some evidence?" I asked.

"Nope. We found her body out back, that big bloody bump on her head," Jin repeated her earlier description. "No trail of blood, just a puddle next to and under her. Come on, I'll show you."

We trudged up the slope to the spot behind the house. Some trampled greenery indicated a body might have fallen there, but at first glance I saw no blood.

As if reading my mind, Jin said, "It rained the day we buried her. There was no more blood to see after that."

For a long moment the three of us stared at the spot, but we learned nothing new.

"You think that . . . Bigfoot hit Nancy over the head?" Tex asked.

Jin nodded. "And then stabbed Brubaker and strangled Brick."

Tex bit his lip and studied Jin. "Did anyone witness the murders?"

"No."

"What makes you think it was Bigfoot, then?"

"The fur," Jin said as if she was getting frustrated at him.

"What fur?" I asked.

"Oh. We found some next to Nancy and on the knife in Brubaker. Didn't spot any near Brick. What we found is back in one of my packs. I thought I would take it to Gril."

"Good idea." I paused. "So you've seen this creature?"

"I have once, I think, but others have, too."

Tex and I exchanged a look. I asked, "How has he been described?"

"Seven feet, brown fur, claws, long beard, furry face."

"And everyone describes the same thing?" Tex asked.

"Yep."

"Why would Bigfoot want to kill any of you?" Tex asked.

Jin gave him the most impatient look I'd seen yet. "The oldest reason in the book, of course."

"Money?" I said.

"Yes. Well, gold."

"Bigfoot needs gold?"

"Doesn't everybody?" Jin shrugged, but her tone told me she was just as suspicious as I, and probably Tex, was about the authenticity of a legendary creature and the possibility that the fur they'd found wasn't natural.

"From the mine?" I nodded in that direction.

Jin nodded.

"Has someone found gold recently?"

"No, but we're all sure there's still more there."

Tex and I hadn't had a moment to discuss these circumstances in private, either, but the next look we shared convinced me that he was thinking the same thing I was—someone in the village was dressing up like Bigfoot and killing other villagers. Neither of us wanted to speak that aloud, though. Not in front of Jin. Not without Gril there, too. If the villagers thought they were being tricked, it was clear they thought it was by someone from the outside.

A noise sounded from behind some trees up the slope. Tex moved himself in between Jin and me and the trees.

"Who goes there?" he asked.

"Just us," a voice called.

Tex looked at Jin.

"That's Bruce and Francis. Trappers who come through a lot."

They appeared from behind the copse of trees. My internal wiring was already vibrating—between running from Walker, the body over Jin's horse, the strange village, and its bizarre tragedies, my skin seemed too tight over my bones, and my heart rate suddenly sped up even more as I watched the men approach. They were both tall, not over seven feet, but tall enough to seem even taller and bigger if they wore furry costumes.

Today they wore orange vests and camo hats, both with shotguns slung over their shoulders—all of this was completely nonthreatening on the surface, but I couldn't help my internal reaction. I kept quiet, though, and tried to calm my breathing as Bruce and Francis made their way toward us.

"Howdy," they said as they stopped to the side of Jin.

"Bruce," the taller one said as he pointed his thumb at himself. "And this is Francis." He gestured. He looked at Tex. "I've seen you around."

"Tex and Beth," he said again.

The greetings were cordial, but I gave the men a furtive once-over. Not a bit of fur was to be seen. Other than height, there were no blaring distinctive features about either of them. They were both middle-aged men with pleasant faces. Bruce had blue eyes, and Francis had brown.

I was overreacting. By a whole bunch. I'd had panic attacks before, and I knew that what I was feeling was a harbinger of one. I needed to stop it before it took over.

"Oh." Francis turned my way. "You're the writer in Benedict."

"I am," I said evenly enough to make everyone think I was doing fine. The fact that he knew who I was didn't ease my nerves.

"What a story." Francis smiled. But then he frowned again. "Your guy got away, though, didn't he?"

I nodded as I gritted my teeth.

"Damnation, I'm sorry about that."

"Writer? Guy got away?" Bruce said.

"I'll tell you all about it later," Francis added.

I was pleased that at least someone out here in the wilds of my new world still didn't know who I was. Surprisingly, a tiny giggle bubbled in my throat. I swallowed away the inappropriate reaction.

"What are y'all up to?" Bruce asked.

In a very matter-of-fact way, Jin told the men about the murders and that Tex and I were investigating. Neither Tex nor I corrected her.

"Damnation," Francis said again. "That's not good."

I would have guessed that both men's surprise and concern about the potential murders were genuine. In fact, they were flummoxed for a few beats.

"Shoot, then," Francis finally spoke again. "We'll leave you to it."

"We pass through here to get to our other set of traps," Bruce said to Tex. "They're over on Mason Ridge."

"Let us know if we can do anything for you, Jin," Francis added.

The two men made a path around us and then walked farther down the hill toward the trail that would take them around and out of the village. We watched them go.

Jin said, "Okay, then, do you want to see where Brubaker was stabbed?"

Tex and I both nodded.

We took another path around the perimeter of the village and came upon a door to a hole in the ground.

"This is an icebox?" Tex asked Jin.

"Yep."

The outside temperature was somewhere in the mid-sixties, I thought. It wasn't raining. I knew what they were talking about, though, and I was suddenly excited to see the inside of it.

Ice caves existed throughout Alaska. I'd once been inside one that I would have described as magical, even though we'd been there to search for clues to a murder. I wish we'd gotten to explore this new icy spot under better—or at least different—circumstances.

Despite the mild weather, the cave was frozen. The ice caves were extensions of the permafrost. Though it was under attack from the climate, it hadn't disappeared completely.

"Has the ice pulled back some?" I asked as Jin reached for the door.

"Not yet. We've been lucky."

"I'd say," Tex added.

Jin pulled the door up like a hatch. We stepped forward together and peered into the dark hole.

"My flashlight is packed on the horse. Either of you have something?" Jin asked.

Tex reached into his backpack and retrieved a small flashlight. He twisted the end and aimed it into the hole.

A ladder led to the depths.

"Brubaker was found right at the bottom of the ladder. On the ground. There's an ice room right there. It's not full now, but we sure use it in the winter months, and it'll get stocked this month and the next."

The floor was made of dirt, and we couldn't see any ice from up top.

"Want to climb down?" Jin asked.

"Sure." Tex looked at me. "Want to come with me?"

I nodded. "I do."

"I'll go first." Tex clenched the flashlight between his teeth and swung his leg over and into the opening.

He descended about twenty feet to the bottom and then aimed the light up again. "Come on down."

The climb down was easy, the ladder solid with evenly spaced rungs. Tex made room for me as I stepped onto the ground. We would have been crowded if he hadn't taken a step deeper into the space.

The biggest differences between this room and the cave that I'd seen a while back were the size and the availability of natural light. This icebox was not lit by anything other than Tex's flashlight, so it didn't shine with the blue colors that made the other one so intriguing. However, that wasn't to say that the about twenty-by-twenty room with its walls made of thick, somewhat grimy ice wasn't fascinating.

And, not surprisingly, it was freezing cold. Literally.

There were some food stores present, probably hunks of frozen elk or other hunted meats set on homemade wood shelves.

"How in the world did they find this place?" I asked Tex, my voice clipped because of the enclosed area.

"Who knows? I've heard of people just falling into them from a small sinkhole."

"It's a wonderful treasure for a group of people who want to live out in the middle of nowhere."

"It is."

Tex turned and aimed the light at the ground at the bottom of the ladder. "Brubaker was stabbed, but there's no sign of blood here, just like where Nancy's body was found. No weather here to wash things away, though."

I stepped back toward the ladder and crouched. "This ground is hard, too. I can't imagine the blood would soak into it quickly. I don't see anything that tells me there ever was blood anywhere around here. Even the meat is well wrapped."

I'd calmed down, thankfully, but the cold seeped into my bones as Tex continued to shine the light all over. My limbs started to quake slightly, but the ice cave seemed undisturbed.

A thud sounded from the tunnel we'd come through. In the dark now, except for his light, Tex and I looked at each other.

"That wasn't the door closing, was it?" I asked.

Tex came around me and shone the light upward. "Dammit." He handed me the flashlight. "Follow me up and shine this toward the door."

"Have we been locked in here?" My voice was high-pitched.

"I'll get us out of here, Beth. You don't need to worry."

If anyone could get us out of a locked icebox, it was Tex, but his words didn't reassure or calm the renewed swell of panic inside me. However, the task of holding the light did keep me from losing it completely.

"Let's go." I aimed perfectly.

Though Tex was a big guy, he was quick and agile. His fast trek up the ladder was impressive. I kept the light moving just ahead of him.

Just as we reached the top, the door flung open.

"Oh. Sorry about that. The wind came up and took it." Jin looked at us evenly. "I was sitting over there a ways and had to make my way back. Sorry."

Tex looked down and back at me. "You okay?"

"I am now." I wasn't quite okay yet, not all the way, but the daylight was better than the cold dark.

It was a good thing I'd been working out so much, or my booming heart might have exploded.

"We done down there?" Tex asked me.

"Oh, yes, most definitely."

We climbed out and wiped the dirt and dust we'd accumulated off our clothing, all the while sharing glances with words we still wouldn't speak in front of Jin.

I inspected the door, noticing no lock. The handle was only to be used as a pull. It didn't latch into place. On its own, there was no way to be locked inside the icebox. Of course, that didn't mean my thriller-writer imagination couldn't conjure up a multitude of other nefarious methods—adding a padlock, placing a heavy weight atop the door . . . my imagination needed to stop its free fall.

"Did you find anything?" Jin asked.

"Not a thing," Tex said. "Did someone clean up the blood?"

"Oh. No. It remained encased in Brubaker's coat. It wasn't messy at all. Not like Nancy's."

Her explanation seemed off, but despite all the research I'd done for my books, I didn't know enough about crime scene logistics to know if blood from a stab wound could possibly stay encased inside a coat.

"Why was he in a thick coat? It's not that cold yet," I asked.

"Beats me. Maybe just because he was headed down to the icebox."

"How'd you get his body out of there?" Tex asked.

"Pulleys." Jin shrugged.

I hadn't taken the time to inspect the tunnel walls, and I wasn't going back inside. However, the information was something we could tell Gril and he could take a better look, see if the tunnel held marks that made using pulleys a possibility.

"Look, Brick was found in our small house, on the floor. There's no evidence there either, and the evidence that might be around his neck could be disappearing by the moment. I can show you, or . . . Time's a-wasting, Tex, and I would think that trying to figure out what happened to Brick by getting his body to some official somewhere is more important than what we're doing here."

Tex hesitated briefly and then nodded. "Okay, okay. Yes, we need to get back to Benedict."

"I don't disagree," Jin said. "And I don't want to wait until tomorrow to get started."

"Let's get going," Tex agreed.

He looked at me. I nodded. I had no desire to stay in that village a minute longer.

Four

We gathered the horse and Brick's body. Jin hadn't planned on riding the animal. The trip to Benedict wouldn't be easy for a horse with a body and a live rider, but she knew how to guide the animal so it wouldn't get hurt along the uneven terrain. The cargo atop it seemed secure enough.

We learned that there were three other horses that the villagers cared for and used. Tex and I were offered use of them to carry our things if we wanted, but we were instructed that we couldn't ride them once we were off the trail. We declined and then slung our heavy packs back over our shoulders again. Tex looked at me as if to ask if I was sure about not accepting the assistance. I nodded.

I was still sore and not as strong as I hoped the entire trip might make me, but that moment of gearing up was the first time I sensed I might be getting more used to everything. I didn't let Tex in on my perceived progress, but despite everything, I couldn't ignore a small bit of excited pride at my tiny improvement.

Tex led the way, I followed behind, and Jin and the horse were behind me. For a few reasons, it was a good idea not to be behind a horse if there were other options. Also keeping Brick downwind was better. Walking into the slight breeze worked to keep the smell at our backs.

Once off the trail, I thought we might end up moving slower than we did on the trip in, but we didn't. In fact, we might have moved a little faster. I asked Tex if that was the case.

"A little. Once you've walked a path, though, a small bit of muscle memory sets in and you can take the same route a little faster the next time, or it just seems like it."

"Muscle memory?" I said.

"Your muscles were taking it all in, your subconscious, too."

"Interesting."

We were mostly silent as we made our way, but I did confirm with Tex that he thought we should camp at the same spot we had the night before. With our late afternoon start today, we would have no choice but to camp somewhere overnight. It might as well be in the small clearing we'd already used. Jin didn't argue, and she told Tex to lead the way.

"Although, I'd like to get up and get into town as soon as possible," she added.

He glanced at me over his shoulder. I gave him a brave thumbs-up. I'd do the best I could. I was terrified about appearing tired in front of either Tex or Jin. It wasn't ego. Okay, maybe it was.

"Sounds like a plan, Jin," Tex called back to her.

For the next few hours, we saw no one else, and the only wildlife we came across was a porcupine, moving slowly and not interested in us or our journey.

The clearing we'd stayed the night before had probably been used for camping by more than a few folks over the years. There was plenty of room to set up a small tent or two and build a safe fire.

As I attended to the fire, Tex got to work on our tent and Jin unpacked and unfolded one of her own. Hers was modern, made to unfurl quickly and easily, to give her enough space to sleep and be sheltered. Tex was intrigued by its easy setup.

"Where'd you get that?" he asked.

"My cousin in Florida sent it to me. It's spiffy, huh?"

"It's great. Nothing like that around Benedict or Brayn."

"I know. I've shopped them both. However, you can't get any better socks than at the mercantile in Benedict."

"True that," Tex confirmed.

I was wearing some of those socks, and though I had nothing similar to compare them to, they sure seemed pretty darn good to me. We'd given our gifts to the villagers before we left, and the socks had been the most popular.

Once the camp was set up and the fire lit, Jin offered to share her dinner of beans and corn bread with us.

"I have more than enough for the three of us. I always pack more food than I need. I can't help myself."

We had our own food, but it seemed impolite not to take her up on her offer, so we thanked her and dug in.

The dinner was delicious, though I was so hungry that anything might have been. For dessert Tex and I shared some of our granola with Jin. It was a homemade treat made by Viola with the guarantee that it would satisfy hunger as well as help salve a sweet tooth. She wasn't wrong.

It was about eight P.M. when we finished cleaning up. The sun hadn't set but was low on the horizon as Tex put the coffee percolator on the fire. We'd all expended so much energy that caffeine wouldn't keep any of us awake enough to worry about drinking it so late, and Tex always drank coffee before bed.

By the time we all had full mugs, a comradery had been solidified. It was natural to build trust quickly out in these wilds. You had to—most everyone would need someone else out here, in one way or another, at some point. Breaking bread, sharing food over a campfire only hastened that connection.

"Jin," Tex said. "You really believe there's a Bigfoot out there killing your friends?"

Jin nodded as she sipped the coffee. "Yes, sir." She looked at him over the fire.

I could see the dusky light glimmer in her eyes, the reflection of the dancing flames. I thought she was serious. But then she shrugged. "But I am also not against the idea that it's a person dressed up in a costume."

Tex nodded. "That does feel like a possibility. You think an outsider wants access to the mine?"

"I do."

"When was the last time gold was found in there? You know me. I'm not going to try to take anyone's anything. It is a question Gril will want an honest answer to. I think it's key to whatever is going on there."

Jin shrugged. "Last year or so."

Tex's eyes got big. "Ah, really, I hadn't heard."

"We've been keeping it a secret, of course. I shouldn't have told the two of you right now, but you're right, Gril will want the truth."

"We won't tell anyone," I said. "I mean, other that whatever Gril needs to investigate."

"I understand." She paused and took a moment to squint out toward the sunset. "We live there, we battle what we battle. Whether it's true or not, we feel like we deserve whatever we find. We know that people want the easy way. Some people feel like they can just take whatever they want."

"You're pretty sure it's an outsider? You don't think the killer could be one of your villagers?" I asked.

"I do not," Jin said quickly and firmly.

I understood fierce loyalty. If someone accused any of my close friends of doing something heinous, my first reaction would be to defend them, probably until the bitter end—even if they were guilty.

"When's the last time someone new moved to the village?" Tex asked.

Jin took another sip of coffee. "Peter Murray moved in last summer."

"What's he look like?" I asked. "Is he a big guy? Do you know anything about his life before he got there?"

Jin's expression turned into something verging on anger. Her guard went up. "He's a big guy."

I nodded and remained silent. She knew what I was getting at just by asking the questions.

Tex said, "What *do* you know about him, his past?"

Jin's eyes slid to Tex. "He's a good man. He's helped us a lot."

"How?" I asked.

Jin sighed. "He's just a nice guy. Fits in with us."

"Was he at the gathering earlier? Which one was he?"

"He wasn't there," she said. "I don't know where he was." She sent Tex a level gaze. "You know how it is." She turned to me. "Lots of people come out here to get away from whatever it was they didn't like so much wherever they were before. They don't always like to tell everything about their past from the lower. They get away."

I'd heard only recently "the lower" used to mean the lower forty-eight.

"I know all about that, hiding from something," I said. "Do you know what he was running from?"

"I didn't say he was running from anything. I said he just wanted to get away."

"Okay." I paused. "Jin, Tex and I aren't trying to be difficult. We just know some of the questions that Gril will want answered. I'm sure he'll want to talk to everyone at Blue Mine, Peter included, and he will ask Peter why he came to Alaska. He knew about my story, my escape. He was the only local who knew for a long time, so the good news is that if Peter wants his story kept secret, Gril knows how to do that."

"Good to know. Thank you." Her mouth pursed tightly and she looked off into the woods. "Well, I do look forward to talking to Gril." She swung her mug out and dumped the few drops of remaining liquid. She stood. "I think I'll hit the hay, but I am going to get up early and get on the trail. That work for you two?"

"Yes, ma'am," Tex said.

I nodded. "See you in the morning."

With that, she turned and made her way into her tent, zipping it up in a way that made me think she wished for a door to slam.

Tex and I looked at each other and shrugged. I didn't know her. I didn't think Tex knew her very well. We didn't know much of anything, and though Gril would want all his questions answered, it was his job more than ours to get those answers. I wished for a private moment where Tex and I could chat, but I wouldn't even risk shared whispers. It would have to wait. The less said in front of Jin, the better.

We finished cleaning up from dinner and then secured the camp as best we could. Tex was concerned about Brick's body. He didn't want the smell to bother us or attract animals, but there weren't many options. Ultimately, he moved the horse a little farther down the path and to a spot under a natural shelter, far enough but not too far away, and in case it should happen to rain. The horse didn't seem to mind, though I worried about it holding the weight of the body overnight.

"Is that cruel?" I asked Tex.

"It's not ideal, but the horse is young and strong, and Jin insisted. She didn't want the horse to have to go through the load up again. We'll get into town early tomorrow. The horse will be fine, but I would like to relieve it of its burden as quickly as possible."

"Okay," I said, thinking through the options of removing the body and then putting it back. I didn't understand what that might mean for the animal, but Jin would.

Tex looked at me. "I know you will be fine, but the horse could carry some of your pack too."

I would carry my own stuff, no matter how tired I got, but I just said, "I'm fine. Thanks. I promise I'll keep up."

Though our sleeping space was tight and side by side, there was nothing romantic about it. I was so tired by the time we zipped up our own tent walls that sleep was right there when I closed my eyes. Tex was always able to fall asleep easily. Neither of us tossed and turned, but I doubted it would have mattered. Fresh air and a trudge through the woods made for deep sleep.

That night, however, turned into something unbridled.

A boom of thunder startled both Tex and me awake. We missed the flash of lightning that had come before it, but there were plenty more to follow—one after another, in quick succession. Rain pelted the tent's canvas; the noise from everything was overwhelming. I'd awakened with a jolt and my heart rate sped up because it was all so loud. I felt like I wanted to plug my ears, but that seemed an over-reaction.

"I need to check on Jin and the horse," Tex said.

Surprisingly agile, he gathered a rain poncho from a storage spot next to his sleeping bag.

"Want me to come?" I asked as I reached for the pack that carried my poncho.

"No. I need you to stay put, Beth. You'll be safe in the tent."

I nodded. "Okay."

The few seconds that he took to unzip, make his way out, and then zip the tent back up again left a small puddle of water inside the opening.

I didn't like being alone in there. I didn't like not knowing ex-actly what was happening outside. Now that I was fully awake, I was anxious to understand what else was going on.

I sat up and pulled my legs from the sleeping bag. It was much colder than I thought. I reached for the pack with the poncho and my other winter gear.

As I gathered it, another flash illuminated the world. Out of the corner of my eye, I thought I saw a shadow play on the opposite tent wall.

I first thought that I was seeing a large man—which could be Tex—but my brain was working to catch up. At second glance, it looked like the figure could be covered in what could be wet dripping fur. I froze in place and told myself I'd just imagined it, that the Bigfoot discussions had wormed their way into my imagination. I waited for the next flash as I watched the wall, my eyes unblinkingly big. It seemed to take forever, though it must have only been a few seconds before the world lit again.

Bright illumination showed a silhouette. It was enough. I knew that, without a doubt, there was a big furry *something* right outside my tent, standing there, seemingly looking in this direction. As the thunder boomed, I put my hand over my mouth, but it was too noisy outside to hear my scream.

Darkness took over again and the silhouette disappeared. I waited another long moment for the next flash. When it came, there was no sign of a backlit creature next to the tent. I breathed heavily until the next flash or two confirmed that it was gone.

I'd lost track of time. I *knew* that Tex hadn't been gone all that long, but it felt like the better part of an hour had passed. It didn't matter, there was no way I could just sit in the tent and wait for him.

I gathered the pack with my gear. I threw on a coat and my poncho and finally pulled my boots up over the mercantile socks I'd worn to bed.

I crawled to the opening and unzipped the flaps so quickly that I had to pull back to catch my breath from the pelting rain hitting my face. I wiped my eyes, pulled the hood up on the poncho, and tried again.

The rain was quite literally pouring from the dark sky—there was darkness all around, in fact. Until the lightning flashed again, but I couldn't make out anything.

"Tex!" I called, but my voice was getting lost in the storm.

I looked toward the spot where Jin's tent should be, but it wasn't there. Had it washed away?

I turned and looked in the direction where Tex and I had taken the horse, but I couldn't see that far, even with the lightning.

"Tex!" I tried again with the same result.

Movement out of the corner of my eye again caused me to turn quickly and peer into the dark trees. With another flash, I saw the creature again—big and furry just like everyone had said.

I couldn't believe my eyes. I couldn't believe much of anything. Maybe I was still fast asleep inside the tent, Tex next to me, and I was dreaming. I wiped the rain from my eyes and waited for the next light. My boots sunk into the pooling mud at my feet, but I was too scared to move, too scared to do anything.

I had to know.

Only another few seconds later, I was certain—the bright white light illuminated the creature again. This time he stood there and stared back at me. He was probably twenty feet away, but he didn't make a move in any direction. We stared at each other.

I was rattled, of course, but I was aware enough to know that I wasn't looking at something wild, something apt to make a decision based upon animal instinct. Though I would have put money on the fact that what I saw was real, I also knew it couldn't be anything more than a person—a man—in a costume.

"Hey!" I finally called, my choked word getting lost in the noise again.

But after the next dark moment gave way to the light, the creature was gone.

"Hey," a voice said as I felt hands on my shoulder.

I shrieked and turned.

Tex put up his hands. "It's me."

I propelled myself into his chest. I liked the idea of being an independent woman in this wicked environment, but I was suddenly overcome with relief that he was there with me.

"Let's get in the tent," he said.

It was messy because we were soaked and muddy, but we got inside and closed the flap. Tex reached for one of my boots. "Let me take those off. It will be better to keep your feet down here."

I turned my leg so he could reach it better. "Jin? The horse?"

"Neither are here. I'm assuming she took off after we went to bed.

Damn, that's probably why she insisted on keeping the body where it was. She had a plan."

"You think they're okay?"

Tex thought a moment. "I do. Jin's been around a long time. She'll know what to do out there." He paused. "Though, I do think she would have been better off waiting for morning. She sure became bothered by our questions, but it didn't cross my mind that she'd leave. It should have." He managed one boot off.

"Tex," I said.

He looked at me with lifted eyebrows and a dripping beard. My tone had been weird. "Yeah?"

"I think . . . I think I saw the creature they were talking about."

"You did?"

I nodded. "It's not a wild thing."

"A guy in a costume?"

"It's a damn good costume, but that could be what I saw."

"Damn. I'm sorry you were scared."

"That obvious, huh?"

"Not bad. Are you okay?"

I nodded. Since Tex was with me, the worst of the terror had mellowed. Besides, though he wouldn't hold any sort of reaction against me, Tex needed me to keep it together. "It can't be real, can it? I mean, a real Bigfoot?"

"No, it can't be. Beth, I've seen more of these woods than practically anyone. I've seen some strange things but nothing like that."

"Strange things? Like what?"

"Not all animals look like what we expect. I've seen an albino wolverine that was fascinating and certainly unlike other wolverines. Animals that have survived some sort of injury that leaves them lame but still able to find a way to eat and stay alive. I've seen people living in places that I was shocked they could survive—"

"Like Blue Mine?"

Tex shook his head and reached for a towel from his pack. "No, more like living in literal holes in the ground with very little shelter. I don't know how some people manage to survive, and I've been trained in survival skills." He held the towel out for me, but I shook my head. He rubbed it over his head and face.

"Why would someone dress in the costume and come out to where we camped, though? In this terrible storm? If they were near the camp, they had to take the same hike we did."

Tex thought a moment, using the towel on his beard again. He looked at me. "Jin is the only reason I can think of."

"They followed her?"

"Probably. They don't even know who we are. We are just collateral at this point. But if someone did follow us as a group, they are wanting to keep track of Jin."

I thought a moment. "Or Brick's body."

"Excellent point." Tex frowned at the zipped tent flaps. "Maybe there's some evidence on the body, though the weather is jeopardizing that."

"You'd like to go back out there?" The rain was still falling but the worst of the storm had passed. For now. The weather was predictably unpredictable.

"I would, but I won't. Not until the sun is up."

"Are you more worried about Jin now?"

"Yes."

"Should we pack up and go?"

"No, not in this weather—"

"You'd go if I wasn't here."

"That's not true. I have too much respect for the elements. Sure, I'm worried about her, but we have to be smart enough to keep ourselves safe, too. In fact, keeping us safe is our number one priority."

I nodded unconfidently.

Tex squinted. "Are you sure you're okay?"

"Yeah." I managed a weak smile. "You're here, so I'm okay. I'm glad I'm not alone, and I'm sure I'll never do this alone, so that's okay. . . ."

"I bet you'd surprise yourself. You'd be just fine."

I half smiled but didn't argue.

"Let's see if we can get a little more sleep. I'd like to take off at first light. There're a couple ways into Benedict from here, but we were on the easiest route. If Jin is, too, we'll either find her there or in town."

"You think she might have gone back to Blue Mine?"

Tex shrugged. "If she did, I'm sure Gril will be happy to ask her all about it there. We'll let him worry about that. We're going back to Benedict and then decide what to do."

Somehow, we did rest. Well, I did. Tex claimed to have slept, but I couldn't be sure. I was relieved to wake up to temporarily clear skies. We hit the trail again.

In a reversal of how I'd felt just a day earlier, now I couldn't wait to get back to Benedict.

Five

The morning, though topped off with a clear blue sky, was frigid. We packed up camp quickly and decided to eat granola as we hiked. Fresh brewed coffee would have been welcome, but we opted for a cold brew made with some stirred instant to save time. The temperature was low enough to see our breaths, but the continual movement warmed me up and kept me going without too much complaint from my muscles.

We worked quickly. Tex wasn't nearly as easy on me as he had been on the way out. We saw no sign of Jin or the horse along the trail, not even obvious foot- or hoofprints. The weather might have erased them, though. And despite the weather, we didn't have to slog through all that much mud.

Mostly, I kept my eyes scanning the woods as we made our way, telling my legs to keep up. They didn't do so badly.

The miles passed by at a quick clip.

I was surprised by how I remembered and predicted some landmarks. There was that strange fallen tree. There should be a cairn up next, a trail guide or maybe a memorial that someone had created for a reason that wasn't clear. When the rock pile came into view, I was pleased I'd remembered it.

We hiked, and hiked, and hiked.

After a couple hours, Tex insisted we rest and eat lunch to fuel us through the rest of the way. He surprised me by noting that we only had an hour or so to go.

"You really were easy on me on the way out," I said as I slung off my pack, torn between being really hungry and afraid I couldn't get my legs going again if we rested even for a short time. I kept both thoughts to myself.

"It's important to ease into these things," Tex said.

"I appreciated that."

After we ate sandwiches and more granola, we set out again, quietly (so as not to jinx ourselves), recognizing our luck at still having clear skies, and me silently glad my muscles hadn't frozen in place during our break. The temperature wasn't anywhere close to warm, but I still didn't feel a chill.

We'd only left two days earlier, but as we came out of the woods next to Benedict's small downtown around midafternoon, my eyes saw the world with a new refreshed vision, like after I'd been on vacation and then walked into my home in St. Louis. Colors were brighter, details more vivid than when I'd left. We took the world around us for granted; it was always good to find a renewed appreciation.

Downtown was an *L* shape, with the Benedict House on one leg and crucial businesses on the other—a café, the mercantile, the bar, and a post office. Parking lots had been improvised at both ends, and they were currently half-filled with trucks and other vehicles.

A swell of contentedness filled my chest when I saw the sites I'd come to love, the places I now called home, but I was also on alert. If he hadn't arrived already, Travis Walker was definitely on his way to this place, not to mention my curiosity regarding whether "Bigfoot" had also made his way to town.

Thoughts of Travis brought back that disquiet of anger in my gut. It wasn't fair that he'd gotten away. It certainly wasn't fair what he'd done to me. How dare he come here? I'd felt plenty of acrimony about him, but this new wave was even bigger, and it interrupted the contentedness I was relishing.

But we were interrupted by a good thing, too, though. My dog, a husky named Gus, had been attending to his morning toilette in the woods not far from where we'd just come. I didn't get a chance to see who was with him before I noticed him sprinting in my direction.

"Hey, boy!" I called.

"Brace yourself. He's coming in hot," Tex said with a happy tone.

Since the moment I'd become Gus's person, I hadn't spent much time away from him. He even traveled with me sometimes when I stayed with Tex in Brayn. When not with me, he and Viola were also the best of friends.

It appeared he might knock me over, but he slowed just in time, coming to a sliding stop right in front of me. He'd been taught not to jump up on people, but today he whined with the desire to do so.

"What's going on? What are you doing here?" I said as I scratched and patted all the good spots.

Viola followed behind Gus and was on her way in this direction.

"Everything okay?" she called.

Viola wore a holstered gun almost all the time. Today she wore two. I was caught off guard by that, despite knowing she'd insisted on doubling down before we left.

Until that piece of horse dung is put away or put down forever, I'll be as ready as I know how to safely be.

The dung in question was, of course, Travis Walker. He didn't have a big fan base.

"Has anyone seen Travis?" I asked.

Viola frowned and then shook her head. "No. No sign of him whatsoever. We're watching closely."

They *would* watch as best they could. They would know everyone coming in and out of Benedict via any plane or the ferry from Juneau. But as I'd come to learn, there were other ways in—more difficult, of course—over terrain that seemed impassable, although if someone was determined and lucky enough, they could make it.

Unfortunately, Travis Walker had been nothing if not determined and lucky.

"I know," I said.

"Why are you here? Did something happen?"

Tex and I shared a look.

"Let's get you two inside. Beth can tell you all about it, but I'd like to find Gril."

Viola's concerned eyes moved between me and Tex a moment before she just said, "Sure."

Tex had parked his truck in the lot next to the Benedict House. Once we were inside and he was on the road, I told Viola that both of us would have a more enjoyable conversation if I took a quick shower before we were in a closed-in space together for any reason.

Gus hung out in my room while Viola put coffee on and whipped up something to eat. The shower was the most amazing one I'd ever taken.

I didn't usually follow the instructions on my shampoo bottle to lather and rinse twice. Typically, I only did it once. Today I went over every part of me *three* times. When I squeaked clean, I hopped out, dried, and got dressed.

My hair had been cut and styled recently—for the first time since my head had been partially shaved for the brain surgery I'd needed after escaping Travis's van. I'd had a subdural hematoma removed. The leftover scar would be impossible to hide, even with long hair, but the woman who'd done the cut knew her way around hair and made the style work with the scar. It still looked good—well, as good as I might ever look again.

I used to have long brown hair, with clear skin, and bright, mostly happy eyes. My hair had turned white in the hospital. My skin was still pretty clear but now held a ruddiness that I'd noticed on some of my fellow Alaskans—when we weren't all tinged with a little gray because of the lack of sun in the winter.

Even though my hair color and cut were completely different than they used to be, it was my eyes that I always thought held the biggest transformation. They were no longer happy. They weren't sad either, but they were guarded. It was something I saw every time I looked at my reflection, still unsettling but not as shocking as it used to be.

Other than my father, no one else here would have known me before Travis, and Dad had left my life when I was a kid. Still, though, my author picture was on the covers of all my books. The only person who had commented on my eyes had been the librarian, Orin.

Yeah, yeah, there's a difference, but everything about you is so much bigger than it used to be.

I'd laughed at his words, noting that I *had* gone up a jeans size.

Orin had laughed at my reaction. *I didn't mean your body. I meant your soul.*

I hadn't been sure what to say to that, but it had felt like a wonderful compliment. I'd just nodded and muttered a quiet thanks.

Once I was ready—clean, dressed, with my easy hair drying in place, I went to my knees and gave Gus some more attention, scratching his neck and behind his ears again. He smiled happily, his blue eyes looking into my more guarded ones. I loved this dog so much, and he sure behaved as if he felt the same.

"Did Viola take good care of you?"

He nodded and whined in the affirmative.

Though I didn't want to leave the Benedict House, I'd concluded that if that ever happened, Viola and I might end up in a custody battle over the dog.

I simply wouldn't leave. Not yet. Maybe not ever.

Since I'd given myself permission to think that way, that I didn't have to go if I didn't want to, I'd experienced a wonderful freedom that could only get better when Travis was behind bars again.

Gus and I made our way to the dining room, where Viola had prepared pancakes and bacon. I wasn't shy about filling my plate.

In between bites, I told her what had happened at Blue Mine as well as the creature who was being blamed for the tragedies, though I held back on telling her what I'd seen in the storm. She knew about the mine and the small population living around it but had never seen the area.

Viola had stuck close to Benedict since running away from Juneau when she was a kid. She and her sister Benny had ridden the ferry over one day and never left. Benny ran the bar, and they had both become beloved as well as respected.

"Then we stepped out of the woods, and there were Gus and you," I said before I took another bite.

Viola nodded. "I think I've heard of the woman, Jin."

"What have you heard?"

"That she runs a tight ship."

"So, she's the one in charge of the village?" I nodded slowly. "That would make sense. I didn't think about it while we were there, but, yes, everyone pretty much did whatever she said."

"I do think she's in charge. Her father was the first one to find gold there."

"Really?"

Viola nodded. "Yep. He's the one who first dynamited the mine. Rumors are he killed a few people because he wanted the gold to himself, though that's not an unusual story considering the time and the distance from any sort of authorities, as well as the craziness of any gold rush."

"What about now? It appears people are being killed again. Does this just happen every once in a while?"

"Not that I've heard."

I gulped some coffee. "What about a Bigfoot killer?"

"Ah, well, I'm sure that's not real, though there are creatures out there that look similar enough to manipulate people's imaginations. I've heard folks mention something over the years, but it was either never confirmed or later explained away when they found the bear or moose they must have seen instead. If they're blaming Bigfoot, then someone's behind it or imaginations are running wild."

I still needed to tell her about my own encounter. In fact, I'd asked Tex to let me tell Gril about that part, too. As it usually did, the light of day transformed scary things seen in the dark into things less frightening. I was still sure I'd seen what I'd seen, but the more time that passed, the more I had *no* doubt it was someone in a costume. It was an important facet of whatever was going on, but I thought that the story coming directly from me would sound much better than someone saying, "Beth saw . . ." I could be more adamant in my own telling that I knew it wasn't real.

I pushed the almost cleared plate back a little. "I need to tell you more."

"I'm listening."

"I saw it."

"It?"

"The . . . person in the suit."

She pushed her plate back, too. "I'm listening."

I told Viola about the details and my reaction. I sounded *almost* like I was convinced it wasn't real. I was going to have to do better with Gril, but I was glad to try the story out on Viola first.

"Yeah, someone is doing this," she said. "It's a person in a costume or a bearskin or something. You are aware of that?"

"I am, but I don't have proof either way, and I have no doubt that I saw a big furry thing."

"You need to tell Gril. It might be something pertinent to his investigation."

"Tex is telling him what the villagers said but not what I saw. I asked to be the one to do that."

She thought a moment. "Let's drive over there. I don't like to be out of the loop, anyway. This will give us a good reason to see what's going on."

"Want me to clean up the kitchen first?"

She shook her head. "Later. I also want to see if Jin made it to town or if she turned back for home. Let's go."

I felt a guilty urgency as we climbed into her truck, Gus finding a comfortable spot in between us. I noticed Viola's eyes scanning constantly.

"Viola, what's going on?"

"I just also don't want to take any chances with anything."

I watched her profile for a moment. "Oh, Viola, I'm so sorry."

"About?"

"Coming back. Now you have to babysit me."

She laughed once without humor. "Beth, you being here is almost a relief. I have my eyes on you and my guns ready. I can handle anyone. I know Tex would keep you safe, but now I can be certain."

I looked around. In any good adventure movie, her words would be the bellwether for an ambush.

But there was no sign of one. There wasn't sign of much of anything or anyone. Once we were out of downtown, it was just us and the trees we passed by on each side of us.

I'd often told myself not to see things in the dark woods that weren't really there. It was easy to let my imagination run wild, but I was determined to keep my wits about me. Viola wasn't telling me the full truth about being glad I was back in town, but she wasn't lying either, really. Everyone was as torn as I'd been about me staying or leaving.

It's why the plan was created and then executed. Gril, Donner, Eddy, Viola, Orin, and even Benny had all agreed to be prepared to fight a battle. And, frankly, win it, whatever that meant.

It wasn't vigilantism, Donner had explained to me. *It was protecting one of our own.*

And no one had hesitated. In fact, everyone had concluded that if Travis was determined to find me, he would, and they wanted him to come to Benedict over anywhere else because they all knew they could "handle the situation" better than anyone else.

It had been three weeks since Detective Majors had called, three weeks since I'd been out on my father's boat with him and Tex, seeing the glaciers for the very first time, and my cell phone connected with the National Geographic ship's tower, managing to find a connection in the middle of the ocean. Detective Majors had been able to reach me and tell me about Travis's escape.

I was still concerned, but as time had gone on, so had life. Other things were now at play. I wasn't sure if things like murders in a mining village and the appearance of Bigfoot were good distractions or bad.

However, that didn't change the involuntary reactions my body had to triggers. There was something about the empty woods, the one of the two paved roads in Benedict ahead of us, that made the inside of my head feel like I was on a Tilt-A-Whirl.

As furtively as possible, I pulled oxygen into my lungs and then let it out slowly. I hadn't been as covert as I'd thought. Gus whined and Viola asked, "You okay?"

"Yeah, I think so. One second I'm fine, the next . . . my feelings change on a dime right now."

"To be expected."

I hoped she was right.

As we pulled next to the cabin that housed the local police, I was happy to see the horse. "That's a relief."

"Yes, except . . . well, last time I saw it, there was a body flung over its back."

"Her husband . . . Brick?"

"Yes."

Viola put the truck in park. "Let's go see what's what."

As the three of us made our way inside, I took stock of the other vehicles. Gril, Donner, Tex, and Eddy as well as Jin must have been inside.

They were all in the open front part of the station, sitting in folding chairs in a circle, appearing casual as they sipped from coffee cups. Everyone's attention was turned toward Jin, whom I only recognized because of her eyes and the fact that she was the only female other than Viola and me.

She'd cleaned up—no visible grime anywhere. Now, she just looked like a middle-aged woman enjoying a coffee. She had short dark-gray hair that fell easily to her jawline and a sharp chin that worked with her bright eyes.

"Beth," Gril said as he stood and made his way toward me.

Though I'd spotted Eddy's car, I didn't see him in the cabin, and, fleetingly, I wondered where he was.

"Hey," I said. I made eye contact with Tex and Donner and nodded at Jin.

"You clean up well," Jin said.

I couldn't think of anything else, so I said, "Thanks. You, too."

Jin laughed. "I get a shower every other month or so."

I wondered where she took the showers, but I didn't ask.

"You okay?" Gril said as he looked at me.

He was trying to relay something. I couldn't figure out what it was, but I would err on the side of an economy of words.

"Jin was telling us about losing Brick's body," Tex said.

"Oh?" I said as my eyes went back to her.

"It was something," she said.

"Come on over," Gril said to Viola and me.

Donner and Tex each grabbed another chair. Viola and I sat with Gus in between us.

"Come here, pup." Jin leaned on her knees and called to Gus.

He didn't move.

"He takes time to warm up to people," I lied as I put my hand on his neck.

Jin nodded and sat back in her chair again. "Who are you?" she asked Viola.

"This is Viola. She helps out with most everything in Benedict," Gril said.

Viola sent Jin a mostly friendly nod.

"You like your guns," Jin said.

"Yes, ma'am," Viola said as she and I each took a cup of coffee that Tex offered. Viola took a sip, keeping her eyes over the rim and locked on Jin's.

To no one's surprise, Jin looked away first.

"Should I start from the beginning again?" she asked Gril.

"Please," he said.

Jin put her tongue in between her teeth and seemed to think a moment. I hadn't noticed her do that before and I wondered if it was a habit or a tell. I watched for her to rub her finger under her chin, a gesture that *had* become quickly familiar.

There was a chance I was working way too hard to understand something, maybe anything. Find answers to ambiguous questions.

"After we all bedded down, my knee told me a storm was coming." Jin tapped her knee with her finger. "It never fails me. If I'd slept, my knee would have fought me hard in the morning and I knew I needed to get to town. I got up and checked on the two of you—"

"How?" I asked. "Did you try to wake us up?"

"I stood outside your tent and asked if you were awake." Jin shrugged. "I didn't want to be loud enough to wake you up if you were snoozing, but if you were alert, then . . . well, you didn't answer so I packed up and took off. I left you a note."

I looked at Tex. He shrugged.

"I unzipped your tent an inch and stuck it in there."

"It could have easily gotten lost in our in-and-out during the storm," Tex said.

That did make sense.

"You were willing to travel in a storm?" I asked Jin.

"Sure. I've done it plenty of times. I know what I'm doing, and I really thought I might get ahead of it, not go through it. And the knee was still working okay." She tapped it again.

I'd already thought that she and the other villagers were a hardy group, but it seemed that common sense would dictate *not* traveling in a storm. What did I know, though?

"I was worried about the horse, too," Jin said as if that explained it.

"I was, too. I was worried about both of you," I said.

"Shoot, I'm going to be fine. The horse would have been okay, too, but I didn't like him having to be out there just getting rained on, and I knew how to navigate the way."

Quickly, I scanned the others to see if what Jin was saying made sense to them. Clearly, she'd made the journey just fine, but I couldn't imagine any one of the other people in that room making the same decision.

No one spoke up, though, told her she was crazy to have done what she did. Everyone's demeanor was neutral, so I turned my eyes back to her as she continued.

"And, we did just fine, until we came to the crick . . ."

"Which creek again?" Gril asked as he reached over to a nearby desk and grabbed a pen and notebook.

"The one about a mile that way out of here." Jin nodded. "I don't know if it has a name."

I couldn't remember passing a creek before about three miles out from Benedict, but I was still constantly surprised by the things I didn't know about or suddenly discovered.

Gril bit his bottom lip a moment. "*Mmm.* I think I know the one you mean, but I'm not sure."

"It's there," Jin said, "It was raining, Gril. The crick was high."

Gril nodded. "Sure. Go on."

Jin continued, "Well, I knew I'd made a bad decision when we found that running water. The storm hit big, and the water kept rising and rising. I tried to find a place to wait it out, but there was no shelter in sight." Jin frowned, looked at the floor in front of her, and shook her head. "Honestly, it was terrifying. I just wanted the horse to be safe, so I held on, we held on, the best we could." Jin looked up and directly at Gril. "That water rose so much that it lifted us up. Just briefly, but enough to knock us silly. Fortunately, the swell passed, and we found the ground again. With a flash of lightning, I saw a spot with some shelter, if we could get to it." Jin shook her head again. "I don't even know how I did it, but I got hold of the horse and got us out of the mess. But—and I didn't see how or when it happened—once we were under cover, I noticed that Brick's body was gone." Jin's eyes filled with tears. "Just gone."

"And that's why you initially made the trip through the storm? To get Brick's body to town?" Donner asked her, irony and sarcasm not well hidden.

"Yes, sir," Jin said. "Somebody's killing us, and I want you all to investigate it. I had to prove that Brick was killed. I didn't know any other way." A couple tears trickled down her cheeks, and she sniffed.

"I'm sorry, Jin," Gril said as he put the pen down.

His tone was genuine. Almost. I knew him well enough to hear something else. I thought he was probably feeling his normal healthy dose of doubt. He never took anything at face value right away. The technique had served him well.

"Jin," Tex said. "I think you should tell Gril about the new guy who came to your village."

Jin's teary eyes snapped up to Tex. "He's a good man, Tex."

"I'm not saying he isn't—"

"Jin," Gril said. "If you want me to investigate, I need to know everything. Who has recently come to the village?"

Jin sniffed again. "I know, I guess. Yeah, his name is Peter Murray."

Gril and Donner reacted quickly. They both sat up straighter and looked at each other.

"Our Peter Murray?" Donner said aloud, but he was looking at Gril.

Gril looked at Jin. "Tell us more about Peter. When did he get there? What does he look like? Did he say where he was from?"

Jin frowned at their reaction, but she must have known she couldn't stop now. "He came to the village a couple months ago, summer. He's tall, dark hair, and big shoulders. Dark eyes. Normal looking. Just a guy."

"A couple months ago? Are you sure?" Donner asked as he stood and made his way to his desk on the other side of the room.

"I think so. Close to that. No more than three months ago, I don't think," Jin said. "Do you all know him? He's never said where he came from."

No one answered as we all watched Donner open a file drawer and sift through it. Shortly, he pulled out a manila folder. As he walked toward Gril, he opened and looked inside the file.

"Nine weeks ago was our first official visit," Donner said before he closed it and handed it to Gril.

"Peter Murray, huh?" Viola said.

"Yeah," Gril said as he perused the file.

"You all know him?" Jin asked again.

Gril thought a moment before he looked up at Jin. "We do. Well, we know someone by that name and description. He disappeared from his cabin a couple months ago. Well, as far as we can tell."

"Disappeared?" Jin shook her head. "He didn't share his background with me, with anyone, as far as I know, but I didn't know he was from Benedict."

I was watching the goings-on and trying to place Peter Murray, but I was sure I hadn't met him. However, there were plenty of tall men with dark hair out in these wilds.

"Who is he?" I asked.

But my question was ignored.

Gril turned to Jin. "I will head back out to the village with you tomorrow. Do you mind sticking around here the rest of today?"

"Not at all. I kind of like it."

I looked at her, something irking me about her tone. She sounded . . . normal, but that was what caught my attention. Until that moment, she'd sounded somehow defensive.

Gril looked at Viola, who must have picked up on his silent message.

"Stay with us at the Benedict House, Jin," Viola offered a beat later.

It did make sense that Jin be under her watchful eye.

"Thank you kindly," Jin said, though now she sounded like her guard was back up.

The Benedict House was a halfway house for "recovering" female felons. I could see in Viola's eyes how she was going to feel about a new "guest" before any further conversations had been had. Though she treated everyone fairly, she had an uncanny knack for knowing how she needed to communicate with her guests so they may move along their path of redemption as fast as possible. Some required a little tough love, but her methods were mostly made of using the right words—not tough as much as spot-on; a productive economy of words, I always thought of it. Though Jin wouldn't be a typical "guest," Viola wouldn't like having so much left in the dark about someone staying under her roof.

My curiosity, however, was now mostly focused on who Peter Murray was and what was going on with him. I was aware enough to appreciate how all these new mysteries were wonderful distractions for my own fear.

But it was only a temporary vacation. As I looked around and wondered what we were all going to do next, as everyone made moves to stand and plans were made for Viola to take Jin with us, that icy fear trickled back into my thoughts. Had Jin brought up Bigfoot? Was it time for me to do so?

I was standing, too, but as I opened my mouth to tell my own part of the story, the front door opened.

"Hey," a voice said from the entryway.

We all turned at once to see my father, Eddy. He was dressed in camo. Even his face was painted green and black.

"There's someone in the woods," he said.

"Are you sure?" Donner said.

"One hundred percent."

Gril took charge immediately. "All right. Donner, you and I will check it out with Eddy. Tex, you stay with everyone else in here." He gave Tex a hard look. "You got this okay?"

Tex reached into his pack and pulled out a gun I didn't know he'd been carrying with him. How had I missed that?

"I got this," he said.

I swallowed hard and fell back to the chair I'd been sitting on. It was a good thing it was still there.

Gril, Donner, and Eddy rushed back out the door as I worked very hard to keep my composure.

Six

Viola made her way to the door and opened it. She peered out before she closed it again and turned the bolt to lock it.

Tex made his way to a window and peered out by lifting one of the closed blinds.

"What's going on?" Jin asked as Viola turned and walked back toward the group.

"My . . ." My throat was suddenly so dry.

Jin took the chair next to me and frowned as she inspected my face. "That guy who took you is here?"

"I don't . . ."

"We don't know, Jin," Viola said firmly. "But we're being cautious."

"Wow. I thought I felt a vibe in here. I knew you'd come to the village because you were running from something. Then Bruce and Francis talking about you . . . I asked and someone at Blue Mine knew your story. Crazy, but I get it now, but I had no idea everyone here was so . . . mobilized. Lucky girl," Jin said.

At the moment I didn't feel so lucky, but I got what she was saying.

I felt like a burden, a pain in the ass, like I should have taken it upon myself, been brave, and just left, so these people whom I cared about didn't have to deal with my crap.

But here we were. And I needed to stop second-guessing it all. I'd made decisions, and it was time to live with them.

"What's . . . ?" I asked, but I still didn't have any saliva.

Tex walked to me, reached for the coffee I'd set on a desk. He handed it to me. I took a gulp as he watched, a concerned glimmer in his eyes. He sat on the corner of the desk and turned to Viola. "What's going on out there? How did Eddy know?"

Viola took a seat on my other side and nodded. "Gril set up a crow's nest."

"How? When?"

"It's amazing what can get done when you get a bunch of people working on it," Viola said.

I didn't know to whom I should ask the next question. I didn't even know what the next question was. I needed to get a grip, but suddenly everyone was looking at me.

I held up a hand and closed my eyes. They all respected the fact that I needed a moment and waited silently.

Stop this. You are fine. You are safe. There are people all around you who are willing to literally kill to keep you safe. Get it together.

I opened my eyes and let out the big pull of air I'd taken in. "I'm sorry. I'm okay."

Tex and Viola's eyes were concerned. Jin's were impatient. I appreciated each and every emotion coming my way. I was also concerned and impatient with myself.

I nodded. "So, they built a tree house or something?"

Viola nodded. "Something like that."

Jin cleared her throat. "Well, hanging here is not my style. I'd like to have joined them. Do any of the rest of you feel like sitting ducks?"

"No," Viola said as one of her hands went to a gun.

"No," Tex added, but he wasn't quite as obvious about his weapon.

"I'm not one to wait for an attack." She stood. "I think I'll go out there."

"Sit down." Viola wasn't one to be argued with, but Jin didn't care.

"Free country," she said as she marched to the door.

"Jin, please," Tex tried.

Jin put one hand on the doorknob and another on the latch as she looked back over her shoulder. "Nope. I'm not good at waiting around. Shoot me if you want."

She knew no one would shoot her, but I was sure Viola was tempted. Still, though, she didn't draw. She and Tex shared a look. She shook her head at him.

"Please, Jin. It's for your safety," Viola added.

Jin unlocked the door, pulled it open, and left, closing it behind her.

Tex hurried to the door and opened it again. "Jin!" he called. He shook his head and closed and locked the door again. "She disappeared quickly. She's headed toward town. I'm not going after her."

Viola and Tex shared another look.

"She lives a different sort of life," Tex said.

Everyone out here lived a different life than what I'd lived before moving here. This sort of scenario wouldn't play out quite the same way in St. Louis.

But that's where Travis had escaped from, so who's to say which method, what procedures were ideal.

"She's an idiot," Viola said. "But I want us together here. I won't go after her either. Gril might see her and set her straight. She didn't take the horse?"

"No." Tex frowned.

"Hard to think she'd leave the area without him," Viola said.

"Should *we* go after her?" I asked.

Another long beat later, Viola and Tex both said, "No."

Tex continued, "She knows how to take care of herself, and she's right, it is a free country."

"And she's free to be an idiot," Viola added.

"I hope she'll be okay," I added.

Viola huffed.

Another few moments passed as I was sure Viola and Tex continued to ponder if one of them should have at least followed Jin.

I tried to shake off the fear and said to Viola, "Tell us about Peter Murray. Who is he?"

She nodded. "Sure. Peter was born in Benedict about thirty years ago. His parents were beloved, always there to help anyone who might need it. When Peter was about seventeen, his parents were killed in a plane accident—"

"A Harvington plane?" I interrupted.

Brothers Fred and Frank Harvington ran the airport and piloted small planes, mostly back and forth from Juneau. Fred had flown me into Benedict, the landing more a downward plunge than something we eased into. It had been terrifying, but I'd heard that they hadn't ever had an accident.

"No," Viola said. "The Murrays were assisting with a rescue out there"—she nodded toward outside—"and the plane they were in went down. The plane and pilot were from Juneau."

"I think I remember that," Tex said.

"It was a terrible tragedy." Viola sighed. "Peter was left an orphan, but with his parents' money in the bank he was fine. He stayed in their home, and we all watched over him until he decided he didn't want to be watched over anymore. He grew up and then turned into a recluse, rarely spotted in town buying supplies."

"Why is there a file on him?" I nodded toward the folder that Gril had dropped onto a nearby desk.

"Right. No one had seen him for a while, so Gril and Donner went out to his place a couple months ago, I guess. The house was empty, with no sign of Peter, which was no big deal, really. Folks enjoy heading out during the summer months, exploring. But Gril and Donner kept checking, and he was never there. One month is curious, but two months is worrisome."

"Was he at the Death Walk?" I asked.

The Death Walk was the yearly event where everyone was supposed to meet downtown to check in after what was usually a long dark winter. It had taken place about three and a half months earlier.

"Yep. In fact, I talked to him briefly," Viola said. "I said hello, and he smiled a little and nodded at me before he walked away, but he was there. He's never been a problem. He's always kept to himself."

I looked at Tex. "I told Viola what I saw." I turned to her. "Would he be someone to don a Bigfoot costume?"

Viola's eyebrows furrowed. "I can't see that. He never causes any trouble, but I don't know him well. I don't think anyone does."

"He just *showed up* at Blue Mine, according to Jin," I said.

"Maybe he wanted a change of scenery." Viola shrugged. "Jin's right, it's a free country."

"I hope Gril finds him," I said. "I can't think if I've even seen him."

"No, there's no reason why you should. He's not around much, and it sounds like he's been over at the mine for a while. Gril and Donner will talk to him out there if they need to. He's not in trouble."

I eyed the file and wondered if Viola's explanation was the reason for the shared looks between Gril and Donner or if there was more. I wouldn't read it without asking first, but I was sure curious.

Tex made his way to the window and peered about.

A moment later he said, "They're on their way back."

"Is someone with them?" I stood and hurried to join him. Viola was right behind me.

"Yes," Tex said, but his tone was weird.

I frowned as he moved out of my way so I could see better. That was probably a clue. Tex didn't stop me from looking at who was being escorted toward the building. He wasn't worried. I had an easy look.

Eddy and Donner led the way. Gril trailed behind, his hand on another person's arm. I sensed he was holding on tight, but none of the four people were angry or upset.

Finally, I saw whom my father had spotted.

"Mill?" I said, my voice cracking.

"That's just what we need," Viola said from behind me.

She wasn't wrong. Mill was a gigantic pain, but she *was* my mother, and she'd been missing for a few months now.

I moved around Tex. I fumbled with the lock but finally got it undone. I pulled the door open and rushed outside.

"Mom!" I said as I stopped on the porch, my hand on the railing.

She looked good. She looked great, in fact. I'd wondered if she was hiding in the woods somewhere, but it seemed that hadn't been the case at all. She looked healthy and as if she'd slept inside comfortably.

She smiled big. "Dolly! You got your hair cut. It looks fantastic!"

Mill Rivers was back in Benedict.

Seven

Though she was probably as healthy as she looked (and she really did seem in good shape), Mill Rivers smoked like a chimney. Gril wouldn't let her light up in the station, and he didn't want us outside, so Mill was relegated to just holding a cigarette between her fingers as she told us all what she'd been up to. Or her version of it. I doubted she told the entire truth about much of anything. It wouldn't be her style.

She had left town with the man who'd first taken care of Gus—Elijah, who, surprisingly, had a history with my family. The discovery had only reinforced that it truly was a small world. Mill shrugged him off now, though.

"Didn't matter. I dumped him at the border," Mill said.

"What border?" Gril asked.

"The one into the lower forty-eight. We hopped on a boat, made our way to Juneau, then down to Seattle."

"That's all possible without being discovered?" I was asking for Mill as well as to learn what Travis's options might be.

"It's not easy," Gril said.

Mill made a *pfft* noise. "Anything is easy with money. Elijah had enough to shut everyone up. Anyhoo, in Washington, we parted ways. I told him I had stuff I needed to do in Missouri, and *that* was the last place he wanted to go. Neither of us were surprised."

Sometimes the easiest explanation is the correct one, or so Occam's Razor theorizes. Though I might have been worried about her safety, imagining all sorts of things she'd gotten herself into, the most obvious thing Mill could have done would have been to go back to where Travis Walker was and kill him. She hadn't managed the second part yet, but she'd gone back to Missouri, with murder on her mind, most likely.

I watched my parents. They hadn't seen each other in decades. My dad couldn't stop staring at my mother, though there wasn't anything loving or contemptuous in his gaze. He was curious, maybe looking at the differences, or maybe wondering why there weren't more.

My mother was working to not look at my father. She was avoiding him, but I knew that wouldn't last forever. She had some things to say, and Mill couldn't contain herself forever. It was going to be loud and vicious at some point, but the setting would have to be different, private, and between the two of them—I would try to worm my way in, though.

For now, and though I couldn't dwell on it, my family was together again, in one room, and no one could have predicted the timing or the Alaskan setting.

"Okay," Gril interrupted. "We have some things to take care of. First of all, where's Jin?" He looked at Viola.

"She said it was a free country and left."

"Did you threaten to shoot her?" Gril asked.

"Yes, but I thought she had a point."

I'd never witnessed any moment of contention between Gril and Viola. I thought we were all about to, but Gril only nodded and didn't question either Tex or me. "I suppose that's correct." He sighed. "All right, Mill, tell us everything else you can when it comes to Walker. I'll deal with Jin later. Also, I'll want more details about what you've been up to, but later is fine on that, too. I think I have a good idea."

"You got it, Chief." She paused. "I saw Travis escape."

"You did?" I said.

Everyone was shocked, sitting up straighter, making curious noises.

"Yep. I was watching the whole thing. When he took off, I tried to follow him. Someone had to be helping him."

"Who?" Gril asked.

"I have no idea," Mill said. "If I knew, I'd've been up in their business so fast, they wouldn't have known what hit them."

"How were you able to watch?"

"I was tailing the van that was set to transport him." She shook her head. "I had to pay big for the timing details, but I knew who to bribe. It worked. Through some binoculars, and from an old manufacturing parking lot a block or two down from where he was being held, I watched as the officer brought Travis out. They kind of disappeared behind the van, but I saw the officer get sick, and then I saw him appear to go into a panic."

"But you didn't actually see where Travis went?"

"No, but not for lack of trying. I hightailed it over to the woods that were on the other side, but it was all for naught. I didn't see a thing."

Gril frowned at Mill. "What do you really think happened to him?"

He was serious about wanting her opinion. She liked having the respect.

My mother was, at best, a piece of work, at worst, a criminal. I didn't think she'd killed anyone yet, though. When she'd shown up in Benedict months earlier, I'd thought her arrival was a very bad idea. It hadn't been a complete disaster, but she never leaves a place as nice as she found it, and she'd left a small wave of discontent behind, mostly because she disappeared without telling anyone she was going, running away from things that she should have faced.

However, despite the upheaval that just comes with Mill Rivers, I'd missed her. More than that, I'd been worried about her. I was irritated at her for causing so much concern, but couldn't help but feel pleased to see that she was alive and well.

Finally, she shook her head. "If I knew, I wouldn't be here, Gril. I'd've taken care of him and then disappeared. I know how to do it, too."

"Were you *actually* going to do something to Walker?" Eddy asked.

Mill looked at him, really let her eyes land on him. For the briefest of instants, I saw something like affection. The knowns: My father had left us when I was a kid, my mother had searched high and low for him. Somehow, she'd figured out he was in Mexico but hadn't come out and told me. She hadn't even taken off to confront him south of the border once she'd finally, after years of searching, learned the truth.

I wondered what they'd said to each other today out in the woods, if anything. Maybe nothing. Yet. But I sure wished I'd been there to witness that first glance, those first beats of reunion.

When he'd first revealed himself to me, I'd punched my dad. Mill might do the same or worse, though I was sure she'd saved her killer intentions only for Walker. But inside this gathering, I thought I had seen a brief beat of real fondness. It hadn't lasted even a full second, but it had been both interesting and a bit heartbreaking to witness.

Finally, Mill answered, "I guess I should plead the Fifth, but you can all figure it out."

"That doesn't really apply to this situation," Gril said.

Mill shrugged. "Whatever."

Gril sighed and looked around at the rest of us. "When it rains, it pours, I suppose. Honestly, I'm not surprised she's not still here, but does anyone know where Jin actually went?"

"Toward town," Tex said.

"Let me guess, she didn't like being stuck behind walls, or something like that?" Gril said.

"That's what she said." Tex nodded.

"All right, we need to get to work," Gril said.

"Gril, I need to tell you something first," I interjected.

My words put a harsh halt on the momentum, but he turned to me patiently. "What's up, Beth?"

I looked at Tex. "Did you or Jin have a chance to tell him about . . . it?"

"Jin did."

"Bigfoot?" Gril said. "Is that what you want to tell me?"

I nodded. "I saw it, but I know it wasn't real. I mean, really a creature. I thought it was a man in a costume."

Gril nodded.

"This is interesting," Mill said.

"That's good," Gril said. "I'm glad you saw . . . whatever it is. That gives Jin's story some credibility. It's good to know." He paused. "Is there more?"

I shook my head, realizing there wasn't any more. There had been no need to be concerned about what someone might think when I shared what I saw. I wasn't sure why I'd turned it into a big deal in my mind, but I was willing to chalk it up to stress.

"All right, we need to get to work," Gril repeated.

"What can I do to help?" Tex asked.

"What can we all do to help?" Viola asked.

Gril took another long moment to look at us.

When he spoke, we all listened intently. "This is what's going to happen. I need to stay in town. Eddy and Donner are going to head back out to Blue Mine in the morning. I'd like an investigation of the village, and I want Peter Murray brought back to town, at least temporarily." Gril's eyes landed hard on Donner. "He's free to live wherever he wants, but something's not right about his exit from Benedict, along with the potential murders, not to mention a Bigfoot sighting. . . . Ask him nicely to come talk to me. If that doesn't work, arrest him. Make something up. I don't want to take the time to go out there, and I need to speak to him."

Donner nodded. Eddy nodded, too, looking surprised. He'd never helped Gril out with anything this serious before. I figured the command was made simply to keep my parents apart for a little longer, maybe give them time to get used to the fact that they were in each other's lives again and delaying the blowup that was bound to happen.

Gril's gaze skimmed over Tex, Mill, Viola, and me. Gus whined at the chief's scrutiny.

"Mill and Beth will stay with Viola. Tex, could you stay at the Benedict House until Donner and Eddy return?"

"Of course."

"If you need to run back to Brayn to check in with your family today, that's okay, but I'd really like you back in Benedict this evening."

"No problem."

"Thank you all," Gril said, his eyes landing again on Mill, as if to drive home the fact that he needed her to behave.

To her credit, Mill nodded soberly.

"Here's what I'm going to do. First of all, I'm going to attempt to catch up with Jin and bring her back. I won't travel far, but I still might be able to find her. I'm going to call a couple of locals to search for the body that fell off her horse, but I might need to call in someone from Juneau to help, too." He frowned. "I'm not overly keen on doing that, because you never really know if you're going to get someone so by the book that we can't get things done. . . . Anyway, let's get to it."

Mobilized, we stood to make our way to the places we were supposed to go. Viola, Mill, and I were to head directly to the Benedict House and would not leave until we were given an all clear at some point.

Tex walked with me outside.

"I don't need to run back to Brayn but I need to talk to Gril a little more. I'll see you at the Benedict House, okay?"

"Sure. I'd love to know what you're talking to Gril about."

"I promise I'll tell you later."

"Deal."

Viola, Mill, Gus, and I hopped into Viola's truck. It was just one bench seat; with Gus we were particularly crowded, but no one seemed to mind.

Mill smelled like peppermint and pine—clean, indicating she hadn't been on the run in the woods.

"When did you get back to Alaska? What path did you take to get to Benedict?" I asked.

"I came into Anchorage, took a boat down to Seward. Hitched from there."

Hitchhikers weren't uncommon in this neck of the woods, but they weren't usually middle-aged and they often carried big packs like those Tex and I had had on our trek.

"Man, this place is still so friendly to hitchhikers," she continued. "Everyone thinks you're a serial killer in the lower forty-eight."

"Mill, what happened to Elijah, really?" Viola asked.

Even at the mention of his name, Gus whined a little.

"Like I said, we parted ways in Seattle. Too much ancient history kept rearing its ugly head. He's out of all of this, Viola. He's moved on, doesn't want anything to do with any of it or us." Mill petted Gus. "He misses his dogs, but not enough to come back. He says he just needs to move on with a new chapter of his life."

"How do you feel about Eddy?" Viola added.

"I feel lots of things about Eddy, none of them good at the moment, but I'm working through it."

"That might not bode well for Eddy?"

"I'm not going to kill Eddy," Mill continued. "But I have a number of things I'd like to discuss with him. Alone. Just the two of us."

"That doesn't seem wise," I said.

Mill's eyes darted to me as if she was going to admonish me, but she must have remembered that I was a grown-up now, too.

"We'll be fine," Mill said with forced calm.

"Good," I said.

"Aw, shoot." Mill smiled. "I'm so tickled to see *you* in person again, I might just forgive your father."

Both Viola and I smiled, albeit tightly. Even Gus seemed to be pleased.

Viola, Mill, and I set up rooms for Mill and Tex. Viola told me she didn't care if Tex and I roomed together—her comment extorting an immature whistle from my mother. I sent Viola a smile, but I didn't commit to any spot where Tex might sleep.

When the rooms were ready, we met in the kitchen and examined the food stores. Viola had been prepared to feed herself for a couple of weeks. With four of us, the food wouldn't last nearly as long, but there was enough for a few days.

Viola took Gus out for another break before she and I started cooking dinner. I thought I'd take the opportunity to find Mill in her room and have whatever heart-to-heart I felt like I needed to have.

I knocked lightly on her door but got no answer. My first panicked thought was that she had run again. I didn't hesitate to turn the knob and push the door wide. She hadn't run. She was fast asleep on the bed, out like a light.

I knew something then; it was something I hadn't felt ever, but it was crystal clear at that moment. Mill was done running, searching. She was tired, in more ways than one. This was it, this was somehow her last adventure. I could only hope that if it was doomed to end in death, it wouldn't be hers.

I closed the door and went to help Viola in the kitchen. We were having stew—the same kind she'd made for Tex and me to take with us on the trip.

As we got to work cutting vegetables, she said, "Well, the gang's all here. How do you feel about that? Your mom and dad?"

"I feel . . . weirdly neutral. Maybe my focus is on other things."

"Good. That's what I wanted to hear. Now, chop this onion."

I did exactly that.

Eight

Tex showed up in time for dinner, but Mill didn't stir. As we ate, we discussed logistics again. Nothing had changed; Viola wanted to make sure things hadn't been misunderstood. I asked Tex what he'd wanted to talk to Gril about, but he said it was the same thing that Viola had wanted—a clarification on what was going on, who was going where.

His answer didn't ring true to me, but I didn't push him on it. Maybe he didn't want to tell me the details in front of Viola. I decided I would ask him later.

As we were cleaning up the dishes, a storm rolled in, promising to be a replay of what Tex and I had gone through the night before. Flashes of light, big cracks of lightning, and booms of thunder.

Tex didn't like it. Viola didn't like it. I understood why—they didn't like the thought of someone using it as cover, a way to hide. After all, no one in their right mind wanted to be out in a storm this big, except maybe someone who wanted to remain unnoticed, or, of course, someone actually not in their right mind.

I liked the storm, but that was probably because I was cocooned inside a place with Viola, Tex, and Mill, who were all good with weapons and didn't seem apprehensive to do whatever might need to be done.

Tex and Viola decided to take turns sitting in the front lobby on watch. They didn't take me up on my offer to watch by myself, but I understood that, too.

I was in the best of hands as I lay in my own bed and looked up at the ceiling. Rain pelted the windows pleasantly enough, but I couldn't sleep. I peered over to the dog bed on the floor. Gus was resting just fine. He was out just like Mill had been since we'd come home.

I swung out of bed and grabbed some sweats and thick socks before I left my room and made my way to the lobby.

"Hey," Tex said as I came into view. "Can't sleep?"

"I can't. I'm certainly tired enough."

"It's been a big few days." Tex grabbed a chair propped against the wall, unfolded it, and patted the seat.

I took it. "Anything going on?"

"Other than your mother's interesting snore, nope, nothing new." Tex smiled.

"Imagine trying to sleep in a car with her doing that." I smiled back at the memory.

"In a car?" Tex asked.

I nodded. "I've told you how we searched for my father."

"Sure."

"Mill didn't always have the money to spring for a hotel room, a tank of gas to get us home, as well as dinner. I think that her actions would probably get the attention of child welfare services today, but back then, it was just all part of the adventure." I bit my lip. "Although my grandfather put a stop to her taking me with her, he never said one bad word about her actions. At least not to me. To her, he surely had a few choice admonitions."

"I would think."

"Yeah."

"Do you remember them as the good old days?" Tex asked.

I pondered. "I don't know. I think we're all so influenced by the events of our childhood. My mother always loved me, or maybe I just thought she did because mothers are supposed to love their children—"

"Oh, she loves you."

I cringed. "Does she? Or does she just like a good obsession?"

Tex shrugged. "I think her love is genuine, but I'm not sure she does it the same way others might."

"Agreed." I smiled. "So, want to tell me what you really wanted to talk to Gril about?"

"Sure. I thought I should go back out to Blue Mine with Donner, and Eddy should stay here. Not because I don't want you to have the best protection possible, but because I don't think Eddy will know how to assist at the village."

"Why wouldn't Eddy know what to do?"

"I believe Jin in that nefarious things have been going on out there, but . . ."

"What?"

"That place has been home to many suspicious mysteries over the years, and Jin has been at the heart of a couple of them."

"Oh. Like what?"

"People seemed to have disappeared on their journey to the mine. I've heard of two men who've gone missing. Jin claimed not to have ever seen them, but some of the other villagers had slightly different memories, all of which changed after maybe Jin had a chance to talk to them."

"Was there any proof?"

"Not one bit. That's part of the reason I was hoping to get Brick's body back here. Maybe a look at what happened to him could help explain what happened to others."

"Smart."

Tex laughed. "No, just able to see the obvious."

I looked down the hallway toward Viola's room before I turned my attention back to Tex. "Should we have stopped Jin from leaving?"

"I've thought about that. Short of physically forcing her, she wasn't sticking around. I don't think it's wise to do that to anyone unless you're more than a little sure they're up to no good. No, I don't think it would have been wise to intervene in her departure more forcefully."

"*Hmm.*"

"But, Beth, I really don't know. Gril wouldn't answer me when I asked him the same question."

"Ah, you also asked him that when you talked to him about you going back out to the mine?"

"I did."

"I'm sorry."

"Sorry? Why? No time for that. We need to be on our toes."

"Right. Still, though. I could have tackled Jin."

"Next time," Tex teased.

"So Gril didn't like your idea of trading places with Eddy?"

"No, and I didn't push him to explain. He's the boss. Here I am, and I'm glad I'm here. I think I would have also regretted going. I would have been worried. . . . This is where I belong."

Startling us both, the front door swung open, with a force made violent with the wind. Tex and I both stood. He put himself in front of me quickly.

Once the door was closed and the rain poncho's hood was pulled down, we were relieved to see that it was Gril.

Tex said, "You okay?"

I stepped around him. "Gril?"

Gril nodded. "I need Viola."

"I'll get her," I volunteered.

I hurried down the hall. Just as I reached for the knob, her door swung open.

"Who's here?" Viola asked. She was still fully dressed and holstered.

"Gril. He asked me to come get you."

She nodded and made her way around me and down the short hall.

"What's up?" she asked.

"The body's been spotted," Gril said.

"The one that Jin brought into town?" Viola asked.

"We think so. It's wrapped the same way, I think."

"Where?" Viola asked. "Did you find Jin?"

"I didn't find Jin, but when I got home, Shane Grady was there waiting for me, said he saw it hooked on a fallen tree branch by his house. He couldn't figure out what to do because of the storm, but since it looked like a body to him, he came and found me."

"He lives right next to a creek," Viola said.

"A creek that's only rising," Gril said. "Don't know if it's part of the same one that swept up Jin, but it's feeling that way."

"Her horse?" Viola asked.

"Safe in a nearby barn. She never did come back for him."

"We need to get that body."

"Tonight, if possible, before it gets carried away."

"What can we do?" Viola asked.

"I'm going to need all of you. Donner and Eddy are gone. You're the ones I have left. Get dressed in your best rain gear and let's go."

"Should I get Mill?"

Gril took a moment to think about the question. "Is she asleep?"

"I can wake her," I said, already starting to walk toward her room, which was right next to mine.

Gril sighed. "No, let her sleep. I don't . . . she's . . ."

"A wild card?" I offered.

"Something like that. But, let's get a move on. Our time is surely limited."

It was only about ten minutes later that the four of us were packed into Gril's truck.

Gus and Mill slept through our departure.

Nine

As the rain did, indeed, continue to pour down, thunder boomed, lightning flashed, and Gril expertly steered his truck down the road back toward the police cabin.

I'd met Shane but had no idea where he lived. I always thought he looked like Einstein, and he often wore bear fur coats and hats. He'd always been friendly enough. However, since he was older, it made sense that he wasn't physically able to wrangle a body off a branch along rising water. It was unlikely anyone could by themselves, particularly in this storm.

Just past the police station, Gril turned onto a dirt—well, currently mud—road. I worried we would get stuck, but I didn't say a word. No one did. We all wanted Gril to focus fully on the task at hand: driving. We forged on.

Benedict wasn't the type of place where you could just hop in your truck and drive around to get a feel for the area. There were too many dirt roads, too many paths to nowhere that ended with near impossible turnarounds. And there was always the threat of weather. Winter, summer, and the few days of fall and spring could all bring rain, some of it light but most of it heavy.

As small as the town was population-wise, it covered a lot of land, and I had neither seen nor experienced most of it because it was so wild. I didn't think I'd ever been this way before, but I couldn't be sure because of the weather blinding the way. All I could really see were flashes of light out the rain-smeared windows.

As the truck slowed to a crawl, the storm lit up a cabin situated directly in front of us. I caught the gasp that made its way into my throat. If I made any noise, no one paid it any attention.

It wasn't a big cabin, but it was set up on a berm—mostly likely because it was near a creek, though I couldn't immediately spot the water.

"Hang on one second. Let me scope things out," Gril commanded the rest of us. He hesitated. "On second thought, come with me, Tex."

Tex nodded and the two of them exited the truck, leaving the insides of the doors dripping from the blowing rain.

I looked at Viola in the seat next to me. "Is this scary or have I just not done anything like this before?"

Viola hesitated a moment. "Oh, I think it's all a bit scary, but we know what we're doing, Beth. You'll be fine."

"How about everybody else?"

"Everybody will be fine," Viola said, though I wondered if I heard a smidgen less confidence in her tone now.

I hoped not.

We waited. We couldn't see where Gril and Tex had gone. The seconds stretched. I didn't realize I'd barely been breathing until Tex opened the passenger door again and I took a deep pull in relief.

"We see the body and we think we can get at it, but we need to be fast," Tex said, raising his voice above the sounds of the storm.

"What can we do?" Viola asked.

"We're going to need all hands, so come on out." He looked at me. "You're covered but you're going to get soaked. It's just the way it is. Try not to let it bother you."

I nodded and gave him a thumbs-up.

"Let's go," Viola said.

Outside, my feet felt immediately unstable in the muddy ground, though I wasn't really sinking as much as just wobbly. I was soaked quickly, and I understood why Tex had warned me. It was discombobulating to think I was prepared for the weather, but the preparations didn't work. Had he not said something I might have spent a distracted moment wondering what I'd done wrong and what I should do to fix it. As it was, I just went with it.

"Stick close to me," Tex said.

As he took off toward the side of the cabin, Viola put her hand on my back and guided me to go next. She followed behind.

I trudged my way, but so did Tex and Viola. Even experienced hikers were bound to have to struggle a little in this mud.

We walked up a slope and then over a small ledge before going down another slope. With a lightning flash, I saw the scene in front of us—but only briefly. I thought I glimpsed Gril next to the fast-moving creek, which I would classify as a river if I were in charge of naming such things. The body was being stopped from floating away by the flimsiest of tree branches. My eyes went wide as I waited for more lightning to confirm what I thought I'd seen, but I didn't need it. Tex flipped the switch on a powerful and apparently waterproof flashlight. I'd seen it before, out in the snow-covered woods as we carefully made our way toward a wrecked vehicle last winter. I wished for snow over this rain.

Gril gave us instructions by raising his voice and using lots of hand and arm movements to explain what we were going to do.

Brick's body could come unhooked from the branch at any second, but Gril didn't seem panicked or rushed. He wanted to be sure that we understood him.

He explained that he'd wrapped a rope around himself and a nearby strong tree. I would be in charge of his rope and Viola would be in charge of Tex's when he did the same thing.

I realized I'd done something like this with Donner when we were crossing some other nearby fast-moving water. The fact that I had a tiny bit of experience under my belt with such a scenario gave me a smatter of confidence. I nodded eagerly as Gril handed me my end of the rope.

Gril and Tex were going to walk as close to the edge of the creek as they could and lasso the body. Together, they decided they could pull it through the water and over to this side. They weren't going to go into the water—at least that was the plan. Viola and I were there to help pull them back if they did. Gril was pretty confident that our assistance was just precautionary.

I took the rope around my assigned tree, and Viola did the same on hers.

So as not to sugarcoat any of this, no matter my small bit of confidence, this was all horrible. The weather made visibility nearly impossible, the ground was muddy and mushy and slippery. Despite my gloves, the rope was slippery, too.

Once I was around the tree, I put my entire focus into holding the rope. That was my job. Watching, or trying to watch, Gril and Tex work wouldn't help them. The only thing that would help would be me holding on tightly, so that's what I did.

I dug in and held on. It pulled taut quickly, so I held on even tighter. So far so good. A pull tugged me a little deeper into the gunk at my feet, but I did not let go. The skin on my hands might have been protected but that didn't stop them from beginning to cramp. A burn came with the cramps, inner and outer. My skin was starting to feel it, too. I gritted my teeth and ramped up to holding on for dear life.

Without warning, I was suddenly propelled backward, the rope hanging limp in my burning and cramping hands. Had Gril come loose from the rope? Had he fallen in the water?

I scrambled up and came around the tree, but I couldn't see much of anything.

I tumbled and slid toward the creek, human forms finally coming into view. They were all there and they were okay. Viola, Tex, Gril, and the body at their feet. It had worked!

Though my panic had turned to glee, my feet were still struggling to gain purchase.

I probably weighed close to a hundred pounds less than Tex, so as I careened toward him uncontrollably, he must have thought he'd be able to stop me. So did I, frankly.

But that's not what happened. As I propelled into him and as he crouched in an attempt to halt my forward motion, he was probably as relieved to be the one to save me as I was. I knew he would stop me. How could he not?

However, instead of coming to a stop, the side of my shoulder hit his calves, like a football tackle, and he was sucked into my movement instead of halting it. Immoveable object, undeniable force or such. I had never been overly fond of physics.

As I would remember it, we were both propelled up and into the air. We flew a little bit before both of us landed in the swelling creek, now a real river, certainly.

It was cold, very cold. I gasped as, at the same time, I instinctually held my breath. Not a good combination. I was being pulled along with a force I couldn't fight. I didn't know which way was up, and I'd only gotten a tiny bit of oxygen into my lungs; water was ruining my entire respiratory system.

I fought, but flailing arms and legs were no match for the rush of water. I tried to see. Mostly, I looked for Tex. I couldn't make out anything except more water.

I didn't know where this "creek" went. Was I headed toward the ocean? Would that mean my body would slow down or speed up? Would a whale eat me?

Was this really the end? Was I going to die? I fought even more fiercely, though I still couldn't accomplish much of anything. I still couldn't find purchase with my feet or my hands. I still could not tell which way was up. I just knew I had to keep trying.

Suddenly, my body slammed into a force so sturdy that whatever air I'd managed to keep in my lungs was expelled along with some water. I made a gurgled *oomph* and continued to attempt to gather my very scattered senses.

I was lifted out of the rushing water. There was still water out here, in the form of the falling rain, but there was also air. I sucked it in and coughed everything out, over and over again.

I figured the person who'd pulled me out of the water was Tex, but I hadn't looked at his face yet. I couldn't do much more than try to breathe for a very long few moments. Finally, I turned to look at my manfriend, but it wasn't him.

It was still dark, and lightning was still flashing. At first, I could only make out the shape of the man who'd rescued me. It wasn't Tex. It was someone smaller, though not tiny. It was a distinctly male form.

A flash illuminated the man's face. He wore not only a raincoat with a hood but also a ski mask. I thought it must be terribly soaked. I could only see his eyes—I knew those eyes.

I emitted a full gasp as I brought my hand up to my mouth. I stumbled backward and strangled out one word, "Travis?"

The man stood there in the storm, statue-like. Though I could only see his eyes, I was sure he was sneering at me. He was going to kill me.

As he spoke, he lifted an arm, but he didn't swing it at me. He pointed. "The man went that way."

And then he turned and walked up the slope and into the darkness. My head swam, my breaths were hitched, but at least I was breathing now.

Had Travis Walker just saved me from the creek?

That could not have been what happened. Could it have?

"Beth!" a voice seemed to carry on the wind. I turned.

Tex was walking toward me. He was just as drenched as I was. He was upright, and I didn't spot any blood on him, either.

Through the muck, we hurried toward each other, and I sunk into his giant bear hug.

"Jesus, I'm so glad you're okay," he said.

"I'm glad you're okay," I said as I nodded into his chest.

We stood there a long moment, but he disengaged. "We need to get back. They are going to be worried."

I nodded. "I have no idea where we are."

"I know. Just stay with me. Okay?"

"Absolutely." I held onto his hand for dear life, literally.

He led us back toward the spot we'd gone into the creek. I would tell him, tell everyone about the man, but not now, not until we were totally safe.

Of course, as we made our way, it all began to feel more and more unreal. What I thought had happened couldn't possibly have. Maybe a man helped me from the water, but it was my imagination that turned him into Travis Walker.

Right?

Ten

No matter how long it seemed I'd been in the water, we hadn't gone that far. Tex had managed to get out by himself and had just kept walking downstream with the hope of finding me. I was grateful he had, and I was okay with him thinking I'd also gotten myself out of the water, at least for now.

We came upon Gril and Viola walking toward us as quickly as the conditions would allow. They were even more relieved to see us than I'd been to see Tex, though there wasn't time for a long reunion. We had to get a body into the back of Gril's truck.

I'd heard about the ungainly weight of a dead body, but I'd never tried to lift one. Even with the four of us, Brick's body was heavy. And, though Jin's wrap was still doing its job fairly well, the whole thing was awkward and seemed to be missing a respectability. But we had to do what we had to do. We finally got Brick loaded up and then we hopped into the truck. We were all soaked to the bone, but none of it mattered.

"Are you two okay?" Gril asked me and Tex after we were all in the truck.

Tex and I both said we were.

"I'm sorry for . . . all that. We will talk about it, but right now, we're going to Powder's and I need to focus on this drive," Gril said as he steered us out of there. "That work?"

We nodded.

Benedict didn't have a morgue and the Harvingtons couldn't fly in this weather, so the doctor's place was the best choice for the body.

After Gril made the proclamation, we were all silent, catching our breaths, fogging up the windows some. I was trying to process it as well as sending some gratitude into the universe.

Viola was the next one to speak. "Damn, that was something, but all's well that ends well, I suppose."

"Yes, ma'am," Tex said. He wasn't in the best of moods, but I knew he didn't dwell on many things. He would move forward from this quickly.

I could see Gril nod, but he didn't comment further.

I debated telling them all then what I thought I'd seen, but I didn't. I couldn't quite get the words out. It was all turning even more unbelievable, and we had a task to attend to. If I mentioned it now, Gril or Viola or even Tex would want to search. I didn't want that. I wanted to get Brick to the doctor's office.

Dr. Powder and his wife were awake when we arrived. Not much startled the doctor, considering what he'd seen during his time in Alaska, but I saw his eyebrows rise as we delivered the body to an examination room.

Once that was done and Gril, Viola, Tex, and I were in the doctor's foyer, which doubled as his waiting room, Gril turned to the rest of us. "Let's get cleaned up and dried off. And then we'll regroup."

We all nodded, and before I could further judge if the timing was right, I couldn't stop myself from saying, "I need to share something. . . ."

"What?" Viola asked.

They all looked at me expectantly.

"I . . ."

"Gril?" Dr. Powder's voice called from the exam room down the hall.

Gril nodded at me as if to ask for a minute. I nodded back, but he'd already turned to head down the hallway.

"What's up?" Viola said. "You okay?"

"I'm fine." I smiled weakly.

Viola squinted and frowned at me. "What, Beth?"

"Viola," Gril called. "Join us, please."

She gave me the same sort of nod Gril had and then made her way down the hallway.

"I feel left out," I said to Tex.

"Might be for the best." He frowned. "What's going on, Beth?"

I kept my voice low. "A weird thing happened to me in the woods."

"Weirder than being swept away through rushing water?"

I nodded.

"What?"

"I . . ." I couldn't bring myself to say it. "I probably imagined it. You know, sometimes being close to death and all . . ."

"Beth, what?" Tex said.

But we were further interrupted by Viola and Gril returning. Tex and I looked at them, both of us hoping they'd share what was going on.

"It's not Brick," Gril said to Tex.

"You know Brick?" Tex asked.

Gril shook his head. "Never met the man, but I know that's not someone who's lived out in a mine village for years." He nodded toward the hallway. "That's Peter Murray in there."

Viola nodded confirmation.

"What happened to him?" Tex asked.

"That's what Dr. Powder is going to try to figure out."

Tex and I shared a look.

"Jin told us the body was Brick. It appeared to be the same one she'd had on the horse. I know without a doubt it was wrapped the same way." I looked at Tex.

"I'm as sure as I can be, too." He looked at Gril. "Jin said it seemed he was strangled, and she was bringing the body into town so you could investigate."

"Or, she was just leaving the village to hide a different body, but lied so you wouldn't be onto her," Viola said.

"That's beginning to seem likely." Gril rubbed his still-wet whiskers. We were all still dripping in the doctor's lobby, a wet path now well forged to and from the examination room.

"Shit," Viola said. "And she's on the run."

"Yes, she is."

Oh, boy, I thought. My additional complication couldn't have come at a worse time. Gril needed to know, but this was going to turn all the disasters into even bigger ones. If it had been real, that was—again, as more time went by, the whole thing seemed a product of my imagination.

"Beth needs to tell us something," Tex said, probably picking up on my anxiety.

"Beth?" Gril said, surprisingly patiently considering everything.

I nodded. "I . . . I think I saw Travis Walker in the woods. I think he saved me."

I was met by silence and furrowed eyebrows all around.

"What?" Viola finally said as she put her hand on my arm.

I nodded. "I know, it sounds totally crazy."

"It does," Gril said as he held up his hand to stop me from continuing, "but, unfortunately, not impossible. Come on, let's all go back to the Benedict House. Let's get cleaned up and get some food in us. Then we'll talk."

Eleven

We did get cleaned up, and we also slept. Before we could talk about anything, Gril commanded the three of us to close our eyes for a few hours, insisting that we couldn't function at the level we needed to without some rest. None of us thought we could sleep, but we all did. Even Gril admitted to catching some Zs on the chair in the lobby.

I woke up as Viola was making breakfast. Gril and Tex were already in the dining room with her.

Mill was still asleep in her bed as we filled our plates with eggs, bacon, and toast. She was setting some sleeping record, which made me understand that her disappearance truly hadn't been fun and games.

"All right, Beth, tell us everything," Gril finally said.

"It's so ridiculous." I grabbed a piece of bacon from my plate. "I really do think I should chalk it up to the trauma of the entire situation."

"So maybe there was no person there at all?" Viola asked.

I chewed the bacon and replayed those moments in my mind. "No, there was a person there. I know the mind can play tricks, but I'm pretty sure I didn't imagine a whole person, just their identity."

I was mostly sure.

"If it was him . . ." Gril began.

"Then he's here. He's made it this far," I ruminated aloud.

"Who?" a voice asked from the dining room doorway.

Mill was now wide awake. Gus was at her side, and he seemed just as curious about the dining room meeting as she was.

"Come on, boy, I'll take you out." Viola stood and signaled Gus to follow her outside.

"Who's here, Beth?" Mill asked.

"Come have something to eat, Mill," Gril offered.

She crossed her arms in front of herself and opened her mouth to say something she probably shouldn't, but Gril was ready.

"Nope," he inserted. "Sit down, Mill."

She opened her mouth again.

"I mean it," he said. "I'll lock you up and you won't get away from me."

I turned to my mother as she sat next to me. "Look, Mill, everyone is doing everything they can to protect me. None of us have time for your crazy."

She looked at me, she looked around the table. If there was a Team Mill, she was the only one on it at the moment.

She turned to Gril. "Has Walker been spotted?"

"We aren't sure, but we are ready either way," Gril said.

"I really don't mean to be a total pain." Mill paused. She usually meant the opposite when she said these sorts of things. "But I sure would like to know what's going on, what's led to this." She forced some conciliatoriness. It was the best she could do.

I relayed the full story as everyone ate. Gril filled in with the details of gathering the body.

"Damn," she said when I was done. Surprising me, she turned to Gril first. "The body is one of yours?"

Gril nodded.

"What are you going to do about that?"

"Investigate."

"You don't have enough people."

"I don't, but I'm going to have to make do unless we want more Juneau people than I'm planning on calling in out here." He looked around the table. "You all know what that would mean, don't you?"

"Abso-fucking-lutely," Mill said. "It means we'd either have to do things by the book or risk getting in trouble."

"That's right."

Mill fell into thought a long moment. "For whatever it's worth, I don't care if I get in trouble. I can be the bad guy. I don't care at all."

"Well, I appreciate that, Mill, but it's impossible to predict how anything is going to go down. It's dangerous, and I don't need you, I don't need anyone, to do things that will make all of this even more dangerous."

Mill nodded. "I hear you, but I hope you hear me, too."

"Every word."

"Okay, then, so what are you going to do? Give me an assignment. I beg you not to tell me not to do anything. I want to stay on your good side, Chief, but I can't do nothing."

"I would never think of it," Gril said. "Here's the plan I have so far. It's subject to continual revision."

We all nodded. I enjoyed the surge of adrenaline that rushed through me. It was good to have a plan. Another plan.

"Beth and I are going to check out Peter Murray's cabin. I hope to hear more from Dr. Powder regarding a cause of death, but I need to check out that cabin and I want Beth with me. Viola is going to stay right here at the Benedict House. Tex, I need you to head back out toward Blue Mine, see if you can catch up with Donner and Eddy. I want them back here. I'm going to *have* to bring Juneau folks in to check out the goings-on out there, but I'd like for them not to spend too much time around Benedict or know about Mill or the possible sighting of Walker. The Juneau people can spend their time at the mine. It means they will be around but maybe not too much in Benedict."

Tex nodded. I nodded. Mill waited with an impatient twist to her mouth.

Finally, Gril said, "Mill, how would you feel about hanging out around town today? The café, the bar, even Toshco. Some people know who you are, but many don't. Wear a hat, disguise yourself a little just in case Walker is around, but keep an ear to the ground of the community."

"Can I wear a gun?" she asked.

Honestly, I was shocked she bothered asking. Though I hadn't seen one on her, surely she was packing.

"No, but you may keep a knife in your pocket. One that folds nicely," Gril said.

"I guess that will have to do," she said.

"Yes, it will have to do."

Viola and Gus returned to the dining room.

"All right, I'll fill Viola in, but you should head out as soon as possible, Tex."

"I can go now," he said.

"Very good." He turned to me. "You okay coming with me?"

"Yes."

"Let me fill Viola in on things and then we'll get going," Gril said. He put his hand on Mill's arm before she stood. "I need you to behave. If you haven't noticed, some of your behavior has been at least indirectly responsible for Walker getting away."

"How's that?"

"You shot him in the leg instead of calling the authorities on him. He ran away."

"Oh. That."

"Mill, please."

"I'll behave."

"Thank you."

Again, we mobilized quickly.

Tex and I shared a brief goodbye. There was a distinct break in the weather, with clear skies and a little sun to help ease the journey to Blue Mine. It was important that he take advantage of Mother Nature's reprieve.

He would be fine, he assured me, and I didn't doubt it.

"Beth, you have to be careful," he said. "Stay with someone all the time."

"Do you believe that I saw someone in the woods?"

"One hundred percent. I also think things can get muddled out there. I've lived here all my life. I've seen all sorts of things."

"Like Bigfoot?" I smiled.

"Well, not a real one, but I might have exposed someone attempting to be one."

"Really?"

"That's a story for another time, but, yes, this is wild country out here. Anything can happen, including Bigfoots and Travis Walkers. That's why we all prepare so much."

I nodded. "Thanks for believing me."

Tex pulled me into a hug. "Now's not the time for sentimental mushiness, but just know that you mean the world to me."

I pulled back and looked up at him. "You mean the world to me, too."

He smiled. I saw it in his eyes. "Remember, I said it first."

I laughed. "I'll remember. Come back safely."

"Stay here safely."

"Will do."

I stood there a long moment and watched him disappear into the woods. I smiled, thinking I couldn't have written a more perfect scene if I tried.

"He's kind of amazing," Mill said behind me.

I jumped and turned. "I don't disagree."

"Quit being scared of committing to him."

I cocked my head at her. "That's not what I'm scared of. What do you know? You haven't been here."

"Then what is it? I see what I see."

I wondered how to explain it. The words tumbled out a moment later. "I can't decide if I need to be Elizabeth Fairchild again or just Beth Rivers. I like Beth better, but I'm not sure my judgment is on track."

Mill shook her head. "It's not a choice. You've never been one or the other. You are both, and you can't force yourself to be anything you aren't anyway. That's not how it works." She reached into her pocket for her cigarettes and a lighter. She took a first pull and let it out. "Ahh, now that's the stuff."

Despite everything, it was good to see her. I walked toward her and gave her a hug. The most surprising part was that she hugged me back.

"Love you, baby girl."

"Love you, Mom."

"Let's go, Beth," Gril called from his truck.

Mill patted my shoulder and we disengaged.

"Don't . . . ," I began, but I stopped myself.

Did I really not want her to do anything drastic? Did I really not want her to hurt or kill Travis Walker?

If it had been him I'd seen in the storm, then he hadn't hurt me, which went against anything I knew or could have predicted.

Still, though, there was no doubt of what he did to me in St. Louis, no different story to go with him keeping me locked in his van, tormenting me for three days. There was no forgiving that, no matter what had happened in the storm.

I didn't want Mill in trouble, but I couldn't control her. No one could. Whatever the penultimate moment of all of this would be, I already processed that it was Mill's last stand. Not that she was necessarily going to go anywhere, but these were the things her life had somehow led up to. She'd been meant to do something . . . explosive.

As I hurried toward Gril's truck, that was the word that played through my mind: *explosive*.

With that, it was the collateral damage I became more worried about. I muttered quietly to myself. "Please, Mill, don't . . ."

Gril didn't hear me. No one did. Gril steered us to Peter Murray's cabin.

Twelve

There was much to discuss, but Gril and I didn't talk as he drove into the woods. I could tell he was deep in thought and figured that if he had something he wanted to bring up, he'd do so. As it was, it was nice to have the downtime. I felt safe with him in the driver's seat, both of us inside the truck.

As furtively as possible, I took some deep breaths and tried to relax.

It might have taken about ten minutes for an old cabin to come into sight. When I saw it, I was motivated to finally speak.

"Oh, boy, that's . . . rough."

"It is. Peter's parents died fifteen or so years ago. He's been here all by himself since then."

"Did you know him well?"

Gril shook his head as he looked through the windshield at the cabin and put the truck into park. "I tried to get to know him. I thought he might want to be more a part of the community." He looked at me. "I was incorrect, at first. We got off on the wrong foot, and he told me to leave him alone. I'd told him I would be out to check on him every once and a while, but for a year he didn't even answer the door. One day, he did. I knocked and it swung open slowly, like in some scary movie or something." Gril smirked. "I went inside, and he was there, asked me if I wanted a glass of iced tea. I said I did, and we sat and talked for about an hour. I did that for about the last five years, at least every other week. He hadn't been home the last little bit, but I didn't chalk it up to much of anything, other than he just wasn't home when I stopped by. It happens." Gril frowned as he fell into thought.

"What did you talk about?"

"Nothing and everything."

"The best kind of conversations."

"Agreed." Gril bit his bottom lip. "Thing was, we gelled, you know. We were both men hiding from our previous lives"—he smiled at me—"a little like you, though maybe less extreme. Anyway, we talked about fishing, stupid politics, bears, all manner of things. The conversations were easy. He was a nice man, and when he disappeared, I worried about him."

"Did he seem like the type of man who would just run off to live at Blue Mine?"

"No. He was the type of man who'd head out on a temporary adventure, but he never struck me as wanting to be anywhere long term other than this place." Gril nodded out the windshield again. "It's not luxurious in there, Beth. It's messy and probably a little too dirty for your tastes, but it was his home, and it was where he wanted to live and, frankly, die."

"I feel like I know him a little now just from what you've said, and I'm sad he's gone."

"Me too." Gril sighed. "Come on, let's take a look, see if we can find anything that might help us understand what in the world happened."

"Okay."

"Although . . ."

"Yeah?"

"Beth, I haven't forgotten what we're doing. You are still priority number one."

I laughed, though I put my hand to my mouth because the noise sounded inappropriate. "I'm sorry. Thank you, Gril. I know and I appreciate everything you do, but, honestly, it's nice to have something else to think about, at least for a few minutes. I'm a little tired of me."

"I understand."

We hopped out of the truck, my feet landing on a foliage-covered gravel driveway. There was so much strewn greenery, probably from the recent storms, that I hadn't noticed we'd driven upon anything but mud and dirt.

"Oh," I said when noise crunched at my feet.

"Peter put the driveway in about three years ago. He got a four-wheeler and wanted something more stable."

"I don't see a four-wheeler."

"I don't, either."

"Gril, there is no way a four-wheeler would make it out to the village, at least the way Tex and I went."

"No, it wouldn't. We'll see if it's behind the house."

Gril led the way up a berm that would have been much easier to maneuver if there had been stairs. At the cabin's porch, he turned and extended a hand. I took it and let him pull me up.

"I don't think this meets building codes," I said.

"No, probably not."

Gril covered the short distance to the front door and pushed down on a handle that didn't have any sort of locking mechanism. He pushed the door so it slowly swung open, maybe just like it had the day Peter had finally welcomed him inside.

"Hello? Anyone here?" Gril called.

We were met with the type of silence that leaves little doubt— there was no one there.

"Come on in," Gril said over his shoulder. "This might be a crime scene of some sort, but it doesn't appear that way right off."

I walked into the cabin and immediately wondered why Gril thought it didn't look like a crime scene.

"This *is* messy."

"This is how it always looks."

There was furniture—a couch and a couple of chairs, but they weren't set up in a common sense way. The couch, covered in worn orange fabric, sat at an angle in a front corner. The two chairs didn't match—one was a wooden kitchen chair and the other a broken-down brown fabric recliner that couldn't possibly recline anymore. All surfaces were covered with clothes, blankets, or coffee mugs. I didn't see any other dishes, though.

That was just one half of the main space. The other half held an old-fashioned wood-burning stove, a sink with a pump, and a refrigerator.

"Electricity?" I asked.

"Nope. He usually kept that running with a generator."

In the middle of the entire space was the main selling point of the house, should Peter have ever wanted to put it on the market. A circular fireplace with an iron grate door. It might have been slightly too big for the space, but it was beautiful as it stretched to a vent in the ceiling, the length of the vent decorated with blue and yellow tiles.

"That is beautiful, but it can't possibly be meeting code either," I said.

"I doubt it, but he never burned the place down and it sure kept it toasty. His father built it."

"I've never seen anything like it."

Gril smiled sadly. "No, I don't suppose I have, either, and I've seen lots of precarious things."

I stepped closer to the fireplace and peered into its pit. "Soot, but not much, and I sense it's all cold and old."

"I thought the same a couple weeks back."

"Does anything appear to have changed since then?"

"Not offhand, but let's keep looking."

I stepped around a pile of dingy pillows on the ground and followed Gril to the kitchen.

"I've looked around some," he said as he reached into his back pocket, "but it's time to dig deep, Beth. Wear these and look into anything that can be looked into."

I took the gloves and snapped them on as if I were a doctor readying for surgery. "What am I looking for?"

"I have absolutely no idea," Gril said.

I nodded and got to work.

I began by opening a coat closet. I'd picked the one spot that was probably more packed than anything else. The space held multiple coats and other winter gear. A top shelf held stacks of hats, gloves, and scarves.

I took every single item out of the closet and searched each pocket. I found a total of seven dollars and sixty-three cents, and uncovered a pair of cross-country skis tucked in the back corner, seemingly unused for even longer than the fireplace. I reloaded the closet, tucking things in and hanging things up better than I'd found them.

I fought a few waves of sadness over Peter Murray's fate, but I didn't find anything in the closet that might explain why his life had ended.

I tackled the sparsely outfitted kitchen next, but there was nothing there, either.

"Do you suppose he just died, that he wasn't killed?" I asked Gril as I joined him in Peter's bedroom, where Gril had been lifting off the bedding and looking into the closet and a nightstand.

"It's a possibility, but at first glance, Dr. Powder doesn't think so."

I crossed my arms in front of myself. "Find anything in here?"

"Nothing, except a candy bar wrapper in the bed, but who doesn't enjoy a good Snickers midnight snack every now and then?"

I nodded. "Did Peter ever talk to you about his parents?"

Gril stopped rifling through the nightstand drawer and stood straight. "Sure."

"Why did they come out to Alaska?"

Gril sent me some raised eyebrows. "Gold. Or the promise of it."

"And it appears Peter died near a gold mine?"

"Exactly."

"Did he ever say anything specific about that mine?"

"No, never."

"That's too bad. That would be a solid lead."

"I agree." Gril sighed. "I haven't found one thing to help us here."

"Me either." I paused and then shrugged. "I didn't look under the couch. I think that's the one spot left."

"Give it a look. I'll spend a little more time in here, then we'll check out back for the four-wheeler as well as anything else."

As I walked down the hallway back to the front room, I caught the view out the front windows. It took my breath away.

As I'd noticed by the slope up to reach the porch, the house was set up on a hill of sorts. It faced out toward the woods, as well as the ocean. I'd had no idea we were that close to the water. The sun was high in the sky, but I knew it was moving toward the direction of the water. The sunsets, when they weren't hidden behind clouds, at least, were surely spectacular.

"Wow," I muttered to myself.

I walked to the windows and stood there, wondering if the view ever got old. I couldn't imagine it did. Movement caught my attention at about mid-distance between me and the ocean. I gasped and braced myself for the possibility of seeing someone, seeing Travis Walker again. Panic was my current default setting.

But it wasn't a person at all. It was a moose. I'd seen plenty of them, including one shortly after landing and deplaning at the Benedict airport. This one, a bull, was making his powerful yet graceful way through the trees. They were huge animals, intimidating and not to be approached in the wild, but I sure enjoyed watching them from a good safe distance. This one turned his head, moving his heavy antlers as easily as if they were one of the hats I'd recently repacked in Peter Murray's coat closet.

Even with all the trees and ground in between us, I thought our eyes made contact. He blinked and nodded, and so did I. I had no idea what we might be communicating to each other, but whatever it was, it was something good. Something right.

I decided I would ponder the moment later. I didn't think I'd be able to forget it.

The moose moved on, and I turned and made my way back to the couch. I got down on the floor and peered underneath. All I found was a layer of dust that wasn't quite thick enough to create bunnies but made me wish for a Swiffer.

Though I'd straightened the winter gear, Gril had made it clear that he didn't want us cleaning anything. There still might be clues in the dust, even if we had no idea what type of clues we were looking for.

I was flat on my stomach as I investigated under the couch. While I was down there, I took in the view of the room from this different angle.

At first, I didn't notice anything different, but after a quick sweep of my eyes over everything, something unexpected niggled at me.

I did another visual scan, this time slowly. And I found what had set off some internal bells. Underneath the pit part of the circular fireplace was an enclosed space, but I thought I might be seeing a seam in the sheet metal it was made of. It might be no big deal to have a door there. Maybe it opened to mechanisms that worked the fireplace. Nevertheless, it appeared to be the very last place to search.

I crawled over there and ran my finger along what was, in fact, a seam.

"Gril!" I called. "Come in here."

"On my way," he said as his footfalls hurried my direction. "Where . . . There you are."

Once he was on the ground next to me, I pointed. "A door?"

"Maybe."

He reached for the seam and pried open the metal. He shone the light from his phone inside the space.

"What have we here?" he said.

A thrill zipped through me. We had found something, I was sure of it.

Gril reached in and grabbed a thick stack of papers contained inside an old worn brown folder. Once it was out of there, he sat up and brushed a thin layer of dust off the top. Printed on the outside of the folder, in thick Magic Marker, were the words GOLD MINE.

"Um," Gril said.

"Um is right." I looked at him. "You and Peter never talked about anything like this?"

"No, we didn't." Gril lifted the file and carried it over to the wobbly kitchen table.

I followed behind. We both sat in the mismatched chairs, which also wobbled as Gril opened the file.

There were probably about a hundred pieces of paper inside. Some of them were receipts, but the items being bought and sold were unclear. Some of the papers were covered in hand-drawn and roughly sketched maps, but they weren't labeled with anything Gril or I recognized.

After looking at one a long moment, I said, "Could this be the *inside* of a mine?"

"Oh," he said. "It very well might be."

"Did Peter's family own a mine? *The* mine? Blue Mine?"

"I don't think so, Beth, but it's difficult to understand those particulars. I'll need to do some research."

"Peter went to claim his gold and they killed him?"

Gril shook his head sadly. "That suddenly seems like a real possibility, doesn't it? I wish he would have talked to me about this stuff."

"Me too."

Gril closed the file, giving it a hard thoughtful look before glancing back up at me. "We need to get back."

His decision seemed abrupt. "Are you worried about the others?"

Gril shook his head yet again. "I'm worried about everyone right now, Beth, but, yes, I think I need to see if Tex, Eddy, and Donner have returned."

"If they haven't?"

"I don't know. It hasn't been quite enough time, but I bet they were moving quickly. Maybe you'll have to come with me to rescue them."

"I'm game. Let's go."

Gril laughed once. "I didn't really mean that. . . ."

"Come on, Gril," I said. "Let's go see what's what."

Thirteen

Before we hurried away from Peter Murray's house with the file, we checked behind the cabin, looking specifically for the four-wheeler. An old shed stood out there but didn't hold much of anything—except for the four-wheeler. It appeared not to have been used for a while, but the key was in the ignition and Gril managed to fire it up before turning it off again.

"Peter didn't take the four-wheeler out to the mine." I stated the obvious.

"Apparently not. Good to know, I guess."

"It really wouldn't be an easy trip from what I saw. The path wasn't quite wide enough."

"No. There are other ways out there, but they take more time. I don't think any of them would be ATV friendly."

We left the four-wheeler where it was, and Gril drove us back to downtown. He walked me inside the Benedict House, making sure Viola knew I was there. Mill was making her way back just as he was leaving again. She was carrying bags of groceries.

"What's new?" she asked Gril as they passed each other in the doorway. Viola and I stood in the lobby.

"You tell me," Gril said. "Did you learn anything out there?"

"In fact, I did." Mill cleared her throat dramatically.

"Mill?" Gril said impatiently.

"The word about Peter Murray has gotten out."

"How?" Gril interjected.

"Believe it or not, I have that answer. Someone named Jemma Crew went to visit the doctor because of an infected cut. She was back in one of the exam rooms, waiting to get examined, when she heard the doctor and his wife talking from another room. She deduced that Peter Murray's dead body was in the other room."

"That's impressive. Thanks, Mill."

"You're welcome." She shrugged. "If you want to know what's going on around here, all you need to do is pick a place and hang out a while. I spent time in the café, in the bar, and in the mercantile, and just listened. I learned a lot of other stuff, but none of it relevant. Well, except maybe one more thing."

Again, she put a dramatic pause into her story, though she didn't clear her throat this time.

"Mill?" Gril said again, more impatiently.

"Someone named Chris Mesh or maybe Mess was talking in the bar. She said she saw something weird in the storm last night, some guy just walking around out there. She admitted that kind of thing happens, but most people hunker down during storms. This guy, dressed all in black winter gear including a ski mask, was wandering around, almost as if he was just out for a walk. She asked if anyone knew who it might have been, but no one claimed to know."

"Really?" I said.

Mill nodded at Gril. "Do you know where Chris lives?"

"Of course." Gril shared a look with Viola and then turned back to Mill. "Not far from Shane's place."

"Isn't that where the body was?" Mill said. She might not have been awake for last night's activities, but she'd caught up.

"Yes."

Everyone looked at me. I knew what they were wondering, mostly because I was wondering it, too. Was the man I saw Travis

Walker or wasn't he? I'd seen the silhouette of the Bigfoot, too. I sure was seeing a lot of weird things.

I couldn't help but think, was it possible this was all one man? Without waiting for any of them to give voice to the questions, I shook my head.

"I don't know, but it's good to know someone else might have seen the guy I thought I did."

"Do you still *think* it was Walker last night?" Mill asked.

I shook my head slowly. "I have absolutely no idea, but I think it's unlikely. If I was sure, I'd feel sure. Wouldn't I?"

Mill shrugged. "Maybe. Maybe not."

"I gotta go," Gril said. "My plan is to be back as quickly as possible. I'm taking Jin's horse, which should speed things up, and get the horse back to where it belongs."

"Jin said the horse couldn't do the terrain with a rider," I said.

Gril squinted. "That's not correct if you choose the right route, but that tells me something else—now I know which way Jin probably went."

I thought back to our time together with Jin. Tex had been suspicious of her from the beginning, but he had never gone into detail and then she disappeared so quickly. But something else altogether occurred to me.

"Gril, is everyone all going different directions out there?"

"Maybe." Gril shrugged, but he noticed the look on my face. "Beth, they're all going to be fine. If anyone knows what they're doing out there, it's Tex and Donner. I promise they are okay. And Eddy's with Donner. He couldn't be in better hands."

Mill huffed a laugh. "Oh, Gril, don't make promises you aren't sure you can keep."

Gril leveled his gaze at Mill. "I'm sure."

Viola had been quiet through their exchange. "What did you bring us?" she finally asked Mill.

"Groceries. Who wants to cook them?"

"We'll figure it out." Viola took the bags. "Thank you for the information." She turned to Gril. "Be careful and be back soon."

"Will do." Gril left, closing the door behind him.

"I'll cook. We will all eat, together in the dining room, and stay here the rest of the evening." Viola transferred the bags to her other arm and then made her way to the front door. She locked the bolt, something she hadn't done much of before but seemed to be doing a lot lately.

"Yes, ma'am," Mill said.

I was surprised there was not one note of sarcasm in her voice.

"What can I do to help?" I asked.

"You can peel or chop something. We'll see what we have." Viola turned and made her way to the kitchen.

"I don't suppose I can run out for a quick smoke?" Mill said before Viola disappeared through the doorway.

"Nope."

"Shit. I should have grabbed one before coming in," Mill muttered.

"Yes, you should have," Viola called. "Come on, ladies. We've got things to discuss."

Mill and I shared a look, our eyebrows rising.

"What do you suppose we need to discuss?" she asked me quietly.

"The potential list is long. Let's find out."

Mill, Gus, and I followed Viola's path.

I soon understood Viola's main goal for having the dinner. Well, keeping us together in one spot was important—she could protect us all much better that way. But the real goal was to talk, even if neither Mill nor I were very good at such a thing.

I'd been in therapy for about six months now. My therapist was located in Spokane, Washington, and specialized in my sort of trauma, specifically the trauma that comes from being taken against one's will. I'd been surprised to hear it was a real specialty.

Leia was great and so subtle that there were moments away from our Zoom meetings when a light came on in my mind and I realized what she'd done there. She'd helped a lot, and I could probably benefit from some time with her every week or so for the rest of my life.

Mill's childhood years were a mystery to me. She never talked about growing up. I might have asked her about it at some point, but I couldn't remember doing so. There might have come a point when I didn't bother anymore.

I'd learned more about her from her father, and even that wasn't much. My grandfather, Dusty Sherwood, had been Milton, Missouri's police chief for most of Mill's life and all of mine. He'd been the best man I'd ever known, taking me under his wing after my father left and attempting to let Mill know how bad a mother she was without actually telling her as much. None of his words were enough to change her behavior. I'd discussed these nuances plenty with Leia. Both she and I gave credit to my grandfather for intervening with his own form of therapy, which was made up of him spending time with me and listening to whatever it was I wanted to say. Protecting me, loving me, letting me be myself.

Still, though, I had some resentments, and for a reason I couldn't understand, it sure seemed that Viola wanted me to air them—*that* night at *that* dinner. I wanted to ask her why, what her purpose was, but when I sent her the questions with my eyes, she didn't respond other than with an expectant gaze that told me to "let it all out—now."

Viola sparked the conversation by being blunt. "Okay, ladies," she said with her hands on her hips, "we need to resolve your issues now, tonight."

Mill and I looked at each other.

"We don't have any issues," Mill said.

Both Viola and I gave my mother scrutinous gazes. Mill caught mine.

"You have issues with me?" she said with genuine uncertainty in her tone.

I hesitated to answer, but Viola's eyes were pushing me forward. "Well. Mill, my childhood was unusual, to say the least."

"*Pftt*. That was your dad's fault."

"Okay, but . . . well, we didn't have to spend so many years searching for him."

"I thought you enjoyed it."

I guessed we were doing this. "Um. Well, I enjoyed traveling with you, but breaking into houses might have been a bit much."

Mill's head moved back and forth as if she was weighing my words. "We never hurt anyone."

"Your father was a police chief, and you were breaking and entering."

"He never knew."

"He knew lots more than he let on. He didn't say it out loud because he knew he would probably have to arrest you. Breaking and entering, even if you don't hurt anyone, is against the law."

"Sure, but I wouldn't have done it if your father hadn't left."

"I think you need to quit blaming him," I said, the volume of my voice rising a little. I cleared my throat. Was that part of my issue? Was I mad at her for *blaming* Eddy? But I was mad at Eddy, too.

Shit.

"How can I not blame him? It was his fault."

I gathered words from somewhere, though I didn't know if they came from my sessions with Leia or some long-ago buried stuff. "You could have chosen to focus on us, the two of us and the family we still were instead of chasing after a missing husband." I paused and my finger moved to my chest. That's where I felt . . . whatever it was I was feeling.

Viola was now working in the kitchen. "That's what I'm talking about," she called.

Mill looked at me with genuine surprise and curiosity. To her credit, for the most part she'd never been someone to blame her mistakes on someone else. She did blame my father, but that wasn't because she wasn't *willing* to take responsibility. It was just the way she saw it. However, the look on her face told me that she was digesting my words, and that they were new words, new ideas to her.

"Well, shit, Beth," she said after a long few moments. "Huh."

"Mom . . ."

Mill held up her hand and sent me a quick, weak smile. "I just need a minute."

Viola came from the kitchen with a big bowl of pasta and set it on the table. "This is going well."

I matched my mother's smile as I looked at Viola, who seemed pleased with herself.

"You know," Mill said, "Your gramps told me I was messing up, but I didn't see it that way. Until this moment, I'm not sure I could see anything that I'd done wrong. Now, though, I feel like while I should blame your father some, maybe I didn't make the best decisions, either."

I reached for the serving utensils inside the bowl because I wasn't sure what to say next. Also, I thought if I tried to speak I might ruin the moment and Mill would change her mind about her responsibility. Or, I'd do what I felt like I should do, tell her it was all good, that she hadn't done anything wrong, play the dutiful daughter. Leia had helped me get past that tendency.

Viola and I had filled our plates and dug into the pasta carbonara she'd thrown together when Mill finally blinked back into the moment.

"Well, then," she said as she, too, reached for a serving spoon. "I'm so sorry, Beth. I truly am."

I chewed and held back tears that burned behind my eyes. It was silly to cry about such a thing, but it was an emotional moment. Thankfully, Mill saved it from going too far.

"Don't get me wrong." She pointed at me with her fork. "I am sorry, but your father was the true jackass here."

"I do not disagree," Viola added. "But here we are, all together, and that was good, Mill."

"In Alaska, of all places," Mill said.

"In Alaska," I said with a nod. "Thank you, Mill. I accept your apology."

"You can't see it coming," Mill spoke one of the thoughts I had frequently had in this strange new life I'd been living.

"Nope. You sure can't." I twirled the pasta around my fork.

As I lay in my bed that night, staring at the ceiling and listening to Gus snore again, I pondered the redemption dinner. That was all it had taken for something inside me to shift. It wasn't a huge change. I had mostly forgiven my mother a long time ago, my time with Leia only assisting with easing any bad feelings. But tonight, there'd been another small shift, and it broke more of that "good girl" bond I'd still hung onto for a while.

I didn't need to make my mother feel better about any of her behavior. We were two individuals, made of human things like making mistakes. But each of us owned our own.

Of course, Viola knew we needed it. She'd run away from Juneau to Benedict when she was a child. Like me, her formal education hadn't extended past high school, but she was one of the most intelligent, informed, and insightful people I'd ever known.

I didn't think I'd be able to sleep. I had so much on my mind and had so much I felt like I needed to get done. I was worried about everyone out in the woods and wished them home. I wanted Travis Walker stopped.

But just as I was wondering if I was ever going to sleep again, I fell right into some deep and only slightly disturbing dreams.

Fourteen

was awakened by Gus's nose on the bed.

"Good morning," I said as I smiled. "What time is it?"

I reached for my phone. I'd slept in until nine. I looked at Gus again.

"Oh, that felt good, but I bet you need to go out."

I hopped out of bed and threw myself together. Once I stepped out into the hallway, I sensed something wasn't right.

I stopped by Mill's room, knocking first and then opening it wide. She wasn't inside and her bed was made.

"Mill?" I called down the hallway as I shut the door.

There was no answer. "Come on, boy."

Gus and I hurried down the hallway toward the other leg of the building. The kitchen and dining room were empty of people, but there was a plate of blueberry muffins sitting on a table as well as a smell of coffee in the air that made my mouth water, but I didn't stop there.

"Viola?" I called.

I knocked on her door, too. There was no answer there, either. I didn't usually just open her door, but I did this morning, finding it empty but her bed put together.

I hurried to her office, relieved to find a note. I read it out loud.

"'Beth—I took Gus out already. I'm running out to see if anyone is back yet. Your mom is here, but don't go anywhere. I won't be gone long. You might be interested in the stuff in the file, though. Gril brought it by for me to look through. Read all you want.'" She'd noted the time she'd written it, which was about half an hour ago.

The note had been placed atop the folder that Gril and I had taken from Peter Murray's house. I wanted to look through it, but I wanted to track down my mother first.

I hurried back down the hallway and checked her room again. It wasn't easy to hide in the small space. The bathroom door was open, proving that was empty, too. I didn't check under the bed, but I knew she wouldn't be there. Unless she was put there.

A horrific scenario played through my mind, and I fell to the ground. Relief spread through me when I saw only a plastic zipped storage container with thick winter quilts underneath.

Gus had gone to his belly and was looking, too. He whined at me.

"It's okay." I petted his head. "She's probably out front having a smoke."

Gus seemed to think that was a viable option.

We both stood again and made our way to the front door. I wasn't supposed to go anywhere, and I figured that even meant I shouldn't step outside. Nevertheless, I opened the door a crack and peered out one side, moved and then peered out the other.

"No Mill," I said to Gus. "As stir-crazy as I think I'm going to go in here, I am not going out there."

Gus thought that was a smart plan. I closed and relocked the door, which made me wonder how Mill had gotten a key—because I was sure I had unlocked this door before looking out.

I shook my head. Mill was the most restless soul I knew. Of course she wasn't hanging around waiting for me to wake up.

"Come on, I have another idea."

We padded back to Viola's office, where a rare creature, a landline phone, sat on the desk. I lifted the handset, always happy to hear a dial tone, and dialed the bar.

"This is Benny," Benny answered.

"Hey, it's Beth."

"Hi. Um, where are you? I thought you were out of town, but I can't keep up with whatever is going on around here."

"I'm in the Benedict House. My mother came back to town."

"I thought I saw her!"

"Where? I mean, this morning?"

"No, yesterday. I'm glad she's okay. Why are you in town? Was that guy found?"

"Not yet. I hate to bother you, Benny, but could you look outside and see if my mom is anywhere out there?"

She hesitated a second, probably wondering why I couldn't handle this task on my own but knowing enough that maybe no request was too off base.

"Sure. Hang on a sec."

I waited as I heard Benny put down the phone and leave her back room. I was tempted to peek out the front door and wave at her, but that might be even stranger than what I'd asked her to do. She came back a moment later.

"No one out there," she said. "Oh, Orin's here. He's been asking me what I've heard about things, but evidently, I don't know much. Can I send him over to talk to you?"

"Of course. Tell him I have coffee and blueberry muffins."

"Viola's blueberry muffins?"

"Yes. I'll have him bring one back to you when we're done visiting."

"I'll take two if there's enough."

"Deal."

We ended the call and I made my way to the front door again. I was anxious, wondering about my mother and wishing Viola had just woken me and taken me with her. Nevertheless, I was thrilled to see Orin.

I opened the door a crack again and watched him make his way. A Willie Nelson look-alike who always smelled like weed because of how he handled the pain from a back injury. Thin and wiry, he wasn't as young as he used to be when he was running secret government missions. Although he was "retired" now, he still had valuable contacts and even participated in covert operations, though just those that require minimum physical involvement.

After he came inside, I shut the door as Gus greeted him happily.

"Hey, boy." He returned Gus's enthusiasm with ear scratches. He looked at me. "What are you doing here? What's going on? You aren't supposed to be here, and I can't find Gril."

"Would you mind taking Gus out one more time before breakfast? Then I'll tell you everything."

"Sure."

Orin and Gus were quick about it, returning only a few minutes later.

Over muffins and lots of coffee, I shared with Orin everything that had gone on over the last few days—including thinking I saw Bigfoot as well as Travis Walker.

"What?" I nudged after he silently seemed to be processing my words.

"Of everything you've said, I'm most shocked and sad about Peter Murray and concerned about the potential Walker spotting."

"Not Bigfoot?"

"Well, only if it's Travis pretending to be one. I've seen plenty of those over the years."

"Real ones?"

"No, but lots of people have used the disguise to try to pull off something else. They wanted to scare someone or something. I don't like what's going on at Blue Mine, and I'm heartbroken about Peter Murray, but I think there needs to be a daytime search of the area where you think you saw Walker."

"I think Gril would like to do that, but he had to get to the others back here. Or . . . well, I don't know exactly what he's doing, but I was instructed to stay here. He said he was taking Jin's horse back out there."

"Jin. *Hmm.*"

"Do you know her?"

"Not even a little bit. Do you know her full name?"

I thought back to when Tex introduced us. "No, but her husband's name is or was Brick depending on whether he's alive or not."

"Let me see what I can find out about her, and the rest of them at the village, too. That place is weird, but there are many weird places around."

"I'm stuck here. I haven't heard the news. I know Walker's escape is *old* news by now, but have you heard anything?"

"I've been monitoring and I'm in touch with Detective Majors—"

"You are?"

"Of course. I keep Gril up to date, too."

"That's great. Okay, so what's new?"

"There have been no verified spottings of him, though the police in Missouri are getting calls every day that he's been seen somewhere."

"Fake?"

"As far as they can tell, yes, fake, but the sheer volume of calls keeps them concerned that they're missing a valid lead. They've hired two new officers just to do initial follow-up on the leads."

"Well, I suppose that's being vigilant."

"I agree." Orin didn't sound happy about it.

"What aren't you telling me?"

"I didn't know your mother was here, either. The police are looking for her, too, and there've been Mill sightings in Missouri as well. Not as many as Walker, but still."

"And Mill's here, at least in town, so everything is pretty much just a mess."

Orin's mouth twisted before he said, "Maybe." He rebounded. "However, I'm very glad your mother is here. I think that's good."

"Wild-card Mill? You're glad?"

"Sure, but the reasons aren't altruistic at all, Beth. She's gutsy and if Walker's here . . ."

"She'll take the fall if something happens to him?"

"That's not as neighborly as I should be."

I laughed. "Orin, she wants to take the fall. I'm not great with her doing so, but if we keep the Juneau authorities out of here, I hope we *can* just get things taken care of." I cringed. "Not that I condone vigilantism."

Orin frowned. "I hear you. I really do."

We sat together for a beat or two in silence, both of us in our own thoughts.

"Oh!" I finally said. "I have a file."

"Okay?"

"Hang on." I hurried back to Viola's office and grabbed Peter Murray's file from her desk.

"What have we here?" Orin said as I sat and placed the file on the table between us.

"This is the file I found under Peter's fireplace."

"Oh. You buried the lede. No, I take that back, there are so many high points, it's impossible to know where to begin. What's in here?"

"I've only taken a cursory glance. Let's see what we find."

"Absolutely." Orin opened the file.

One of the sketches that we thought might be a map or the layout of a mine was on the top of the pile. Orin studied it and then moved it to the side as we went through the other pages.

I wanted to inventory the items. Since I didn't have an eidetic memory like Orin did, I gathered a notebook and a pen. Once we went through all the papers, Orin separated them into piles on the table.

What we found:

There were seventy-three pieces of paper in the folder.

1. Fourteen sketches of what Orin decided were indeed details of a mine. Only one mine. Orin put the drawings in the order he guessed they'd been created, which was basically

from least detailed to most detailed. He didn't know if it was Blue Mine or some other one. There was no label.

2. Thirty pieces of paper were receipts that spanned three decades. The first one was dated August of 1989 and the most recent one was dated four months ago. All of them were for equipment and gear, though not all of it mining, some just camping. One was for the four-wheeler. Peter had purchased it two years ago in Juneau, and it had cost him $5,225.00. He must have brought it over on the ferry.

3. There were twelve copies of pictures inside the file. Verified by Orin, they were pictures of Peter and his parents over the first sixteen years of his life before they died.

4. Four pieces of paper held unclear notes, one of them saying, "Television show from early sixties." Another said, "Roaming is knowing."

5. Finally, the last thirteen pieces were covered in what must have been Peter's handwriting, probably written shortly after he lost his parents. They were the words of a young person in a lot of pain and were too difficult and felt too personal to read. Nevertheless, we did. Every word.

"Well, that was awful," Orin said when we'd finished.

I sniffed away a few tears. "He was so heartbroken."

"I wasn't here yet, but I heard about the tragedy. I tried to get to know him, but just a little. He was not welcoming to company."

"That's what Gril said. He finally made headway about a year ago, though." I put my hand over the journal pages and took a moment to send peace out into the universe for Peter Murray. "Orin, there's nothing here about *owning* a mine. How does one own a mine in the wilds of Alaska anyway? Did his parents pay for one? Did he? Gril said they had enough in their bank account to allow Peter to live in the house just fine. He was sixteen when they died but everyone just left him alone."

"That's not unusual. If folks thought he was okay, no one would want to cause him more hassle."

"Yeah, I've noticed. It's both good and bad."

"Better than being all bad, I say." Orin took a breath. "So, yes, you can buy a mine in Alaska. They aren't cheap, though. Last I researched, I think they were a quarter to a half million dollars. Offhand, I don't know what they were back in the late eighties, early nineties. I will look, though. I will see if I can find a record of ownership anywhere. There's a chance the Murrays just moved out here and found a mine on their own, dug without doing any sort of proper paperwork or paying for anything."

"How long could someone get away with that out here?"

"Depends. Our law enforcement was pretty bad when the Murrays got here. They would have taken bribes. I'm sure they did. Maybe the Murrays bribed them. I will look at that, too."

"I'm not fond of sticking around here all day. I'd like to do some of my own research. Maybe Viola would let me come to the library."

"I could protect you." In what had become a signature move of his, Orin flexed his thin wiry arm. He didn't carry weapons, claiming that that wasn't his specialty.

I smiled. "I have no doubt."

The front door opened.

"Viola? Mill? Orin and I are in the dining room," I called out.

Viola came around and without greeting Orin said, "Where's your mother?"

"I don't know."

"Shit. Again?"

"I don't know. Is anyone back yet?"

"No, not yet."

"What's up, Viola? You know they can all take care of themselves," Orin said.

Viola nodded.

"Are you worried about Mill?" Orin asked.

"Kind of."

Orin and I shared a look.

"What's going on?" I asked. "What did you find out there?"

"Nothing. Really."

"That doesn't sound like nothing-nothing," Orin said.

Viola considered us and then sat down in a chair. She looked at me. "I drove around the area where you thought you saw Walker."

"Oh. And?" I tried to keep my voice level, but it wasn't easy.

"I saw a tent."

My heart sunk into my stomach. "Oh. Okay. More validation that I did see someone."

Orin put his hand over mine on the table. "That doesn't necessarily mean anything. There are some tents out there sometimes."

"I know, but I did see someone, that much I'm sure of. I just . . . I don't know. Did you explore the tent?"

Viola nodded with too much vehemence. "There was a receipt in the pack with a lantern. It was purchased from a store in St. Louis."

"That's . . ."

"Good!" Orin interjected. Viola and I looked at him. "If we know it's him, we can take care of him."

The front door swung open. I jumped at the sound and Viola jetted out of her chair to peer into the hallway. I watched her body relax a little.

"Mill, where'd you go?"

"Out for a smoke."

"I asked you not to leave."

"It was just a smoke. Or six."

"Come in here. We need to talk."

"Yes, ma'am."

It appeared that another plan was in the works.

Fifteen

Orin suggested that we move to his house. It was a fortress, or at least it could be. He didn't "arm" everything all the time, but he could. He was sure we'd be safer there. Voila decided that was a brilliant plan and wondered aloud why we hadn't thought of it before.

However, Orin had to run to the library first to make sure someone could watch and then lock up the place later. Viola already had a key to his place. That's what people did around Benedict, share their house keys with those they could trust. So much was done in Benedict in the name of "just in case," and though Orin wasn't quite as active as he used to be in his top-secret world, if he was called to action, there was always a chance he wouldn't make it back. The risk came with the job, he'd say with a shrug.

"It seems like a key to a fortress wouldn't just look like a regular key," I said as I noted the one Viola found on her key ring.

"Well, that key just unlocks the front door," Orin said. "The good stuff is on the inside and I don't have all of those keys."

He gave Viola a rearming code and then took off. As he was leaving, Mill asked if she could smoke in his house. He told her no and she sighed heavily.

"Pack some bags, ladies. Grab Gus's stuff, too," Viola said.

We did exactly that. It was only fifteen minutes later that we piled into Viola's truck.

As she drove toward Orin's, I realized we were also headed toward the area where I thought I'd seen Walker.

"Could we drive by the tent?" I asked.

"No," Viola said. "You won't be able to see it the direction I'm going."

Mill turned to me. "If that bozo is here, Bethie, you need to get behind those fortress walls. He's a slippery mother." She paused. "Viola, will he know anything about Orin's place? I mean, the news story about Beth showed Benedict's downtown and made it clear where she lived, but do people just know about Orin's place?"

"Yes, but the community won't tell much of anything to any stranger."

"The word is out locally then?"

"The word is out in the world," Viola said. "Walker's escape was a big news story."

"No, yeah, I mean, does everyone know that he's threatened to come here? I don't remember that part being in the news. His note. I knew he'd be up to something, but I didn't learn about the note until you guys told me."

"We haven't shared the news about the note."

"And, someone who bought a lantern in St. Louis is out here camping in the woods?"

"It appears so."

"Well, that's not Travis," Mill continued.

"What makes you say that?" Viola asked as I looked at my mother.

"Travis Walker isn't going to buy any sort of camping gear, either here or in St. Louis."

"You don't think so?" I said.

"No, he's a primitive sort. If he can't have his van, he'll find an-other one, or some shitty vehicle that will get him where he needs to go, but he's not going to prepare like most people would. He doesn't think that way."

I pondered that. Somewhere along the way—probably because of my therapy with Leia—something changed in the way I thought about my days in Travis's van. Right after my time in the hospital and when I first came to Benedict, I didn't remember them. But as time went on, everything came back to me—or at least I thought it was everything. As Leia had pointed out, "You might not remember what you don't remember." When things started swimming up to the surface at first, I would look at the memories with trepidation. I didn't want to give in to them because they were painful. They were still pretty terrible, but now I could think about them without too much anxiety.

I allowed my thoughts to run through that time frequently. I did it now. My mother was correct—Travis Walker was, in his mind, self-reliant and able to improvise.

"I think you're right," I said.

"I know I'm right."

Viola asked, "Do you think you know who is out there?"

"I think it's a . . ."

Mill and Viola spoke at the same time. "Copycat."

"What?" I said.

"Or a hero wannabe," Mill said.

"Yeah. I hear you," Viola said.

"Let me at him. I'll get it figured out," Mill said.

Viola shook her head. "Nope. We're going underground, so to speak, until others return."

"This guy is living some delusion," Mill continued. "He needs to be stopped even if he thinks he's not out to do harm."

Viola nodded. "You might be right. I'll check it out after I get you two to Orin's."

A part of me wished I was with the others. Investigating whatever was going on out there seemed better than sitting around thinking about myself. But hiding at Orin's certainly sounded safer, though I was beginning to have doubts about this plan. It felt too locked away, too reactive instead of proactive.

"His eyes," I said. "They sure looked like Walker's."

"Maybe he knows that and is using it to his twisted advantage." Mill *tsk*ed and shook her head. "People are nutsaroni."

"Yes, they are," Viola added. She looked at Mill quickly in the mirror. "I'll let you do your thing when some of the others get back. Until then, stick with us. Stop smoking for now."

"Well, that sounds awful, but I'll do as you ask." She hesitated. "Or I'll try my best."

"I suppose that's *all* I can ask."

Mill sent me a nod full of promise and confidence. I saw that the fingers on her smoking hand twitched. She hadn't run away. She had just been taking a break. She sounded more sincere than I remembered her ever sounding. She was trying.

I appreciated it, even as I still didn't quite trust it all the way.

Surprisingly, Viola grumbled and then turned the steering wheel. "Yeah, I think we'll take a quick look." She looked at Mill again. "I don't want you out here on your own, and I don't want to leave the two of you alone at Orin's."

"Nice. Thank you, Viola," Mill said, a smile to her voice.

It was unlike Viola to change her mind about much of anything. I studied her profile. She was concerned, but about which problem I couldn't be sure, and I didn't ask. I was glad we were taking a look, too.

In response to Mill, she grumbled again.

"It's not too muddy," I offered as the truck bounced over the uneven ground.

"Yeah, not too bad, mud-wise. Hold on." Viola's attention was on the narrow path ahead.

I'd been down a few of these types of byways—not a road but a natural break in the woods that someone had taken advantage of to create access for themselves and anyone else who came along.

This one was the kind that forced you to hold on to something so you didn't suffer whiplash or a slipped disc in your back.

"Yeehaw!" Mill called.

Viola slowed the truck. "Here we are."

I had to follow the direction of her gaze to notice the tent. It was well hidden behind thick trees, but a flash of canvas finally caught my eye.

There was no sign of anyone.

"Stay here." Viola moved the truck into Park.

"You sure?" Mill asked. "Beth can stay here, lock the doors. Let me come with you."

Under any other circumstances, Viola would have told Mill no, but today she nodded. "Let's go."

As Mill got out, I jumped out, too.

"Beth?" Mill said. Viola just looked at me.

"I'm not going to sit in a truck alone. I don't care what either of you order me to do," I said.

Mill nodded. So did Viola, but the look on her face was more displeased than Mill's. She sighed and turned to lead the way to the tent. Mill, Gus, and I followed behind.

"Hello!" Viola called. "Who's in the tent? Show yourself. We're Benedict police," she lied.

No one responded.

We took high steps, lifting our legs because of the thick brush and the wet earth underneath it all. It was messy out here, but I'd seen it worse.

Viola stopped and looked at Mill and me. "Give me just a minute to do the initial check. Join me in a second. If something happens to me, get in the truck and get the hell out of here."

"Yes, ma'am," Mill said immediately.

I nodded, but I didn't want anything to happen to Viola, to anyone. I told myself to keep it together.

Viola drew one of her guns and high-stepped it toward the tent. "Who's there?"

Again, no one answered.

"No one's here," Mill said quietly. I didn't think she was speaking to anyone but herself. Her eyes scrutinized the entire area.

Viola unzipped the flap, and Mill and I moved up beside her.

"Any bodies in there?" Mill asked.

"Nope. Neither alive nor dead."

Viola had retrieved a flashlight from one of her pockets and was shining it inside. Mill and I peered over her shoulders.

The tent was full of supplies similar to what Tex and I had set up during our own camping, though Tex had owned most of our items for at least a few years, some since he'd been a kid. At first glance, I could tell that the items in this tent—the tent itself, too—were all new, still shiny and without the wear and tear of use, even after being set up through at least one bad storm.

One sleeping bag, two lanterns, two small lockboxes probably packed with food, and a folded-away green cooker with a matching coffeepot sat in a corner.

The sleeping bag was rumpled, not rolled up for the day's hike like Tex and I had done in the mornings.

"There's a water bottle in there," Mill noted.

Behind the pillow at the far end of the tent was, indeed, a half-empty water bottle.

"Yeah." Viola continued to move the light around.

"I'm going to go get it just in case DNA is needed at some point," Mill said.

She moved past me and Viola, who didn't stop her. So as not to make a mess with any gunk on her boots, Mill went down on her hands and knees and crawled ten feet to the back. Once there, she didn't immediately retrieve the bottle. Instead, she lifted the sleeping bag, ruffling it a little. Then she grabbed the pillow, which made crinkle noises.

"What have we here?" She peered inside the pillowcase.

Viola didn't stop her from doing any of it.

"What's there?" Viola asked.

Mill dumped the papers onto the sleeping bag. Even from my vantage point at the flap, I could tell what had been inside the pillowcase: copies of newspaper articles. Though I couldn't immediately see the specifics, I caught a glimpse of a picture. My hair before its new haircut. Me after Travis had been arrested and my story had been spread widely.

"All about Beth," Mill said.

"From what newspaper?"

Mill examined the mastheads then looked up at us. "All of them are from *The Kansas City Star.*"

"That's pretty close to St. Louis, right?" Viola said.

"Four hours up I-70. I've done the trip a time or two," Mill answered.

I had been to Kansas City, too, but I didn't comment. I swallowed hard. I'd been fine a few minutes earlier, able to think about my days with Travis without completely freaking out. As I looked at the articles on the sleeping bag, though, I shuddered. Why did someone have a pillowcase full of articles about me?

"Just about me?" I managed to say without sounding strange.

"Yep. They go back a little." Mill set the approximately twenty articles out on the sleeping bag. "To when your first book hit it big."

I nodded. I'd been lucky with my first book, and the subsequent ones had managed to do just as well, if not better. Lots of people like to read scary stuff. I liked to write it, but living it wasn't as much fun.

"Well, that's creepy as shit," Viola said.

Mill shrugged. "I don't know. These aren't the actual newspapers, just copies. If this person has been obsessed with Beth for a long time, they'd probably be the genuine articles, maybe inside a scrapbook. These are recent copies. I'm deducing that someone has a hero complex, not an obsession with her."

"Sounds like a criminal profile," Viola said.

"I've studied."

Viola and I looked at Mill, our eyebrows furrowed.

"Well, YouTube. You can learn about anything on YouTube."

"Right," Viola said.

"Nonetheless, this person is here because of me or for me, or something. It seems pretty obvious," I said.

"And he got to save you in the river," Viola said.

"I bet that made his day," Mill added flatly. She looked up. "This isn't Travis, Beth. I'm sure of it."

I nodded.

"In fact . . . Well, it's too bad we can't talk to him. He might be odd, but I bet he'd calm down if he met you."

"I'm not thrilled about that plan," I said.

Mill shrugged. "I'm just saying, I really don't think this guy is violent. Something's not . . . I can't make all the pieces fit, but I'll think about it." She looked at Viola. "Should we stay out here and wait for him? I can just stay by myself. I can find my way back."

Viola looked at me and then Mill again. "Let's get to Orin's. We'll regroup. You're not staying out here alone, Mill."

Mill didn't argue and exited the tent. We all looked around as we made our way to the truck. There was still no sign of anyone. At the truck, we stopped and took another moment to listen, too, noticing no unusual noises, nothing that sounded as if someone was nearby.

I had Mill and Viola with me so I wasn't overly bothered, but a little leftover panic buzzed through my limbs. However, Mill hadn't lied. She wasn't making up a story about her "profile." If she'd thought anything different, she'd've said so.

We hopped back into the truck and made our way to Orin's.

Sixteen

Viola let us into Orin's house and then went through the motions of arming it. She knew what code to key into Orin's main post to make all the doors and windows lock with swooshing and clanking noises. The computer's middle of three screens displayed views from different outdoor cameras. We could see anyone approach from any angle.

"Paranoid much?" Mill shrugged. "I mean, I like it, but . . ."

"It's helpful," Viola said. "Orin made sure that Gril, Donner, and I knew the ins and outs around here. This place even has a safe room. I can't believe we didn't just send you over here, Beth."

"I can't believe you know computers so well," I said.

Viola shrugged. "It helps to have a connection better than dial-up."

"I see that."

Hiding at Orin's hadn't even been discussed, and I was sure Viola remembered the plans we'd talked about as well as I did. The plan was that Tex and I would leave for a bit and ultimately someone would take Travis down, possibly kill him. I wasn't sure I was a fan of this new plan of hiding. I loved Orin's place, but I didn't think this was where I belonged.

Everyone else sure seemed to think it was a good idea.

All of this, everything about what Travis had done to me, had to end. It was long past time for all of this to be over. But this didn't feel like the right way to accomplish it. I'd left town with Tex to get away and hide, sure, but it was also supposed to give me time to think through possibilities and options. Though so many other things had interrupted any thinking about me I'd needed to do, my subconscious had been working on the problem.

"I don't think I want to be in a safe room," I said. "Sounds claustrophobic."

"Yeah, me neither," Mill said.

"I don't think anyone will force anyone into a safe room, but it's a good option to have on the table." Viola scanned the screen with the camera views.

"Viola, I'm not sure about this," I said.

She looked at me. "Why? It's the safest option."

I realized something then that rattled me. I didn't want to take the safest route. It was a ridiculous notion because who doesn't want to be safe? I needed to understand it myself better before I tried to tell Viola, so I just said, "I'm not sure."

Viola nodded and turned her attention back to the screen.

I could tell Mill was feeling the same way I was. It might be laughable that she and I were on the same page here, but there wasn't much humor to be found.

The rest of the house's main level included a kitchen and living room. Machine parts were scattered everywhere, leaving the scent of a mechanic's garage throughout. It reminded me of my grandfather's tinkering on his cars, and I wondered if Mill felt the same.

The middle level of the three-story home was less cluttered and held three bedrooms. The top floor was a great place to relax, maybe watch the big-screen television or play some of the old-fashioned video games, like Pac-Man and Asteroids. Asteroids was my favorite.

"Can we head out onto the roof? I noticed a satellite dish up there and it seemed mostly flat," Mill asked.

"Sure," Viola said.

I'd been on the roof. Mill was in for a treat. Viola led the way up the last flight of stairs. There was a ladder up and through a hatched door that wasn't attached to the alarm system. We left Gus in the recreation room and climbed up the ladder. Once we were all through the hatch, Viola pointed out that the door was camouflaged and you had to know where to grab or you would have no idea that it's there.

"There's a fire pole down the side if you're adventurous." Viola nodded toward the back of the room where there was, indeed, a fire pole.

"He's a regular James Bond," Mill said, though her tone was still doubtful.

Mill liked Orin, had even told me she was glad I had someone like him in my life, but she was naturally suspicious and never subtle.

Viola and I shared a look at Mill's tone. I shook my head, hoping to relay that Mill was just being Mill. Viola nodded.

Not only was the home three stories tall, but it also sat atop a small hill. It had been designed as a fortress, but, according to Orin, not because a fortress was needed, it was just the way he knew how to do things. He'd been trained to put safety first. This was ultimate safety, though probably overdone.

We walked around the roof, Mill nodding approvingly at the distant views, including the one of the ocean off the back. It was a good distance away, framed by trees and topped by pillowy clouds today, but beautiful, stunning, and never-ending. Not as good a view as Peter Murray's, I noted to myself.

My new hometown of Benedict was as close to the ocean as a person could get and not be swallowed up by the tides. I forgot that sometimes. This former landlubber living in the middle of the lower forty-eight had seen the ocean, but now I lived next to it. It was part of my life, and I liked remembering that.

Damn Travis Walker for trying to ruin that.

Orin kept outdoor furniture on the roof, comfortable enough for a barbecue or reading a good book. We didn't sit, though. We walked around, all of us scanning the countryside.

For a long time, we saw no one and no wildlife, which was disappointing.

Orin's truck was the first sign of life we saw coming our way. He turned onto his drive and then stopped next to Viola's truck.

"We're up here," Viola called when he got out of the truck. "House is armed."

Orin pulled his cell phone out of his pocket and slid his finger across the screen. We heard the house disarm with repeat swooshes and clunks and also felt a slight movement to the entire structure.

"Come down," Orin said.

None of us chose the fire pole. It seemed too frivolous, considering the circumstances.

"While I was at the library, I did a little research. I found Peter's mine," Orin said as we joined him in the kitchen.

I scratched Gus's ears as we listened to Orin.

"Peter's parents bought a mine about three miles into the area we call the West Tundra—"

"That's rough, but there is a small clearing," Viola said.

"That's where it is. Peter never went to probate court to get everything put into his name. He was young and everyone around here just went along as if things were his, but he should have gone to court, just as a formality, to put everything in his name."

"I should have intervened," Viola said. "Gril wasn't here yet."

"From what I heard, Peter might not have listened to anyone back then. Anyway . . ."

"There's an old law about a mine being forfeited if not worked for a certain amount of time," Viola said. "I feel like this might be where you're going."

"Correct." Orin nodded. "That's where I think the problem comes in. I found out that a few months ago, Peter wrote a letter to officials in Juneau, telling them that someone else had been working in the mine and he wanted them out."

"Did he write down who was working it?" I asked hopefully.

Orin shook his head. "He didn't, and I can't understand why. The letters to the Juneau folks are vague and uncertain."

"Did you talk to someone in Juneau or just hack your way into some computers?"

"Well, I did leave messages for people, but I haven't heard back. I did a little hacking to see the back-and-forth."

Mill made a noise that sounded like she was impressed.

Orin continued, "I'm going to go check out the mine. I just wanted to give you all an update and see if anyone has made it back. No one was at the police station."

"No one back yet, as far as I know," Viola said.

"I'm coming with you," I said.

"What? If you go, we all have to go," Mill said.

"Not true." I did not want to stay here. "If I go with Orin, it will get me out of here, which was the original plan anyway. I . . . don't want to hide here."

"Beth?" Viola said.

I looked at her. What I was going to say wasn't just about me but about everyone else's safety, too. It was going to sound selfish, but I couldn't change the way I felt. "I can't do it. I can hike through the woods, walk out of Benedict, but I can't just wait here. I'd rather . . . I don't know, Viola, but this isn't what I want to do. I need to keep moving, not standing still."

Viola's eyes transformed from confusion to understanding quickly. "All right. I get it."

"I think I'll go back into town," Mill said. "Come with me, Viola. Travis Walker isn't going to come out here, unless he thinks Beth is here. I think I'd rather be in town myself."

"Okay," Orin finally said. "I get it, too, but I'm not sure I like it."

"None of us like any of this," Mill said sternly.

We looked at her.

"Am I wrong?"

"It's okay, Mill." Viola looked around at the rest of us. "I think we all get it."

I nodded and crouched to Gus. "Go with Viola. I'll see you later."

Gus trusted me enough to know I would get back to him soon.

So, after less than an hour at the safest place in or near Benedict, maybe Alaska, we left again, Gus going with Viola and Mill, and me going with Orin.

I had no sense that I was doing the wrong thing, or that I was doing the right thing. I was doing what I needed to do and that was good enough for me.

Seventeen

According to my quick search for a definition, a tundra is "a treeless level or rolling ground found in cold regions." It took Orin about twenty minutes to drive to the tundra that held the Murrays' mine.

Grass covered the West Tundra.

"Does someone mow this?" I asked, though I realized it was probably a silly question. The short green grass in the area probably just didn't get much of a growing season.

"No, but it seems so because it's so much less wild than everything else you see out here."

"Something about this is familiar."

"Yeah?"

I nodded as Orin steered his truck over open land, no clear road in sight. I couldn't place why this wide open space triggered something inside me. It was almost a memory but not quite. I hoped it would come to me, as I had to put the lion's share of my focus on holding on for the bumpy ride.

"Look up there." Orin nodded forward.

I zoned in on a small amount of fencing, old wood slats up on four posts that made about a six-foot-by-six-foot square.

"The mine is in the ground?"

"Yes. This area is packed with gold and copper."

"What? Why aren't there more mines?"

There was not another person or structure in sight. I didn't spot any other fences, no vehicles, just the open tundra. Something else sparked in my memory.

"Is there a name for this place, not just a location?"

"Fallen Rock."

"That's it! I remember a news story."

I watched Orin's profile and could spot his eyebrows furrow. "What news story?"

"I know something you don't? How is that possible?"

"Maybe I just need a reminder."

"There's a river around here. . . ."

"Yes. Only about a tenth of mile that way. See the trees?"

"I do."

"It's right over there. You'll hear the river when we get out— Oh, wait, I remember," Orin said. "There was a story about three months ago about no mining out here because there are so many salmon running that river."

"It was a small story." I thought back to what I'd read. It had been only a quarter page or so in the Juneau paper. A picture of the area had been included, which is probably why it looked familiar to me. "I think the article might have even talked about Peter's mine." I paused. "You know what, I think they said the Murray mine, but that meant absolutely nothing to me when I read it. Honestly, I didn't even know it was this close to Benedict. What are we, only about ten miles from town?"

"That's right, though it wasn't a new story. It was a reiteration that the Alaskan government wouldn't be allowing mining out here because of the salmon that run so close. This river contains one of the biggest runs in the state. I'm pretty sure the story resurfaces every few years for one reason or another."

"This time maybe because Peter Murray was trying to stake his claim?"

"Maybe."

"A mine is here, though, has been since the Murrays came to town, apparently. There's paperwork that they own it. That article might have done something to push Peter to finally try to do something about all of it, though leaving town for the other mine seems odd. Maybe he was trying to reclaim it or something after so much time and thought he could ask folks at Blue Mine."

"I'll get more details, but I think you are right. It's too much of a coincidence that that's about when Peter disappeared. Since we're here, let's take a look at the mine shaft."

"Officials haven't closed it off?"

"Probably not. The old fencing might have been the extent of their efforts."

We got out of the truck and walked the last twenty feet or so. We stepped over the mostly fallen slats and leaned and peered inside carefully.

"Let's not get too close," Orin said.

"Right, but I'd sure like to see the inside."

"We can get *that* close, but keep back at least a couple feet from the opening."

"Will do." I extended my hand in his direction. "Hold on."

"If we were smart, we'd gear up and do this more safely."

"Are we going to be that smart?"

If Tex was with us, we would take all safety measures available— and all the gear would be there for us, in Tex's truck or backpack. Orin's stealth and talent was more about his brains than the equipment he carried with him, though I knew he'd taken plenty of physical risks over the years of his top-secret missions.

Orin took my hand. "We'll be okay."

It turned out to be much ado about nothing. The shaft's hole was about three feet in diameter. As we peered in, all we could see was darkness. Orin grabbed a nearby rock and threw it in. We waited quietly but didn't hear any sort of landing. Then we cupped our hands around our mouths and called down, "Helloooo!"

Echoes returned as expected, but neither of us knew if there was a way to measure a distance based upon the level of return volume or repetitions of the word.

We stepped back from the hole.

"Could the government stop Peter if his family truly owned the mine?" I asked.

"Probably, particularly since Peter didn't take the step of going to probate court. I would think all that would do, though, is delay things, but that salmon run is pretty valuable. Maybe this area wasn't as important when his parents bought the mine, but since it is now, red tape was being unfurled to keep Peter from mining. That's all just a guess. I'm wondering what the government told his parents. This mine hasn't given up its riches, I don't think. I'm pretty sure nothing more than this hole has been dug. I need to research."

"Gold and copper, huh?"

"Lots and lots of both."

"Greed is such a motivator, Orin. Why haven't more people come out here and just dug holes?"

Orin shrugged. "It's Alaska? Intimidating, maybe?"

"Greed, though," I repeated.

"I wouldn't be surprised if that's what's at work here. If that's why Peter was killed."

"At the other mine?"

"There's the mystery. What was he doing there? What does Blue Mine have to do with this one?"

"Good questions." I put my hands on my hips and looked around.

This wasn't like the mine where Jin had come from. This was just a hole in the ground. I didn't spot any tire tracks over the tundra. Even the path Orin and I had taken seemed mostly undisturbed, the grass only somewhat flat now. This was rugged land. Even the grass fought back.

As I spun in a slow circle and scanned the whole area, the sun briefly broke free from the fast-moving clouds above. Something on the ground, almost hidden by the grass, glinted about ten feet away.

I made my way to the spot quickly, hoping not to lose sight of the spot.

"What's up?" Orin asked.

"I saw something." I put my hands on my thighs and looked down at the ground. "Right over here, I think."

Orin came up beside me and struck the same pose.

"The sun caught something." I pointed at a thin silver rod next to Orin's toe. "There. What's that?"

Orin retrieved the object and held it up. "A pair of glasses."

"No," I said.

"Uh, yes."

"No, I know. Yes, it's a pair of glasses, but, Orin, they belong to Jin, I'm sure of it. I saw her wearing them. They were on a chain around her neck."

The glasses were the worse for wear, bent frame with one cracked lens and one missing. They might have been old the last time I'd seen them, but at least they'd been intact, I was pretty sure.

"Jin? The woman from the other mine." But it wasn't a question; he knew who we were talking about, but his tone told me he wished he knew a lot more than just her name.

I nodded as I inspected the glasses, hoping they might actually tell me something other than that they were pretty beaten up. I looked up at Orin. "I don't see any blood, at least, but these have been through a wringer. I hope Jin is okay."

"Well, though you might have seen her wearing glasses like these, they very well could be someone else's. I think the mercantile sells these readers."

"Oh. I didn't know. That would make sense."

I thought back to the moment Jin reached for her glasses but didn't put them on. I had no idea if they were for close or distant vision.

"They could be anybody's, then," I said. "But, what if they are Jin's? If she came this way, why? And, more importantly, is she hurt? Something happened to destroy these. Would this be a reasonable route to get to her mine?"

Orin thought for a moment. "It's doable but circuitous. Let's look around a little." Orin set off in one direction over the tundra.

I went the other way. "Jin?" I called, though it seemed a waste of effort. The word was met with only the wind and an obstinate cloud parked over the sun. I called back to Orin, "She ran off back in town. Maybe she chose the circuitous route so she wouldn't be found."

"Seems a possibility."

I came upon an old beer can but didn't see anything else unusual. There was no one out there with us, at least where we could see them. If anyone was around, they were being silent and didn't want to be found.

There was something about finding the glasses where we had—so near the mine shaft—that I couldn't let go of the idea that Jin had indeed been in this area. Or maybe it was just me pushing a narrative. She lived near a mine and had been transporting Peter Murray's body. She'd run away. Jin and Peter were somehow tied together.

I needed not to assume, though. It was too easy to miss something important if your mind was already made up.

"I don't know," Orin said as we came together again. "I didn't see anything or anyone."

I held up the beer can. "This is all I found."

"Always good to get rid of some trash. . . ." Orin frowned as he looked around again.

"What?"

"No other trash? Your earlier words struck a nerve with me. Why haven't more people been out here?"

"Maybe people have just picked up after themselves."

"Maybe." Orin looked at me. "I'll do more research. For now, let's get you back to town. I'm hoping someone else returned and maybe found Jin along the way."

We hurried to the truck and made our way back to Benedict.

Eighteen

As Benedict's downtown came into view, I was relieved to see Viola's truck parked next to the Benedict House. I didn't think she and Mill would go anywhere else, but it was still good to see that they were where they were supposed to be. Or at least the vehicle I'd last seen them in was.

"Drop me off here," I said before Orin could pull closer to the Benedict House. "I want to run into the mercantile and look at the readers."

"Good plan."

I hopped out of Orin's truck and waved as he turned and redirected the truck toward the library. He'd been deep in thought on the ride, so much so that I didn't want to disturb him. I'd kept quiet, too. I didn't think he noticed my wave goodbye—he didn't return it.

With a singular focus, I hurried inside. I hadn't forgotten that even though I didn't want to hide in Orin's house, I didn't need to make myself an easy target, particularly if I was alone. The mercantile—simply named just as the POST OFFICE, BAR, and CAFÉ— was owned by a sixty-something guy named Randy. Everyone liked him. He ran a good shop and embraced top-notch customer service.

"Beth!" he called as I came in. He did a double take. "I thought you weren't supposed to be around town for a few days."

"Hey, Randy. Change of plans." I made my way to the counter he stood behind. I didn't spot anyone else, so if the two dressing rooms were empty, we were alone. Still, I kept my voice low, just in case.

Randy turned and gave me his full attention. "Good to see you. What can I do for you?"

I grabbed the glasses from my pocket. "Do these look like something you sell?"

The answer came before he could speak. He grabbed his own readers from his shirt pocket so he could better see the pair that I held. They were identical.

"Yes, ma'am." He waggled the pair he'd put on his nose. "Why? Do you need a new pair?"

I shook my head. "They aren't mine. Orin and I were out looking around and found them. I just wondered if this is where they were purchased."

"Well, they're pretty generic, but if you found them around Benedict, chances are good they were bought here. Why does it matter?"

"I don't know yet, but thanks for confirming. Could I ask you some more questions?"

"Sure." He took off the glasses.

"Do you know about the Blue Mine area?"

"Of course."

"People from there shop here?"

"Sure do. All the time."

I nodded. "Do you know a woman named Jin?"

"I do." He almost frowned.

"What's she like?"

Randy squinted at me. "Why are you asking these questions, Beth?"

"There's a lot going on, but she was just here in town. . . ."

"I know. She stopped by . . . oh, day before yesterday, I think."

"She did? What did she buy?"

Randy looked at me with furrowed brows.

"Right," I said. "She brought a body into town, claiming it was her husband, Brick, but it turned out to be Peter Murray."

"Our Peter Murray?"

"Yes. Dr. Powder is trying to determine a cause of death, but at first glance, it could be murder."

Randy's mouth made an O. "That's terrible."

I nodded. "What did Jin buy?"

"Camping stuff."

"Shoot."

"You think she's on the run?"

"I don't know what to think, Randy, but I can't imagine she'd need more camping gear to head back to Blue Mine. She left without taking the pack she'd brought with her, but she could make the trip quickly. Maybe she just wanted a tent for the one night she might have to spend in the elements."

Randy shook his head. "It was more than a tent. It was full gear, times two."

"Two?"

"I know her husband, Brick, too. I asked if they were planning a trip."

"What did she say?"

"She didn't come out and give me an answer." He paused. "She was in a hurry, though."

"Okay, well, normally I'd suggest you call Gril, but he's every which direction. I'll tell him what you said. Maybe he'll come in. Can you think of anything else she might have said or done that he should know?"

Randy rubbed his chin. "She asked if there'd been any change in the ferry schedule since a couple months ago. I told her there hadn't been."

"She hopped on the ferry?"

"I don't know, Beth. All I know is that she asked about it."

Had Gril gotten ahold of the maritime folks? I had no idea, but he'd been so set on heading back out to the mine, I thought maybe he hadn't.

"Randy, I don't know who to call to ask for ferry manifests. Do you?"

"I do, but I don't think they'll listen to me."

"Could you try? Tell them Gril is busy but you are sure he'll want to see them as soon as possible, that if Jin and Brick board, they might want to . . . I don't know, wait or something?"

"Absolutely. I can try." He turned and grabbed a satchel that was on the back counter. "I'll head down there right now."

"You can't call? Oh, of course you can't call." Randy didn't have a landline. "Maybe you could use Benny's phone?"

I would have offered to make the call for him, but if they wouldn't listen to Randy, they certainly wouldn't listen to me. I was sorry he'd have to close the shop, but hopefully it wouldn't be for long.

We left the store together. I watched as he locked the door and then turned to make his way to his truck. The dock wasn't far but far enough that walking would take significantly longer.

I looked out into the woods, where Gril, not to mention the others, had gone. I wished them all back, safe and sound. Where was Jin? Where was Travis? Was anyone watching me?

A chill ran up my arms as I glanced across to the other leg of the buildings where the Benedict House stood. Something registered and I did a double take.

What was on the door? That wasn't blood, was it?

I took off in a run.

Nineteen

I didn't have far to go, but for an instant it felt like I was in the middle of one of those dreams where you are trying to get somewhere but obstacles keep getting in your way, pulling you backward. I made it, though, and was shocked to see that the swath of red was, indeed, blood, or red paint. No, it was definitely blood.

I turned the knob and burst through the front door. "Viola! Mill!" I yelled as I made my way down the hallway that held Viola's office and room.

"In the dining room," Viola called back.

No one warned me, told me not to go in, but it wouldn't have done any good anyway. I came to a stop outside the dining room and took in the horror.

Tex was sitting on a chair, bleeding.

"What the—"

"I'm fine," he said.

I hurried to him. Viola was on one side, tending to his upper arm; Mill was on his other side, frowning at the entire scene.

"He was shot," Mill said.

"Shot!" I exclaimed. "What?"

"Stop yelling, Beth," Viola said.

I hadn't known I was so loud. I tried to lower my voice as I looked at Tex. "What happened?"

"Someone shot at me. The bullet went through my arm. I'm fine."

"Where? How?" I said.

"Beth," Mill said. "Tex is fine. He's lost a little blood, but he's going to be okay. Okay?"

What did she know? I looked at Tex.

"Mill is correct. I'm going to be fine. I'm not happy and am going to find who did this," he said. "But I'm fine."

"Yeah," Viola muttered as she continued first aid on the arm.

Tex had bled onto the floor and his arm was still somewhat covered in it, but there was nothing gushing.

"Should I call the doctor?" I asked.

"I already did," Mill said. "I used Viola's phone."

"Beth, really, I'm going to be okay," Tex said. "I promise."

I could see both pain and anger in his eyes, but they were open and clear. He was fully conscious. He was making sense.

"Tell me what happened."

The front door opened, and Dr. Powder hurried to the dining room.

"Everyone but Tex, get out," he commanded. "I have this."

Reluctantly, I followed Viola and Mill out of the dining room and to Viola's office.

I could feel that my eyes were still wide with . . . I wasn't sure if it was anger or fear. Maybe both. I needed to calm down, though, that much I was certain of. I took some deep breaths.

Mill frowned at me somewhat sympathetically. Viola directed me to sit down. Once we all had chairs, Viola said, "He was on his way back, not far from here. Just in the woods where Gus likes to do his business."

"Just out there?" I asked. "Why was he coming back?"

Viola nodded. "He'd gone one direction, but came back to check on all of us before taking another shot in a different direction. He wasn't sure which way everyone else had gone and he didn't want to pick the wrong route."

"He was coming back this way, and someone shot him? Could it have been a hunter, a misfire?" Such things happened.

"It will be investigated at some point," Viola said.

Mill huffed.

Viola glanced at Mill, a flash of anger in her eyes, but she mellowed quickly. "Yeah, you might be right, Mill. We may never know what happened." Viola sighed deeply. "However, the good news is that Tex is going to be okay. It wasn't a graze, but almost."

I swallowed. Tex had been shot. He had scars from minor injuries over his lifetime, acquired via his outdoorsy ways. But even with guns always in the vicinity, he'd never been hit by any sort of bullet.

I couldn't help but feel like this injury had something to do with me, with Travis Walker. Was my kidnapper really hiding in the woods on the edge of downtown, shooting people?

That didn't make a lot of sense, but what did? My life since Travis had been mostly unbelievable.

"Beth, he's fine. We'll move on," Mill said.

She could be so right and so wrong at the exact same time.

You survived, Beth. Don't give him any more than he already took. The words that Mill had said to me as I'd lain in the hospital bed, coming out of brain surgery, all those lights, all those eyes looking at me, wondering if I was going to be okay. They'd had to open my skull, after all. The brain surgeon had told Mill, "I am optimistic." But that had been the most he would give up.

And then I *was* fine. A few headaches later, at least.

The day before I made plans to escape the hospital, a man and a woman—I can't remember their names—walked into my hospital room, armed with a clipboard and some big attitudes. They were there to prove I was going to need some time in rehab—that's what they'd told Mill. In typical Mill fashion, she'd huffed at them and told them they were being ridiculous, that I was fine.

She sat in a chair as they approached my bed with "I told you so" eyes, even before I'd taken the test.

They began with "Beth, can you count backward from one hundred, by threes?"

I was slow but no slower than I'd usually be with numbers. They stopped me when they were sure I could handle the task.

They asked me to memorize things, who political officials were, what year it was.

I aced the test. And, to their credit, they told my mother that I was fine and wouldn't need rehabilitation. She was right. She didn't handle it graciously, but I didn't care.

I wasn't aware of my expression as I looked at her now, but she blanched and then smiled briefly as if to ease something, so I tried to relax my tense face. It was work.

Tex was going to be fine. Yes, he'd been shot, but there was no changing that now. Now, we just needed to be grateful he'd be okay.

"He's fine," Mill repeated.

"Got it." I nodded confidently. "Yes. Got it."

"Good." Viola grabbed a pen and a yellow pad and started sketching. She marked a spot on the edge of the same road I took to the old hunting shed where I worked. When I'd first arrived in Benedict and my identity was a secret, Gril had set me up there, giving me the title of publisher of the *Petition,* the local "newspaper." I could take my typewriter and not only create *Petition* editions but work on my novels without someone wondering why I was doing all that typing.

"What's that?" Mill asked.

"It's where Tex said he was when he was shot."

"Wait, what was he doing there?" I asked. "Even if he took a different way, he should have been coming from the woods about fifty yards that way." I put my finger on the map. "I mean, it's not far off, but it's a little."

"He stopped by your shed, just wanted to make sure everything was fine there."

I hadn't even thought to give Tex a key to the shed. As far as I knew, Gril and I were the only ones who had one.

"Was everything okay?" I asked.

"As far as he could tell. He didn't see Orin's car at the library or he would have gone over there, too, just to let Orin know what was going on and ask if he knew anything else. Now"—Viola put the pen on the paper again—"considering angles and trajectories, I think the person who shot Tex was here."

"People aren't supposed to be hunting there," I noted.

"Nope, but that doesn't mean they don't. It's rare out here because so many people know what they're doing, but accidents happen—"

"But whoever shot Tex ran off. He said he looked," Mill interrupted.

Viola nodded. "He didn't look long. He was bleeding and knew he needed to get some help."

"I'll go take a gander." Mill sat up straighter. "Can I have a weapon?"

"No," Viola said. "But I have two. I'm going to head out there. I know some ins and outs that strangers wouldn't."

"You're not going by yourself," I said. "If Tex is going to be fine, he'll go with you. No, Viola, you aren't going out there by yourself."

"I'll be fine, Beth, and, frankly, you don't get to decide."

"No," Mill added, "but Beth is right, and you know it. You shouldn't go out there alone. Tex needs a little time, but I bet he'd be ready to search tomorrow."

"Tomorrow's too late." Viola clicked the pen.

"I agree. I'll go with you." Mill's expression was frozen in assurance.

"No—" I said.

Mill put her hand up in my direction. "You aren't the decider, Beth,"

"But—"

Mill looked at me. "It's the best we can do. Tex should rest today. He'll bounce back, but even big guys aren't superhuman. Who else is going to go with Viola? You don't get to say you again. Not an option."

"Why not?" Anger was beginning to boil under my skin.

"Because it's you who Travis wants."

"That means I should go."

"Nope," Viola said. "That means you stay hidden. I wish you'd go back to Orin's. I wish we hadn't left. I've had time to think about it—"

I crossed my arms in front of myself. "No."

"Fine," Viola conceded. "Then stay here and take care of Tex."

I opened my mouth to speak again, but Viola jumped in with a sternness I'd seen her express but never with me before. "Enough."

I hated all of this so much, but I knew who was in charge, and I trusted her implicitly, even if she was making me so angry at the moment.

As if he knew what I needed right then, Gus whined and nudged my leg with his nose. He looked up at me with his beautiful intelligent eyes.

My heart . . . well, it didn't melt, but it did relax a little.

"All right." I petted his side. "I will do as everyone says."

"Good," Mill and Viola said together.

I really meant it. I wasn't lying just to appease them.

Then again, things change.

Twenty

had no idea where Gril, Donner, and Eddy were, but my imagination had me hoping they weren't in the woods somewhere, shot down and alone.

Gus and I saw Viola and Mill off at the edge of the woods. As if Viola had instructed him, when Gus had done his thing, he directed me back inside the Benedict House. I found my way to the room Tex was resting in—he was fast asleep. Dr. Powder was sitting in a chair, reading with his glasses perched on his nose. Not surprisingly, they were identical to the pair I had in my pocket.

He closed the book on his lap and smiled at me. "He's fine," he whispered. "He'll be a little sore, but there's no permanent damage."

"I'm relieved." I pointed at his glasses. "Did you get those at the mercantile?"

Dr. Powder took them off his nose. "I . . . probably. We have a few of them around the house. We have both needed them for ten years or so now, but at least we can still see far away."

I took the pair out of my pocket. "Orin and I found these."

Dr. Powder peered at my hand. "Yes, they look the same." He sat back in his chair and frowned. "Care to tell me what's been going on? I'll be here a while."

"Sure."

"Hang on. Let's take some chairs out to the hallway and talk there. Tex needs to sleep."

We gathered chairs from the dining room and set them in the hallway between the dining room and Tex's room.

As everyone else did now, Dr. Powder knew who I was, but he hadn't pushed me to tell him more. He'd made it clear that he was there for me if I needed anything. Today, he listened intently as I told him what was currently happening around Benedict, as well as some of the things that had occurred during my time in the van.

When I hit a lull, he said, "You want to kill him?"

"I want him gone. I don't think I can stop my mother from trying to kill him," I finally said.

Dr. Powder nodded. "That would be on her, then. But I would like for you to really think about it a minute. Is the glory of killing your kidnapper something that will sustain you through the rest of your life, or is regret a real possibility?" Dr. Powder smiled sadly.

"I don't know. I don't think I can stop the others."

Dr. Powder nodded. "I know Gril, Viola, Donner, even Tex pretty well. They'll do the right thing, whatever that may be. So will your father, I think."

"You didn't include my mother in that."

"No, I didn't."

A silence that held more than words hung between us for a good long moment.

"Right," I finally said. "Right."

"At least she's currently with Viola. She'll keep your mother in line."

"I hope."

Mill had outsmarted even the best of them, but Dr. Powder was correct, Viola could keep almost anyone in line.

"I appreciate the conversation," I said.

"Anytime." He put his hands on his thighs. "For now, though, I think I'll go sit with my patient a bit. He's past the worst of it, but I just want to be nearby for a while."

"I'm not much of a cook, but I could round up some food."

"I could eat."

I walked Dr. Powder back to Tex's room, finding him resting easily. No fever, no look of pain on his face.

"You gave him some good stuff?" I asked the doctor.

"Yes, but he'll be on ibuprofen only by tomorrow. I wanted him to rest. I didn't think he would unless I intervened."

I kissed Tex's forehead and smoothed his hair before I left the room. In the doorway, I turned, though. "I won't go anywhere, but I'd like to open the door and look outside."

Dr. Powder's eyebrows furrowed. "That doesn't seem wise."

"I realize that, but I think I need to."

Dr. Powder frowned and nodded. "I get it. Make it quick and don't step out there too far."

"Will do."

I was glad to have Gus by my side and grateful that Dr. Powder didn't join us.

I put my hand on the handle and took a deep breath. I opened the door but stayed inside.

From there I could see almost all of Benedict's downtown. Nothing seemed out of place. Lights were on in windows, including the mercantile. People were parking vehicles or walking down the boardwalk. And there was someone walking out of the bar. I knew the man by sight but not by name. He was friendly and always had a quick smile.

The woods where Tex had been shot were to the left. From inside I couldn't see much of them. I took a tentative step and then leaned to peer outside.

Gus whined at me. "We aren't going out right now, but we will soon."

He'd been out already, and I could tell he wasn't in need of another visit so soon. When he was, though, I would have to take him. Or maybe Dr. Powder would insist upon doing it.

I didn't see anyone out there. The sun hadn't set all the way yet, but the thick woods were dark, unwelcoming.

They hadn't been unwelcoming until Tex had been shot inside them. Before they were just dark and mysterious, filled with promises of adventure. I looked at Gus. I wanted them to go back to the way they were. I would work on my attitude, and we would tackle them together a little later.

"You okay?" I asked Gus.

He sat comfortably.

"We'll try it later."

He seemed content with that answer.

I closed the door, and we made our way to the kitchen.

Twenty-one

Beth?"

I opened my eyes and sat up quickly. "Tex. Hey, you okay?" I silently berated myself. I'd told Dr. Powder I wouldn't fall asleep.

"I'm fine." He smiled. "You are always adorable when you wake up."

I rolled my crusty eyes. "You are feeling better."

"I am. A little sore, but I'm ready to get back to whatever it is we need to do."

I looked at the time. "Dr. Powder left only a couple hours ago, declaring you out of the woods. We tried very hard not to turn that into some dark humor. You know, because you were shot in the woods."

"I get it." He smiled. "I like it, and I'm glad I'm out of all the woods. For the moment. I think I need to head back into them again."

I squinted at him. "I'm not thrilled by that idea. Neither is Dr. Powder. He was clear."

Tex nodded. "I understand, but I'll be fine. I let someone get the best of me and I shouldn't have."

"What could you have done differently?" I asked, genuinely curious.

"I got into my head. As I made my way back to town, I was thinking instead of paying attention to the world around me."

"That's one of your outdoor rules—always be aware."

"It is. And I broke it. Even if someone was hiding, Beth, when I pay attention, no one can get away with anything. I'm keenly aware. I see well, I hear well. I know what to listen for, what to look for. I just let my guard down."

"I'm sorry you got shot."

"Me too, but I'm also pretty angry about it. I'll figure out who did it. It might have been an accident, but that means that someone was careless. I will do what needs to be done."

"Tex," I said, remembering the conversation I'd had with Dr. Powder. "Could you truly kill someone?"

"If they were a threat, then yes, but that's not what I'm talking about here. Unless they were trying to kill me. We'll see."

"What if you just came upon Travis inside the mercantile, would you kill him?"

"No, I would tackle him, tie him up, and take him to the authorities."

"That's not what my mother would do."

"I'm aware of that."

"I even think my father would do the right thing, and Travis Walker betrayed him more than once over the decades."

Tex nodded. "Your father is a good man. He's made some bad choices over the years, but that doesn't make him bad. Your mother is a good person, too. She's just a little more . . . tightly wound."

"That's one way to look at it." I sat up and glanced at Gus, still asleep on the floor next to the bed. He'd been awake with me throughout the night, but he still hadn't gone outside. It didn't appear urgent. I looked back at Tex. "Hungry?"

"Starving." He sat up as if he was going to get out of bed.

"No, stay. I cooked mac and cheese last night. This morning, I'm ready to tackle eggs and bacon. How's that sound?"

"Perfect."

I left Gus where he was and did a quick search of the place. Neither Mill nor Viola were in their rooms, but it was just a cursory look. I hadn't heard or seen anyone return.

I made my way to the kitchen. Blue-box mac and cheese had been easy and delicious, but good scrambled eggs could be a trick. It was one of Viola's guests, a man named Chaz, who told me that good scrambled eggs were easy if you just kept the eggs moving in the pan.

If I didn't burn the toast, it would be okay.

I didn't burn anything, and the eggs were perfect. I set up a tray and carried everything in to Tex. He'd fallen asleep again. I stood in the doorway a moment and watched him breathe—I determined quickly that he seemed comfortable.

Not so much Gus. Finally, he needed to get outside.

I set the tray on a side table and signaled to Gus, who joined me with no hesitation.

Quickly, I put on boots and gathered a jacket, even though I wasn't going to step far from the doorway. I didn't want to take my eyes off him to come back inside for gear if it became necessary.

When I opened the door, he ran toward his favorite spots. Though thick with enough trees to keep the woods still somewhat dark, in the light of the full sun and no clouds, I could see more than I could the night before.

I didn't spot anyone but Gus out there. In fact, I didn't see anyone downtown either, though there were a few vehicles. People were around but inside.

Usually Gus stayed on the perimeter, but he seemed to be inside the trees a little more than normal. I didn't like it, so I stepped outside.

"The day I need you to stay close . . . ," I muttered. I put my hands around my mouth. "Gus!" I called. "Come on closer, boy."

From the moment that Gus and I became a team, he had come to me when I called. We hit it off immediately.

I raised my voice even more. "Gus?!"

No sound came for a long time. Finally, though, I heard a bark. It wasn't a yelp; he didn't sound like he was in pain. But he was far away, farther than he normally went.

I didn't think about it. I didn't consider waking Tex. I didn't even think about closing the Benedict House's front door. I took off toward the woods.

"Gus?" I yelled again as I stopped at the edge of the trees.

Another long moment passed, and another faraway bark reached me.

I had no doubt something was wrong, and he needed me. I still didn't think about what I was doing before I set off and into the woods.

If it had rained the night before, I'd slept through it. Inside the woods the ground was mushy and the air cooler. I had an irrational thought that maybe Gus was stuck in mud somewhere. Gus had never been stuck in anything—he was strong. Nevertheless, that was where my head went.

Panic kept me moving. I kept calling to Gus. He didn't answer every time, but I still heard infrequent barks.

I'd been in here plenty of times. I knew I was about a tenth of a mile away from an opening, an area that Orin told me had been cleared because someone had wanted to use the land as a pasture for cows. Those plans hadn't come to fruition, so the area had been turned into a place where people would go for picnics on warmer sunny days—there weren't many, so it didn't see many people or picnics.

I hurried in that direction and propelled myself out and into the open.

"Gus?"

I took in as much of the space as I could. Light and shadows played tricks on my vision, but I finally spotted him.

He was across the valley on the edge of it and more woods. He was sitting like a good boy, not in any obvious distress.

But he was being held by his collar by someone. I opened my

mouth to yell to the person to let go of my dog, but my voice became as frozen as my legs suddenly seemed to be.

I knew that person, even as they wore dark clothes and a ski mask. Fear spider-walked through my limbs. It was the man who'd saved me from the rushing water.

It was Travis Walker.

I swallowed gallons of fear that started to churn in my gut. Travis Walker couldn't have my dog. I would only allow him to take Gus over my dead body.

I took a deep breath and then stepped toward them. So be it.

Twenty-two

et go of my dog!" I yelled as my legs finally came awake and
began sprinting.

The man didn't let go of Gus. Instead, he lifted his hand in a halt
gesture. "Beth!"

The voice was familiar, but I didn't think he sounded like Travis.
Who did he sound like?

"Let. Him. Go." I stopped ten feet away from them, but I was still
thinking of charging.

"Beth," the voice said calmly. "I'm not going to hurt him or you.
I'm going to take off this mask. You'll see."

I was not only breathing fast but also loudly, a wild gravelly
sound coming from my throat.

The man reached for the ski mask and then pulled it off his head.
The mustache as well as shock of blond hair caught me off guard. This
wasn't Travis Walker. But it took me a few beats to realize exactly who
it was.

Finally, I said, "Stellan?"

He nodded. "Beth."

I couldn't immediately work out why the Milton, Missouri, police
chief, Stellan Graystone, was in Alaska. I was too angry and scared

to realize that there was probably only one explanation, and it had to do with me. Well, Travis mostly, but me, too.

"Give me my dog," I said.

"Of course," Stellan said. "He came to me, and I only held onto him so you would come out here and we could talk."

When Gus was finally by my side, I held onto his collar just like Stellan had.

"You probably know where I live, Stellan. You could have knocked on the door."

He shook his head. "Not really, Beth. Not if I want to stay under the radar. I didn't even want you to know, but I need to tell someone what I saw. I thought maybe you'd keep my secret, and then your dog came my way. It seemed fortuitous, I guess."

"You saved me from the water?"

"I did. I'm camping out that way. That seemed fortuitous, too."

"That was fucking terrifying! I thought you were Travis."

"I don't know why. I saved you. I wasn't a threat."

"The ski mask!"

"Like I said, I'm staying hidden. Travis is smaller than me, Beth. Your imagination turned me into him."

I looked at Stellan. He was right. There was no similarity.

"Why do you have articles about me in your tent?"

"Just going over things again, Beth. You are the pride of Milton. I thought you might need some extra protection. I'm here, and I decided to do whatever needs to be done."

I shook my head as surprising hot tears filled my eyes. I'd been so scared for Gus. So much had happened, and here was the man who'd taken my grandfather's job as police chief in my small hometown after Gramps had died.

I'd run away to Alaska to hide from Travis, but everyone had found me. Even Travis, though I did have the presence of mind to be grateful that he wasn't the one whom Gus had run to.

I wiped at one tear that had fallen, but then stifled the others. "Too many people are protecting me, and yet . . . What did you see?"

Stellan nodded. "I'll tell you everything, Beth. I think it's good that you know what I'm doing here and what prompted me to make the trip, but I need to ask you to promise not to tell anyone."

"I'm not going to promise anything." I saw disappointment flash in his eyes.

He'd been the one to find Travis when the first hunt had been on, tackling him in a gas station as Travis arrogantly filled his van's tank, the same van he'd kept me locked inside of, in the town where I'd grown up.

"Okay, okay," I relented. "Let's talk. Tell me what you need to tell me. If I feel like you're doing something I can't keep to myself, I'll let you know, but I'll . . . try to keep your secret."

Relief relaxed his features. "Thanks, Beth. Thanks."

I thought about Tex back at the Benedict House. He was going to absolutely freak out when he woke up. Stellan and I needed to make this a quick conversation so I could get back.

"Is there somewhere private we could go?" Stellan asked.

"This is about as private as it gets."

Stellan nodded again.

We sat on a couple of exposed flat boulders just inside the trees. I'd calmed substantially but was now anxious to get this over with and get back to Tex.

"Talk to me, Stellan," I said.

Stellan Graystone was a powerful man, both in build and position within his community. About ten years older than me, he'd been the successful high school quarterback, the golden boy of Milton, Missouri. My grandfather had died when I was sixteen and Stellan was twenty-six. He'd been given the job my grandfather had been so good at.

From age sixteen to twenty-three, I'd lived in an apartment in St. Louis, a place I paid for with the money I earned from a waitressing job as well as an inheritance from my grandfather. I'd spent my nights at my computer.

For a long time, I wrote about my father leaving the family, my mother's obsession with finding him, my grandfather and his death. Words were the tools I used for working through my emotions, even happy ones. It was what I knew.

I'd never gone to college and didn't have any desire to do so. I could have waitressed for the rest of my life and been content with writing at night as therapy.

But then I had an idea for a story, a scary one. I wrote it and had Mill read it. Though she was my mother, she wasn't one to blow smoke up anyone's anything. She told me it was good. She told me to use a pen name because my words were so chilling, to find an agent, and get it published.

I didn't think she was handing out false praise, but I didn't have any desire to be published—well, at that time.

Mill took it upon herself to find me an agent, who then found a publisher for the book.

But after my grandfather died and Stellan Graystone took his job, his desk, that damn ugly noisy chair, I had no desire to walk back into the station. I'd talked to Stellan over the phone over the years, particularly after Travis Walker came into my life.

I hadn't seen him for over a decade. Though I would have recognized him anywhere without the ski mask, he was definitely marked by the passing of time, the stress of the job.

It took him a long minute to start talking, but he garnered my full attention. "It's my fault he got away."

"What?" I knew for a fact that it wasn't. "Stellan, that's not true."

"I knew, Beth. I knew."

"What did you know?"

"I knew he would get away."

"You couldn't possibly."

"I did. I knew." Stellan gritted his teeth and shook his head. "I don't know who helped him, but I think it was someone in Milton."

"Okay, that someone wasn't you, Stellan." I paused. "No, no one has even hinted that you had anything to do with it."

He gave me a level look. "But I did, Beth." He held up a hand to keep me from protesting again. "I received some . . . I'll call it 'intel,' though that feels a little too cloak-and-dagger for Milton, Missouri." He reached into his jacket pocket and pulled out a folded piece of paper and handed it to me. "I got this."

I unfolded and read the chicken scratch handwriting. "'He's going to get out. Once he's done with Beth, he'll come after you. You won't catch him.'"

I swallowed hard. "This needs context to mean anything, Stellan."

"What other context could it be?"

"Somebody making stuff up. Some criminal wannabe. People like attention."

"I could have done more than think it was a stupid prank, lie, diversion, whatever I thought it was, whatever excuse I used not to follow through with it. At all. I could have at least tried for finger-prints."

I nodded. "Why didn't you?"

"I really didn't think it was real. How in the world could some-one like Travis Walker escape custody?"

"I would have thought the same thing," I said.

"Well, you aren't a police chief. I am."

I nodded again, thinking about what my grandfather would have done. If he was still alive . . . well, Mill would have some strong competition for her murderous mission. My grandfather wouldn't have disregarded the note, but he might not have done much. He might not have checked for fingerprints, but he would have at least taken some time to think about it, wonder who'd sent it.

"Other than fingerprinting, which I bet would have turned up nothing, how could you have figured it out?"

"I could have asked around. Milton isn't big enough to have too many troublemakers to investigate. Someone would have recognized this handwriting."

He wasn't wrong, and that's what my grandfather would have done. He would have probably asked a few people.

"So that's why you're here, because you didn't ask around?"

Stellan laughed once, without humor. "That's the simple answer. However, I'm here to put an end to it."

"I just had this sort of conversation with the local doctor. He made me really think about the consequences that could come with drastic action."

"I'm more focused on the consequences we are all living with because I didn't take drastic action sooner."

Kind of a fair point, I thought, but I didn't say it aloud.

"So you came up here, set up a tent, and then saved me from drowning? How did that happen?"

"I was there. I saw you. At the time I didn't want you to know I was here."

"Why did you want me to know now?"

"I saw what happened to your friend, that big guy?"

"Tex?" Guilt about leaving him without any idea what I was doing tightened in my throat.

"He was shot accidentally."

"By?"

"You aren't going to believe this."

"Travis?"

"No. Bigfoot."

"Oh." I'd almost forgotten all about the mythological creature's sightings. "Someone in a costume."

"Yeah, I think so, but he had a gun, too, and he was lurking out there in the woods. After he shot Tex, he ran that way."

Stellan pointed toward the direction of the mine, but there were many miles between here and there. It wasn't possible to know for sure where he might have gone, but at least we knew he was up to no good.

"That's great, Stellan. It's good to have a witness."

"I can't come forward, Beth."

"That's trickier."

"I know this, too. It's not Travis in that costume. He's not that big."

"Others have said the same."

"I debated following him, but I wanted to make sure Tex was okay, so I went that way instead. Want me to try to grab the guy in the costume, too?"

I sighed. "I want you to go home, Stellan. There are so many people looking for Travis and"—I rolled my eyes—"Bigfoot. I don't want you caught in the fray. I wish you'd told Gril you were here."

"Beth, I'm not here."

"It's impossible not to leave a trail."

Stellan smiled. "I have ways."

I sighed again. "Please, go home. You're going to get hurt and I don't want anyone else to worry about. Please."

"No."

A thought flashed through my mind. "Detective Majors isn't here, too? She's not coming up here, is she?"

"Not to my knowledge."

I made a mental note to try to call her and ask her to stay away.

"Both of my parents are here."

"I saw," Stellan said. "I've been watching the downtown. Your father looks great. Your mother does, too. I had a feeling she might reappear."

"Is she in trouble in Missouri?"

"Officials want to talk to her, but there's no real evidence that she's done anything wrong. I have no doubt that she's been up to no good, but I have no warrant for her arrest."

"My dad?"

"Nope. Your grandfather made sure nothing would stick with your father. Even if it did, the statute of limitations would be long over."

It was an answer I already had but was good to hear again. "I guess that's a relief, even in the middle of everything else."

"Will you keep my presence here a secret?"

"I don't know how I'm going to do that and let everyone know what you saw."

"Call me an anonymous source?"

I frowned. "I'll try, but no promises. I just wish you would go home."

Stellan smiled wryly. "I will eventually."

"You're going to get hurt," I repeated my concern.

"I'll be fine."

I stood. "*Someone* is going to get hurt and that worries me terribly. I need to get back. I just ran off." Gus stood next to me. "If you'd hurt my dog, I'd've killed you. I know that I could have."

"I would never hurt a dog. I'm sorry you thought that might be possible. I really just wanted you to know what happened to Tex." Stellan stood, too. "Is he . . . are you two a couple?"

"Yes, we are."

"Are you happy here?"

"I've never been happier," I said. "Despite all of this. I can't wait for it all to be over so I can go back to that happiness."

"What if it being over means that Travis hurts you?"

The words punched me in the gut. I'd been afraid, but I'd never really thought anything could happen to me. There were too many people on my side. I had a great team. But, of course, Travis was a real threat.

"I'll be fine," I said.

"Me too."

I nodded. "I need to get back."

"I'm walking with you part way."

"I would appreciate that. In fact, you could come in and meet Tex if you'd like."

"Maybe some other time, when I'm really here."

As we made our way through the woods, we were silent. Gus seemed happy for the adventure. I thought about what all of this was leading to. What was really going to happen?

While I appreciated my team, this was beginning to feel like too much. Was it possible to have too many people doing this?

Yes, it was, I decided. I was going to tell Gril about Stellan the second I saw him. I was going to tell Tex, too. I sped up as I thought more about how panicked he would be if he'd awakened. Gus sensed my concern and started trotting. Stellan kept up just fine.

Stellan stayed behind at the edge of the woods, not hiding behind anything. I didn't have far to cover to get to the front door, but though he stood guard, he chose not to walk with Gus and me the rest of the way.

Once at the door, I turned to wave in his direction, but he was gone by the time I pushed on the knob. For an instant, I had the sensation that I'd imagined it all. Stellan Graystone couldn't possibly be hiding out in the Alaska woods, could he?

If I'd remembered that I hadn't shut the door, I would have been bothered by the fact that it was now closed, but that memory didn't come to me until later. I did notice that someone had cleaned off the blood.

"Tex," I called as Gus and I made our way in. At that point I didn't care if I woke him up. "Tex."

There was no answer. I hurried to his room quickly, I peered inside. The covers were rumpled, but there was no Tex.

"Oh, no."

I started off in a run up and down the two legs of the building, calling Tex's name the whole way. There was no answer—except for my noisy and fast heartbeat in my head. Where had he gone?

"Come on," I said to Gus. "We'll find him."

We stepped outside and made a beeline for the bar. Tex knew I liked to hang out and chat with Benny. I burst through the door.

Benny squinted at the encroaching light. "Beth! There you are. Tex was here a few minutes ago looking for you."

"Where did he go?"

"I . . . I have no idea. Why?"

"Viola? Mill?"

"I haven't seen them. What . . . ?"

But I closed the door before she could finish the question.

Gus and I opened every door in downtown Benedict, but Tex wasn't inside anywhere. Neither were Viola nor my mother. Tex's truck had been parked in the Benedict House's lot and it was still there, so he hadn't driven away. I wondered what Viola and my mother were up to this morning, but I was most concerned about Tex.

He was on foot somewhere. Not downtown, but he must have been close enough by. I hadn't been gone that long.

He'd shown me how to track, but I hadn't digested much more than the different sorts of footprints. I could tell a deer from a moose from a bear. I knew human footprints, of course, and I knew the print Tex's boots made.

Standing on the boardwalk, I looked toward the woods Gus and I had just come from. It was a big world. It was easy to miss things—except Tex didn't miss much.

"He went out there looking for us," I said to Gus.

Gus whined at my desperate tone.

"I know. I agree," I responded.

Even Mill had taught me that if we ever got separated in a place like the grocery store or a mall, I was to stay put. She would find me.

The one who knows what they're doing is the one who searches. Everybody else stays right where they are, she would say.

Now, though, the people who knew what they were doing were all out there attending to other emergencies. I was the one who should stay right where she was.

I knew this.

"I gotta go," I said to Gus.

I didn't think he agreed with my plan.

"You can't come with me. I don't want you to get hurt. Come on."

We hurried back to the bar.

I opened the door again.

"Beth? What's going on?"

"Benny, can you watch Gus?"

"Of course, but, hang on, don't you dare leave without telling me what's going on."

"I don't have time."

"Yes, you do." Benny's tone left no room for argument.

"I really don't. I need to find Tex and then I'll be back."

"Wait. Where is everybody?"

"It's a long story, Benny, and I really need to find Tex. Please."

Benny's frown was pinched. "I don't like this, Beth."

"I'll be careful."

Benny shook her head. "Come back quickly and tell me what's going on."

"I will." I knew I probably wouldn't be back soon, but I hoped.

Benny nodded, and I scratched Gus's ears one more time. "Be good."

Tears filled my eyes as I left the bar. This had all gone so wrong. And it was all my fault.

Twenty-three

geared up. I gathered the hiking equipment I'd had with Tex. My boots were good, my pack was full. I had enough water to last a few days, although I hoped I wouldn't need that much.

What I didn't have was a weapon.

I remedied that by grabbing a knife from Viola's office. She kept a few in her desk, sharpened and sheathed. They were under the false bottom of a drawer, but she'd shown me the hiding place—just in case. I figured this was the type of case to which she'd been referring.

I threaded the sheath of the hunting knife through my belt and arranged it to my side. I wrote a note to everyone and left it on the front counter, the spot where people would check in and get their key when the Benedict House used to be a small hotel. I hoped that's where anyone who was searching for me would look.

I hurried to the kitchen and grabbed a few extra granola bars and then left the Benedict House. I left the door unlocked because that was usually the way it was.

As I set off into the woods, I thought to myself: What if we'd all just stayed put? What if we were all just there inside the Benedict

House, waiting for Travis to find us? It would be smarter than what we'd done, better even than waiting at Orin's, in my opinion. Hindsight.

If Tex and I hadn't set out a week earlier, we wouldn't have known about the body on the back of Jin's horse. Since she'd lied about the body's identity, I didn't think she'd told the truth about anything. She was probably taking Peter's body out to the woods where it could disappear forever. There was a very good chance that no one would have ever found him. At least we'd prevented that.

Lots of people got lost in Alaska and many were never found. It was, according to some, one of the charms of this wonderful yet primitive place.

As I began down the path that Tex had chosen five days ago, I wasn't scared—well, not for myself. I was worried about everyone else. I could search in many directions, but I'd decided on heading toward Blue Mine. That's where I thought I'd ultimately find everyone, and Tex would think I'd thought that, too. I hoped.

What had I done? How had I allowed so many people to be pulled into the orbit of my trouble? I could have prevented all of this.

"Come and get me, Travis," I muttered. I stopped walking and looked around. There was no sign of anyone or any wildlife. I put my hands next to my mouth. "Come and get me, Travis!"

My voice flew through the woods, but the silence that followed was heavy and full of . . . anger. I was so angry. I'd been too busy to notice it much, but I felt it now. A hot fury in my gut and throat.

I set off walking again, burning energy, adrenaline, and the simmering anger. I was either going to make it to the North Pole in record time or drop to the ground when I came down off everything that was churning inside. I wished to talk to Leia, but that wasn't possible.

I slowed my speed a little to something steady and less frantic. I didn't need to burn myself out too soon.

I walked and walked but still didn't come upon anyone. Were

they all at the mine, or were some of them headed back in this direction? What paths had everyone chosen? I hoped to find Tex first, but he might have taken off in a run and he might not have even come into these woods. Why hadn't he just stayed put? Why hadn't I?

I realized too late that I should have seen if I could find Stellan again, have him come with me. He would have, no matter that he was trying to hide from everyone himself.

I took another moment to stop and look behind me, calculating if I should go back and attempt a search. I decided not to.

But the time I spent looking behind me gave me a new view. I should have been checking my six, but I hadn't. My sole purpose had been to go forward.

As I glanced down that way, my eyes caught movement amid some trees. There were trees everywhere, but the play of shadow that I'd noticed was in the middle of a tight copse of about ten skinny trunks.

I could have imagined it. It could have been the sun finding its way through the thick overgrowth and into my line of vision. It could have been an animal. Or it could have been nothing. I kept my eyes trained on the spot for a long minute. Nothing else moved.

Interrupting the stillness, a breeze whispered through the trees, rustling leaves and cooling my sweaty cheeks. I told myself that I must have imagined the movement, but I wasn't sure I believed it.

The moment brought me back to something steadier than my still somewhat manic march. I had to be safe in all ways out here. I could do this. Tex had taught me. In fact, Gril, Donner, and Viola had proffered lessons as well.

I was in better shape, in all the ways that mattered in the wilds of Alaska. I could make my way—smartly and safely. I patted the knife at my waist and continued.

It didn't take much longer for the adrenaline to lessen and my heart rate to calm, but I didn't feel the expected exhaustion. I was okay. I wasn't quite as out of control as I'd been, but my footfalls were steady.

I'd asked Tex about the likelihood of running into other people out on the trail. He'd shrugged and said, "Sometimes, but not always."

I remained alert, but the differences of taking this journey alone as opposed to when I was with Tex were glaring, though not all bad.

I had moments of feeling lost, but then I'd tell myself that I couldn't be, that this path was easy (relatively so, at least) and I just needed to keep my head clear. That—keeping my thoughts from running rampant—wasn't easy, though. When my imagination wasn't trying to turn noises and shadows into things they weren't, memories of my time with Travis would surface.

I didn't think I had remembered everything that had happened over those three days, but I did have most of it. He'd tied me up, hurt me, yelled at me, didn't give me food or water, but he hadn't been able to rape me. That had been one of the first things to become clear to me, and I was grateful for it.

Though he'd verbally abused me, I still didn't remember all the things he'd said. I had managed to escape after three days, so whatever I'd endured didn't dig as deep as if he'd been able to dole out his cruelty for a longer time.

As I tried to clear my head, snippets of his monologues rang in my mind.

I stopped walking and turned my focus to the words in my head. A sentence had played through my mind, but I hadn't quite caught all of it. I closed my eyes and worked to bring it back. We'd been in the van but stopped somewhere—where?

Travis had been ranting, which was nothing new, but though I hadn't known about his connection with my parents until much later, I thought I was remembering him telling me something about his connection to them.

Trauma can cause amnesia, but I knew that another part of the reason I couldn't recall everything was because I'd tuned him out pretty early on. I'd tried yelling, screaming, threatening, begging, and even reasoning with him, but I knew within a couple of hours that he wasn't going to listen to anything I said, so I'd made the choice to not listen to his vile abuse. React as little as possible.

But it was the second day, I thought, that he'd said something about Eddy and Mill. What was it? I focused even harder, my head tilting toward the past, my eyes still closed in the cool woodsy air of the present.

"Stupid idiots, your parents. Eddy and Mill Rivers are the biggest shysters I know. They got away with everything. Not me, though. No, I had to figure it out on my own."

Those might not have been the exact words, but they were close.

I opened my eyes. "Huh."

I knew my father had been involved in some terrible activities, including drug running through our small Missouri town, but until she'd started breaking into houses as we searched for him, I hadn't thought Mill was involved in anything illegal.

I hadn't asked Travis what he meant, and as odd as it seemed at this very moment, I wished I had. Had I known I would manage an escape three days into my captivity, I might have actually talked to him, tried to understand his crazy, maybe used him as a research subject for my books.

But I hadn't known. All I'd thought was that I was either going to die or, worse, this insane human was going to keep me forever and do whatever he wanted to me. I needed to get away, kill him, or kill myself before he could inflict more horror.

I resumed walking, but as my eyes opened, I realized it was getting darker. I glanced at the time, surprised by how long I'd been on the trail.

I needed to set up camp. I would have rather flipped on my

flashlight and continued through the night, but Tex had explained how that wasn't a good idea because of nocturnal creatures as well as possible rain, which was even more debilitating in the dark, as I'd already witnessed firsthand.

I'd never set up my tent by myself, though I remembered the steps needed to get it done. I was sweating so much by the time I was done that I was afraid I'd get chilled if I didn't change clothes and get into my sleeping bag.

Once I zipped the flap shut, I crawled into my bag and grabbed some water and granola bars.

As I ate, I pondered if I'd be able to trap and skin a rabbit. It was done all the time out here, for food. I hadn't learned how to do that part of surviving outdoors, but that was my own fault. Tex would have taught me how to hunt anything.

As I sat in my tent with my granola bars, I still didn't think I'd ever be interested in hunting, but I wasn't very hungry yet, either.

On my first trip with Tex, I'd brought along a paperback, thinking I could read at night in the tent. It created an idyllic scene in my head. However, I'd been too tired to do anything but sleep. I felt the same tonight. Though the night noises seemed louder than when I'd been with Tex, I was tired enough to close my eyes and give in to the pull of exhaustion.

When a noise awakened me, it seemed like I'd only been asleep for a few minutes, but it was light enough outside to make me think the sun was rising. I must have gotten a good eight hours in.

I sat up and tried to figure out what I'd heard. The snap of a twig was nothing new out here, but sometimes it sounded like a heavier-than-normal footfall. Was that what I'd heard?

Maybe.

I listened hard. Though there were no more snapping noises, there was another sound that I was sure I knew. There was an animal close outside my tent.

I was hoping for something small, but chances were that it wasn't anything smaller than a bear or a moose. I could handle this. Could I handle this?

I had no choice but to try.

Slowly and carefully, I unzipped the flap and peered out. I saw only the woods. I didn't need a fire last night, though it was chilly this morning. It would warm up enough in an hour or so, but as I stuck my head out from the tent, I could see my breath.

Nothing came into view, so I crawled out a little more. I needed to understand what I was dealing with.

Nothing. Not even a bug was in sight. I sniffed and didn't smell the rank that came with the wild animals. If the wind was right, you could smell them a literal mile away.

Still nothing.

I turned in a circle and looked deeper in every direction. A flash of color—light blue—caught my eye. It was in a tree on the trail ahead about thirty feet, in the direction I would be heading once I packed up camp. I squinted but couldn't make out exactly what it was. I grabbed my boots and slipped them on quickly, without tying the laces, and made my way to the object.

I recognized it about ten feet before I reached it.

"No," I said as my hand went to my mouth. I wanted to scream, but the torrent of fear growing inside me froze me momentarily into place. I couldn't be seeing what I thought I was seeing.

When I'd first come to Benedict, I'd needed to search for something in the woods. I was new enough to this world that I was worried I might get lost. I'd put my socks in trees to mark the path I'd taken. At the time I realized it was an odd thing to choose, but my options were limited.

Still, though, I didn't think deeply about why I might choose a sock, why the idea came to me so easily.

Now, I remembered another moment in Travis's van. When he'd taken me from my home, I'd been wearing light blue socks with Mickey Mouse embroidered on the back. Mill had given them to me.

I knew that if the police found them, if they showed them to Mill, she would know it was me communicating with her, maybe leaving a trail.

It had been a long shot, of course. Just leaving the socks didn't mean much of anything if all the rest of the pieces of the puzzle weren't also in place. The police and Mill would have had to see them, make the connection.

But Travis had caught me.

We'd stopped in a gas station somewhere in Missouri in the middle of the night. My mouth was gagged but there were no other cars in sight, no one else at the pumps. I was in the passenger seat with my hands tied in front of me, my ankles zip-tied together.

As Travis pumped the gas, I hurriedly managed off a shoe. I reached over with my bound hands and got a dirty sock off my foot, too. As I sat up again, I could see that Travis was still on the other side of the van, whistling as the gas gulped into the vehicle.

The window didn't close all the way, leaving a perpetual quarter inch opening at the top. It made for a noisy and hot-aired ride, but I'd become grateful to have another sound besides Travis's voice to listen to.

As quickly as I could, I lifted the sock to the gap above the window, but my hurried pace caused it to drop back on the floor. I had to try again. I bent over and gathered the sock and brought it back up to the gap.

By the time I managed part of it through the opening, Travis was there, looking in at me through the window.

He shook his head, opened the door, and grabbed the sock from my fingers.

"Stupid girl. Stupid, stupid, stupid." He took the sock from my hand and punched me in the jaw.

I blacked out, waking up some time later as we were on yet another dark road and Travis was singing along with an oldies radio station. "Johnny Angel" was the song.

I remembered it all so clearly now—the urgency to get the sock out of the window, the hot humidity, the immediate blackness of losing consciousness.

Now, I told my legs to get into gear, get this over with. Get that sock now hanging from a tree branch in Alaska. If this was one of the same socks I'd worn in the van, then there was no more doubt— Travis was here. There was no other reasonable explanation.

I took one step, two, and then closed the distance to the branch. I reached up and gathered the sock. It wasn't tangled there, but just placed. For a long moment I just looked at it in my hand. I needed to turn it over and see if Mickey was embroidered on its back heel, but I could feel the threads in my hand. I knew that something was there.

Finally, I looked. There he was. The mouse's smile had never looked so sinister.

Air whooshed out of my lungs, and I wondered if I would ever be able to breathe again. Noises came from my throat—gurgled watery sounds. I registered that tears had started falling from my eyes, even though I didn't feel like I was crying as much as drowning.

I crumpled to the ground, sitting on the damp earth. I wanted to disappear. I wanted to have never existed.

But the voice in my head changed. Travis got pushed out while others made their way in. Mill telling me I was going to be fine. Leia, proud of how far I'd come. Tex and his kind gentle-giant ways. Gril—so serious and so much like a father figure. My dad and I had been finding our way.

I'd been finding my way, and I had relished it. I had people who wanted to fight for me to keep living this life that I loved so much.

I was willing to fight, too. I had no choice, but maybe that's why it had become so important to me. That's why I hadn't left Benedict. This was my life, the way it was supposed to be lived.

But no one gets to live the way they want without at least some fight.

I stood and wiped my face, sniffed away the tears. I looked all around. There was no one else in sight, but now I knew. I knew he was here. Maybe, in one way or another, he had been the whole time. Renting space in my head had kept him with me.

He must have gotten here shortly after he escaped in Missouri. He could have moved that fast.

"Come out, Travis," I yelled. "Let's get this over with."

The only answer I received was the wind rustling the leaves. It sounded like laughter.

Twenty-four

packed up quickly. I'd never moved with such accurate precision. The fear that could have crippled me (did for a few minutes) seemed to do the opposite. I was energized and hyper-focused.

I spent only the briefest of seconds considering turning around and heading back to Benedict. It would have been what everybody else would have wanted, but as much as I tried to figure out the right thing, I couldn't make myself do it.

Whatever fray or fire was ahead, I was walking directly into it.

I was extra alert as I set out. I hadn't called out to Travis again. I set my face in a firm expression that hopefully said I wasn't afraid of him.

I wasn't. And I was.

I didn't want to be killed, but living while looking over your shoulder isn't ideal. Whatever the end would be, it was time for it.

If I didn't run into him, I could make it to the mine by this evening if I moved fast. I still hoped to cross paths with someone headed back this way or maybe just find others there. I wouldn't mind not doing this alone, even if I knew I was the one who had to take care of things.

What were they doing out here? Where exactly was everyone?

As the questions rang through my mind, I stopped, freezing into place again with a new horror. What if Travis had killed them all, one at a time as they'd made their way?

"Oh, God," I muttered quietly.

I knew I couldn't let that thought fill my head fully. It would do more than paralyze me: it might make me want to give up. I would be so disappointed in myself if I did that, and so would everybody else.

"Please be okay," I said, again quietly.

Though my legs now felt heavy, I moved them and continued forward.

A plan came to me, and I slowed down a little again. I began to look for signs of earlier trouble—blood or broken brush—but I didn't spot anything suspicious, which made me doubly hope everyone was okay. If they were, it was clear that Travis's sole mission was to get to me.

I had enough strength and energy to continue to the mine, but I stopped early and made camp again instead. This time, I moved slowly, purposefully. Travis was watching, I was sure, but he was good at staying hidden.

I kept the knife sheathed at my side. It wasn't hidden, but I didn't think Travis was afraid of my little old hunting knife. I did wish for a gun.

I made a small fire and I sat by it, eating granola bars, wondering if I was being watched.

As I'd had time to process the sock, I'd wondered if maybe Travis hadn't seen me grab it. I was sure he'd put it there, but that didn't mean he was right there watching me. I'd heard a twig break—that combined with the sock made me automatically assume that Travis was nearby.

But he hadn't shown himself, and the moment I found the sock would have given him a distinct advantage over me.

If he was out here, what was he waiting for? No one was with me. It was a gift, really. I was on a proverbial silver platter.

As I cleaned up, I waited, but no one showed themselves. I was happy to see the darkness take over. Another time, that might have pushed me over some edge—wasn't everyone afraid of the dark?

Not tonight.

I climbed into my tent and zipped it closed. I lay down on top of the sleeping bag. I wasn't even tempted to fall asleep. I wasn't tired. I was wired. I'd stopped early to keep my stores of energy, and I still felt good.

About half an hour into complete darkness, I made my move. Slowly, as quietly as possible, I crawled to the back of my tent—it wasn't a big shelter, only about eight feet long. I stuffed my sleeping bag with whatever I had with the hope of making it look like I was sleeping. I'd never snuck out of the house as a teenager. I felt silly, immature, doing what I was doing, but it still seemed like a good enough idea.

Dressed in my warm gear and with the knife at my side, I unzipped an almost hidden back flap. You couldn't immediately see the zipper and the opening wasn't huge, but it offered another way out if that ever became necessary. Tex had shared with me reasons why a tent might need a hidden back flap—escape from weather or wildlife or just a way to ventilate.

I'd set up the tent close to the trees. I didn't think I was going to be able to fool anyone really, particularly not anyone who was used to being out here. If they knew anything about tents, they would know about the model I had purchased from the mercantile in Benedict.

It was my only plan.

It took a long time to furtively unzip the back and then squeeze my way out and into the trees. I wasn't as quiet as I'd hoped, but it couldn't be helped. I was doing my best.

Sweat trickled down my back underneath my coat, and I knew that I would cool off quickly once I wasn't working so hard—maybe too quickly. It was colder out here than I thought it was going to be—not freezing but cool enough to make me shiver if I was out for very long.

Maybe it would only be a short time.

I crouched in the small space between the tent and some trees. It was a tight fit. I was protected by the trees, but I was also trapped by them. They might keep a bear or moose out, but if a human or something small came at me, they could reach me. I couldn't get up and out of here quickly.

It was as I was considering a good escape route that the fruits of my plan began to show themselves. I heard the distinct noise of someone or something coming my direction.

That was quick, I thought. I stilled myself and worked to quiet my breathing and my noisy heartbeat in my ears.

My muscles wanted to rebel, but I managed to keep them under control. Somehow, I found a weird zen and told myself I was the predator, not the prey.

The noises grew closer. Someone or something was making its way to my tent. I'd set myself up as bait and it seemed to have worked.

Now what, though?

Would the person go into the tent? Was it Travis? Did they think they had trapped me?

I hoped they had.

I unsheathed the knife. It was so dark that it was impossible to see who was on the other side of the tent—the side with the front flap. Slowly, I stood from the crouch. It must not have taken long but it felt like time stretched.

It sounded as if the person was right at the tent flap now.

I needed to make my move. I held the knife in my hand, blade down and ready to stab. I wasn't going to manage stealth at this point, so I needed to be fast.

I stepped out from the cage of trees and took long fast strides to the front of the tent. As I came around, a light flipped on and shone in my eyes, stopping me in my tracks.

If I was any sort of survivalist, any sort of fighter, I wouldn't have let the light stop me. I would have gone in for the kill. But, unfortunately, that wasn't me. Not until I knew who exactly I was killing.

"Stop!" a voice said. "I'm not going to hurt you."

It was a male voice, but I didn't think it belonged to Travis.

"Who are you?"

"My name is Brick. I live out here, near a place called Blue Mine."

"Are you Jin's husband?"

The man hesitated. "Common-law maybe, but we've never formalized anything."

"Show me your face." The light was still in my eyes.

"Okay, but you're going to . . . well, okay." Slowly, the light turned toward the man's face.

Though his head was exposed, his body was covered in a furry costume.

"You're the Bigfoot?" I said.

He nodded. "Yes, ma'am. Just trying to scare people away from the mine. I'm not here to hurt you. I promise."

"Just scare me away."

"Well, no. I've been watching you and I wanted to make sure you were okay. I took this off"—he was holding the head of the costume—"so we could talk. I was worried about you."

"You hurt my boyfriend."

Brick's eyebrows furrowed. "What?"

"You shot him, hit his arm."

"Oh, no. I didn't . . . it was an accident. I can explain. I promise."

"I . . . this . . . this is all too weird, Brick."

"I'm fully aware of that, but I'm also thinking I don't know all that's going on. I promise you I don't deserve killing, whatever you might think."

When I stared at him but didn't say anything for a long moment, he tried a different tack. "Do you know what in the hell is going on between Benedict and the mine?"

"A lot."

"I figured. Care to tell me? I'll get a fire going. You'll have to trust me, but I promise I'm harmless, and I really was worried about you."

"Why did you shoot Tex?"

He lifted his hands. They were covered in fur gloves and at the moment struck me as so ridiculous that I rolled my eyes.

He said, "It was an accident. I was aiming for a rabbit. I didn't bring much food with me. I've been afraid to go back to the mine to get anything. I was hungry. I'm so sorry." He paused. "Is he . . . okay?"

I didn't want to answer immediately, but after a few seconds I nodded. "He'll be fine."

"Good. I'll apologize to him in person if that will help."

"Did you know about Peter Murray?"

Brick deflated. "You mean his demise?"

"Yes, that's what I mean."

"Yeah, I know about Peter. And Gunter, Nancy, and Brubaker, too. Do you know about them?"

I nodded. "I do. What's going on at that mine?"

"What's your name?" Brick asked.

The question was so sincere, I was sure he had no clue who I was. He didn't know my story.

"Beth," I said.

"Beth, can we light a fire, make some coffee or something, and just talk? Maybe we can help each other. I sure could use some intel and I think you might know more than I do. I'm not going to hurt you, I promise, but I'll sit far away, and you can keep the knife out." He frowned at the weapon. "If you want."

I looked at the knife in my hand. Even in the glow from the flashlight that was mostly aimed toward Brick, I could see my white-knuckled grip. I wasn't going to put the weapon away. If I had my way, I was never going to be unprepared again.

"You do the fire. I'll keep the knife out, but I have enough coffee for both of us." I had some food, too—mostly granola bars—but I didn't immediately offer it.

Brick nodded. "I have a pack over behind that tree over there. Let me grab it."

As he made his way in that direction, I opened the front flap of my tent and grabbed the lantern I'd set inside. I flipped it on and watched as he returned with his pack.

After he took off the rest of the costume, Brick did as he said he would. He stayed on the other side of the pit as he started a fire and then put together a percolator with coffee I tossed to him. I noticed the rifle he'd shot Tex with attached to the pack, but he showed me that it was unloaded and not ready to fire.

Brick might have been in his forties, but he had the look that many folks out here had—a little worn from the cold weather and hard work needed just to survive. I'd come to think of it as the "Alaskan tan," which was the opposite of a suntan, tinged more with gray than any other color.

He was a handsome man, but he could have used a good haircut and shave. His brown hair was scraggly and his beard unkempt, though that look wasn't unfamiliar, either. It was easy to not care about how you looked when you were focused on getting through a cold snap.

I understood how things happened, and I thought he'd probably been busy playing Bigfoot for a while.

I was irritated by the act but curious enough for answers that I was okay sharing a fire and some coffee.

He poured some into each of our mugs and handed mine back over. I took it and then tossed him some granola.

"Thank you," he said before he ate it quickly.

"What are you doing, Brick? You know this is strange, right?"

Brick shrugged. "It's as strange as it gets. That was the point."

"You all found some gold." It was both a question and a statement.

"You could say that."

"Lots of gold?"

"I think so."

"I guess I just don't understand all the rules, but doesn't the gold belong to you all anyway?"

"It does, but someone doesn't like that idea and they're killing people to get rid of us."

I didn't know this man at all, but he didn't seem that threatening. It might just be a good act. I wasn't ready to let my guard down.

"Someone out here in the woods is killing people at Blue Mine?" I asked.

"Jin and I thought it would be worthwhile to attempt to scare people away. We don't think the killer is one of us."

"Doesn't that make the most sense, though?" I swallowed some of the strong coffee.

Brick shook his head. "None of our problems started until an outsider moved in."

"Peter Murray?"

"Yep."

"Who is dead now, too, so . . ."

"I see what you're saying, but we, Jin and me, think that his arrival caused other outsiders to pay attention to us. We think Peter brought the killer, though likely didn't know what he'd done. We didn't know where he was from. He didn't say and we didn't push to know."

"Nobody from Benedict knew where he'd gone. Until his body was . . . recovered, folks in Benedict had been looking for him. He was a loner. I don't think anyone followed him out to your mine. Do you know why he was there?"

"Sure. Of course. He said that his folks left him a mine of his own, but he didn't know what to do with it. He wanted some guidance."

"I've seen where his mine is located. It's just a hole in the ground."

"That's what he said."

"You all welcomed him?"

"Sure. Well, we're always wary of strangers, but he was a nice man." Sadness pulled at his features.

"You knew he'd died?"

His eyes snapped up to mine. "I knew he'd been killed."

"Why would Jin have told everyone it was you on the horse?"

Brick shrugged. "I'm not sure. She didn't share her plans with me, but I know her well enough to guess. Did someone from Benedict surprise her?"

I nodded. "Well, yes, I guess. My friend Tex and I were planning to pass through, but Jin was coming out toward us with the body on the horse. She claimed she was bringing it to Benedict and that it was you."

"I bet that she was bringing Peter back to Benedict because she wondered if that was his home." He paused.

"Why didn't she just say that?"

"I don't know." His eyes unfocused as he stared into the fire. "No, that's not right." He looked at me. "She didn't know Peter was from Benedict. None of us did. I doubt he told her."

"So, she was just getting rid of the body, and we interrupted?"

Brick sighed. "Probably. It's . . . well, we didn't want to be bothered. I guess if she told you it was her husband, it might all make more sense. As much as we liked Peter, we didn't know much about him."

"She claimed she wanted the murders investigated, was coming to find Gril."

"She lied. We mind our own business. She was just telling you that then."

"Peter was killed there."

"But not by one of us. She had to come up with a good story for you."

A memory came to me. As Jin was introducing me and Tex to the villagers, she did emphasize Brick's name. From this vantage point, it seemed like too much, like she was telling them to play along.

"I saw you that night, in the storm. You didn't go back to Benedict with her?"

"I saw you, too, but I took off after that. She went on her own. Then she took off from Benedict."

Brick laughed. "Of course she did. If you hear what I'm saying, you know we don't want the authorities in our business. We were going to solve the murders ourselves. The costume was part of the plan. I've been watching and trying to be scary."

"Even to your fellow villagers?"

"Of course. Jin and I can keep a secret better than us and a bunch of others, too."

I took another swig of coffee. "Man, that must be a lot of gold."

"It is, and . . . I'm the first to admit, we shouldn't have worked so hard to hide it. Look at what's happened because of it. Things are only getting worse." He shook his head. "We got in too deep and look at it now."

"Tell me more about Peter."

"I don't know much, but he was anxious to learn how to mine, and we taught him."

"Was he a quick learner?"

"He was." Brick's eyebrows furrowed. "He was quiet, though. Did what he had to do and then went to his tent in the evenings, didn't like socializing."

"Did anyone resent him there? I mean, you were trying to hide the gold. Why would anyone want Peter there?"

Brick half smiled. "All I can say is, he was one of us. You can tell."

I nodded. I knew exactly what he meant.

"Peter wasn't there to hurt us. He wasn't there to steal from us. We knew that immediately. He offered his help, too, and we took him up on it."

"Did you hear the story of his parents?"

"No."

I told him about Peter's parents and the way they'd died.

"Tragedy," Brick said.

"Yes."

He looked at me. "There's a lot of that out here, you know that, right? I mean, it's the greatest place in the world and I wouldn't want to be anywhere else, but it's rough."

As I sat around a fire on a cold Alaskan night, across from a man pretending to be Bigfoot, I couldn't argue with what he said.

"You *really* don't think someone from the mine is the killer?"

"I don't. Neither does anyone else there."

"Have you seen people from Benedict headed out toward the mine over the last day or so?"

"I have, all manner of folks. Lots of people pass through. I spotted Gril two days ago. A couple others, too, but I don't know who they are. I thought I'd work to keep people away, but it appears the opposite is happening."

"Do you think Jin went back to the mine?"

"Lots of places she could have gone. Maybe she's back there. I don't know." Brick shrugged.

"Well, it's time to stop with the costume, I think."

"I don't disagree."

"I could use some help and you owe me, I figure." I looked at Brick. "Though I'm not the safest person to be around."

"That's interesting. What's that mean?"

I took a deep breath. "Have you ever heard of Beth Rivers?"

"No, never."

"It's a long story then."

"I think we have some time. I'm not afraid. Tell me if you want."

I reached into my pocket and pulled out the sock. "Let's start with this and go backward. Did you see who put this on a tree branch a ways back?"

"A tree? It's a sock?"

"A very specific sock."

"Okay. No, I didn't see anyone do that. I didn't even see the sock until now."

I nodded. "He's good. I don't know how he got so good, but he's so good at hiding."

"Who's he?"

"Travis Walker. Heard of him?"

"Never."

"You don't pay attention to the news."

"Not a bit of it. I think the news is just as crooked as the criminals."

"Yeah, can't argue there."

"Who is he?"

"He kidnapped me just over a year ago now. He kept me in his van for three days. I escaped and then ran up here to Benedict."

Brick blinked and studied me a long moment. "Yeah?"

I nodded. "Yeah."

"Let me pour you another cup before you get into it." Brick stood and grabbed the pot to fill my mug.

Again, I took a moment to acknowledge to myself that I did not know this man, that he had been wearing a costume and trying to scare people away from a mine where murders had been occurring, that he'd "accidentally" shot Tex. Nevertheless, I told him my story.

From the very beginning.

Twenty-five

By the time I finished I was exhausted, and Brick had added more wood to the fire—twice.

He remained mostly silent as I spoke, his reactions clear by the changing expressions on his face.

The juxtaposition of his personality with Jin's seemed so opposites-attract, I worked through that a little, wondered about their relationship.

Brick was a sensitive man even if he had shot Tex. Jin was harsh. I suspected the environment had more to do with both their personalities than anything else.

Once I was finished and the fire had died down to mostly embers, Brick said, "Sleep, Beth. Rest. I'll watch tonight. No one will hurt you."

"You need your rest, too."

Brick smiled wryly. "If you think I could sleep after what you just told me . . . I'll be fine."

"Wait. Don't . . . don't make a move to look for Travis tonight, okay?"

"I won't. I'm a reasonable man." He winked at me and nodded at the costume on the ground next to his sleeping bag.

I smiled. "I see that."

"You know, the thing about living out by the mine is that we sometimes forget there's a whole world out there. Benedict isn't all that big, but I need to make the trip there more often. I should pay attention to the news. I should get to know folks better."

"I don't know. Maybe it would be better not to know what I went through."

"More pleasant, sure, but not the way it should be. The things that happened to you should have never happened, Beth. It's criminal, of course, but it's also inhuman and I don't want to bury my head when it comes to right and wrong." He shook his head again. "We protect our people."

"I don't want anyone hurt. . . ."

"Everything's going to be fine. I promise."

I wanted to ask how he could make such a promise, but I knew he couldn't, really; no one could. I liked his confidence, though, and I didn't want to see it falter.

We said good night and I made my way into my tent. I felt safe with him out there. I didn't want him to get hurt, either, but I was convinced that he could handle himself. I hoped so. I needed some rest.

I slept like the dead, rocklike and dreamless.

I awakened the next morning to the smell of coffee.

I stuck my head out of the tent and looked at Brick. "Everything okay?"

"Absolutely. Come on out. We'll eat and then I'll walk with you either to the mine or back to Benedict if you want."

"I have bacon."

"You've been holding out." Brick smiled. "Sounds great."

"I need to go to the mine after breakfast, see what happened to everybody."

"That's what we'll do."

There wasn't much conversation as we ate and then packed up camp. Brick was now all business, even as he hid the Bigfoot costume in a naturally carved-out space in an old tree truck.

Once that was done, he looked at me. "The ridiculousness of this idea"—he nodded toward the costume—"is so glaring now. There are many more things going on here that warrant serious focus. I apologize for any concern this might have caused you or your friends."

"I don't think . . . no one thought it was really Bigfoot."

"No?" Brick smiled. "Shocking."

His pack was smaller than mine, having been depleted of his supplies. He offered for us to switch, but my pride wouldn't allow me.

"It takes time to figure out the necessities and how to pack them appropriately. You will."

I wanted to say that I hoped so, but I wasn't sure how much more hiking and camping I needed in my life.

"You mentioned the police chief from Milton was out here, too?" Brick asked over his shoulder.

"Yes, I saw him yesterday. He asked me not to tell anyone he was here, but fewer secrets seem wiser than more."

"I haven't seen him, but I think I've seen everyone else you mentioned, except for Walker."

"I wondered if maybe I imagined the whole encounter with Stellan—the one where he saved me from the water, too. They seemed . . . unreal."

"Really?"

"Well, they were real. I'm not given to making such things up, but he's been pretty stealthy."

"Even from me, and he doesn't know I've been watching everyone."

"He saw you shoot Tex—"

"Which was an accident," Brick hurried to say. "I will apologize to him, face whatever legal consequences."

"I bet an apology will do." I wasn't sure, but once Tex got to know the man behind the costume, I thought he might forgive him.

"We'll see, I guess. Anyway, maybe Stellan is some sort of outdoor survivalist and particularly good at hiding."

"I don't know if he has an outdoorsy background, but it wouldn't surprise me. Small-town Missouri guy."

"Got it. Let me know if you spot him. I'll point out anyone I hear or see."

"Deal."

Something wavered inside me. Brick's curiosity about Stellan wasn't completely unusual, but his tone had turned funny. He'd been open and friendly, but now his voice sounded tight and a tiny bit unsure. He had reminded me of so many of the people I'd met in Alaska—certain they were ready for anything. Now, though, not as much.

I decided to chalk it up to the fact that we were no longer sitting around a campfire but taking a journey with a purpose. With him in front of me, I couldn't see his face.

I didn't want to distrust him, but it wasn't good to fully trust anyone so quickly.

I was too trustworthy as it was. I'd opened the door for Travis.

I didn't want to think about any of that now. I just wanted to get to the mine.

Twenty-six

A big wave of relief swept through me when we saw Viola walking toward us only a half an hour or so later.

"That's my landlord," I said as I hurried and made my way around Brick. He stepped out of the way so I could pass.

"What are you doing out here, Beth?" she asked first. "Tex okay?"

"Yes, Tex is . . . was fine. I'm looking for . . . where is everyone?"

Viola frowned and sighed. "Gril and Donner are at the mine, trying to figure out what's been going on. Juneau folks haven't shown up yet."

"Tex?"

"What? I haven't seen him. I thought he was with you."

"Long story." I swallowed hard. "My parents?"

"Damn your mother. When we started out, she said she was going to first look around a little for who shot Tex, out by your shed. Then she didn't come back. Before you ask, no, I don't think she's lost, not totally anyway. I think she has a plan, even if the rest of us aren't included. I thought she might have gone to the mine. Before we set out, she made sure I lined out the route we were taking, so I went that way, too."

"But she wasn't there?"

"No. Then when I told everyone that she had slipped my watch, your father took off to search for her. Who knows where the hell everyone has gone."

"They don't know the woods," I said.

"That's what I thought." She shrugged. "But I can't imagine your mother would think that was a problem. She thinks she knows everything better than everyone else."

Viola wasn't wrong. I asked, "Are you headed back to Benedict?"

She looked at me, at Brick, and back at me. "I was. . . ."

I introduced the two of them.

"You're Jin's man?"

"I suppose so."

In her typical no-nonsense tone, she said, "She claimed you were dead."

"I was too busy being Bigfoot to be dead."

Viola nodded. "Right. Well, I'm sure there's more to that story—"

I didn't think I should tell her that Brick was the one to shoot Tex. Viola was not in a good mood and she still had one gun holstered at her waist. The truth would come out later, when everything else was solved. I sent Brick a look to convey that we were going to keep his confession a secret for now. He frowned and nodded.

He looked at Viola. "Is Jin at the mine?"

"No, sir. No one can find her, either. Damnation."

"I don't think the killer is part of the mine community," Brick said.

"Well, I'm not sure Gril feels the same, and he's the boss on that one until the Juneau folks make it out there, if they ever do."

"Juneau. That's just what we need." Brick stepped around Viola and me. His demeanor was less friendly and even more businesslike now. He turned and looked at me. "I need to get back. Do you want to come with me or go with Viola?"

It wasn't an easy decision, but I decided to go with Viola simply because Tex hadn't been spotted—maybe he was still in town.

Gril and Donner could take care of themselves. My parents . . . who knew where they'd gone, but it wasn't logical for me to search for them. It made sense that Brick would want to try to find Jin.

Without anything else more than another nod, Brick turned and set off for the mine. We watched him walk away.

"That was Bigfoot?" she said.

I put my hand on her arm. "Come on. I'll tell you everything, but let's get home or at least get closer."

She frowned and considered my words. Finally, she shook her head. "Let's get going."

We moved quickly. I *was* gaining strength, but I was also somewhat weary. I thought about dropping my pack somewhere to lighten my load, but I would have been disappointed in myself.

We were moving much faster than I had with anyone else.

"You are in deceptively good shape," I said, working hard to keep up.

"I've lived here all my life, Beth. Though I didn't visit the mine before now, I've walked these woods hundreds of times. I know them like the back of my hand." She paused. "That's not to say I couldn't get lost. Things change. Trees are felled, mud slides, water gets rerouted. You have to be alert and careful, and in good shape, too."

"I'm trying," I said a little breathlessly.

Viola stopped and looked at me. "Let's take a break. We'll rest and then get home."

I shook my head. "Nope, let's keep going."

We set off again, though Viola took it a little slower. I told her about Brick shooting Tex accidentally. She'd had no comment, but the expression on her face told me it was wise I hadn't shared when Brick was nearby.

Then I broke my not-really-a-promise to Stellan again and told Viola I'd seen him.

"Well, he can do what he wants, I suppose, but I don't like that he hasn't checked in with Gril. Shoot, we'd've probably welcomed his help."

"Probably."

"If we see him out here, I'm bringing him in."

I wondered how that would go, but I knew Viola would work out the logistics. I just hoped no guns would be fired.

The unknown in front of us kept us moving at what I only recently would have said was an impossible pace. I got so warm, I had to take off an outer layer. Viola's cheeks got rosy, but as far as I could tell, she didn't have one bit of trouble breathing.

One thing about being in the middle of the woods was that even though you know there's civilization out there somewhere that you once left behind and are headed toward again, the woods can trick you into thinking you might be wrong. Maybe there's only woods and you'll never find civilization again. Well, my imagination could do such things. I doubted that Viola felt the same.

I was relieved when we came to Benedict and it was still there, its small downtown a welcome sight. I set off toward the bar. Viola was close behind.

I set my pack on the boardwalk outside the bar and went to open the door. I hesitated, but at the moment I wasn't aware why—later I would think that it was my gut sensing that something wasn't right.

I pulled the door open and went inside. The bar was always so dark that you couldn't see clearly for a second or so when you entered from the outside.

I blinked and moved my eyes to the spot behind the bar, hoping to find Benny there.

I did, but she wasn't happy to see me.

More precisely, she wasn't happy about anything. Her frown was all encompassing.

I took in the scene. My hand went to my mouth, and I had to work to keep my knees from buckling.

Benny was behind the bar, but Tex was sitting on one of the chairs, holding a gun to a man's head. The man was faced away from me and the bar was so dark . . . it had to be Travis.

Twenty-seven

Viola pushed herself around me.

"Put the gun down, Tex," she said as she drew her own.

"Not until Gril gets here and arrests him."

Neither Tex nor Viola was going to holster their weapons.

"I'm not who you all apparently think I am," the man said. He turned his head a minuscule amount so I could better see his profile. "It's me, Beth."

"Stellan!" I explained. "Okay, everybody, this is Stellan Graystone, the police chief from Milton."

"Yeah?" Viola asked.

"Come around and take a good look," Tex said. "Be sure."

I hurried around the outer perimeter of the bar. "Yes, I'm sure. Please, lower your weapons."

Slowly and almost regrettably, both Tex and Viola did as I asked.

"Thank you," Stellan said to me. He scooted his chair a little farther away from Tex and then turned to face the room. He lifted his hands. "I'm on your side."

Both Viola and Tex had seen pictures of Travis. I didn't know what research they'd done on their own, but I'd shown them the pictures that had been included with the articles and news stories.

We'd passed around a couple copies at the meeting where we discussed what I should do.

"Why did you think this was Travis?" I asked Tex.

"I didn't say I thought he was Travis." Tex sent Stellan a sour look.

"Okay. What happened?" I asked. "Why did you consider him a threat?"

"He was slinking around out there. He's set up camp with copies of articles about you in his tent."

I nodded. "Yeah, I know." I sighed. That's where Tex must have gone—to figure out who'd been out there, camping and saving me from fast-moving water.

I didn't know where to begin, so I just jumped in. "I'm sorry I ran off from the Benedict House, but I was talking to *him* in the woods. When I came back . . ."

Tex nodded. "Yeah, I was gone, looking for you, then this guy and I found each other." He smiled weakly at me. "We got our wires crossed, but you're okay so I'm okay. I still don't like this guy."

I nodded, mostly just to take another moment to diffuse the charged atmosphere in the room. "How's your arm?"

"Good as new." Tex smiled again, though I could tell he was in some pain. How could he not be?

"Look, let's talk," Stellan interrupted. "I've been hiding out there over a week—"

"He's the one who pulled me from the river," I interrupted. I'd already shared that part with Viola.

Tex nodded and looked at Stellan again. "I wondered. Thank you kindly for saving Beth."

"Glad I was there." Stellan paused. "But how did you sneak up on me today? I didn't hear you until you were right there."

Tex nodded but didn't answer.

I spoke up in defense of someone who didn't need my help, but I couldn't stop myself. "Tex has been in these woods all his life."

Tex nodded and reached into his pocket. "He was putting this on a tree limb."

I looked at the item that Tex had retrieved. It couldn't be. It was the other Mickey Mouse sock. But there was no *other* Mickey Mouse sock. I'd been found with one still on my foot. Since I escaped the hospital before being released, I never received a bag full of the items I'd been wearing when they brought me in. My thoughts darted— what if I'd asked Mill if she'd been given my things? I hadn't even thought about it, and she was now missing, or at least was somewhere unknown.

First and foremost, this meant that maybe Travis Walker hadn't made his way here.

"Beth, let me explain . . ." Stellan lifted his hands.

My eyebrows came together as I looked at him and tried to understand more deeply what was going on. I reached into my pocket and retrieved the sock I'd found. "Has it been you the whole time?"

"Beth . . ."

I marched to him and without being completely aware of what I was doing, I lifted my arm. I brought it down and slapped him hard. He didn't duck. He didn't fight back. No one made a move to stop me from doing further damage, but it was enough. For now.

I stepped back. "Tell us what's going on."

His hand on his cheek, Stellan nodded. "That's what I've been trying to do."

A few beats after my burst of violence, Viola took over. "Let's all take a breath." She looked at Stellan. "Are you armed?"

He had a knife in his pocket that he immediately handed over to her. "That's it, I promise."

"You were going to overtake Travis with a knife?" Viola asked him.

"And the element of surprise." He hesitated. "I didn't realize how frequently guns are shot off around here. I didn't want to garner the attention a gunshot would bring, but no one would have noticed, probably."

Viola turned to her sister behind the counter. "Benny, how about some ice waters all around?"

"Yes, ma'am."

Benny delivered the waters as the other four of us sat around a table, though not in a cozy fashion. We were all back from the table a bit, each of us seeming to want or need our own space.

"I haven't seen Travis," Stellan repeated. "I haven't seen any sign that he's even been here. I came here to . . . take care of him."

"Kill him," Viola said. There was no question in her tone.

"I suppose, yes. I'm a lawman, though. I'm here . . . well, I was here secretly. No one in Missouri knows where I went."

"You bought a plane ticket, you have your phone, you can run, but you can't hide. You should know that," Viola said.

"I used a false identity. I deal with criminals. I regifted some of their paperwork to myself. It's pretty easy to get a plane ticket that way. My cell phone is at home. I don't even have a burner out here. There was nothing for anyone to know I was here. I wanted to take care of things anonymously."

"So, now you're a criminal, too?" I said. "Stellan, it's not worth it. My grandfather would be so . . ."

Stellan looked at me. I saw the red mark my hand had made on his cheek. I wasn't proud of my reaction, but I doubted I would ever regret it too much. I had been about to say, "disappointed," but that didn't feel honest. I remained silent.

Stellan shook his head slowly and answered anyway. "You know he wouldn't be. In fact, he would have probably been the one to find you when Travis took you. He and his hound-dog instincts would have figured it out before anyone else, Beth. You know that."

What I *knew* was that his words made a good story. The legend of the old-timer cop, the man made of grit and smarts who solved almost everything put in his way.

That was all it was, though, a good story. We could only guess what my grandfather would have done. It was impossible to know.

"How did you know about the socks?" I asked.

"The items in the van. It's all in the report. There was one sock in the van. I guessed that you were wearing the other one when you escaped. I didn't have any access to the items you wore to the hospital. I thought it might work to bait Travis. If he's around, I thought it would bring him out from hiding."

I nodded and told them all the story of my attempt to leave a breadcrumb sock trail.

"So all I did was traumatize you?" Stellan said when I finished.

I shook my head. "It was a good idea, but it would have been even better if you'd given me a heads-up, told me when we met out there."

"Didn't even cross my mind to tell you, which seems ridiculous now."

"Have you seen *any* sign at all that Travis Walker is out there?" Viola asked Stellan.

"Not one." He looked at Tex. "I'm good, too. Maybe not as good as this guy, but I'm pretty good."

"I haven't seen any sign, either," Tex added.

"Maybe you and I should team up and head out together?" Stellan said.

"No!" I exclaimed. I cleared my throat as everyone looked at me. "No. Enough. He's not out there. His threat did what it was intended to do: scare me, cause a ruckus, make me—make us all—paranoid and afraid. This can't go on. We all need to get back to living our lives." I lifted my hand as all of them opened their mouths to argue. "No, don't bother. Enough *is* enough. I want everyone to come back here. I want the murders at Blue Mine solved—that's where the focus should be, anyway. I will live smart." I looked at Tex and Viola. "Work with me on guns. I'll carry responsibly, but we are going to go back to living our lives!"

I watched as the other people around the table deflated a little, but it wasn't in disappointment, it was in understanding. *That was a win,* I thought.

"She's right, and you all know it," Benny said from behind the bar.

If it hadn't seemed too casual, I would have lifted my glass of water and saluted her.

"I'm not leaving yet," Stellan said.

"You're not staying out there in the woods. The lodge is open, as well as other places. I'd rather you went home, though," I said.

"I'd rather stay in the woods."

"Not if you don't want me to report you," Viola said to him.

Anger flashed in Stellan's eyes, but it diluted quickly when he saw the return expression on Viola's face.

"You may have a room at the Benedict House. You are welcome to stay with the rest of us."

"Mill has a room there," I added.

"That should be fun," Stellan said with no effort to hide his sarcasm.

"So, we're agreed, then? We are going to go back to normal. The second everyone else gets back into town, we'll share the plan with them." I paused. "If my parents don't return, we'll just let them figure it out, out there. I just can't care what they do."

I didn't really feel that, but I was currently fed up enough to say it and mean it for a second or two.

"Okay, Beth, I get it," Viola said. "If we're all careful and aware, we really should just go back to our lives."

"You don't get to leave, though," Benny said from behind the bar. "Beth, you stay here. This is your home. We protect our own. Maybe we don't need to be so vigilante about it, but it's what we do, and we will keep doing it."

I nodded and blinked away some sudden and surprising tears. I loved this place, and I loved these people. Other than a maniac and potential killer on the loose and hunting for me, my life was pretty good.

Twenty-eight

Have you ever seen anything like it?" I asked Orin.

"Not out here, I haven't," he said.

Only three days had passed since I'd proclaimed that we were all going to go back to living our lives, but Benedict and its surrounding areas had seen a complete transformation. In a way, it, like so many other things, was all my fault.

The world might not have ever heard of Benedict, Alaska, were it not for me and my story. Sure, Glacier Bay National Park was well known, but the tiny town attached to it wasn't on the tip of anyone's tongue. In fact, even my story had only been a small blip on the world's radar when it had first blown through a few months earlier. But when Benedict, Alaska, garnered worldwide attention again, it struck a familiar nerve, and even more attention was given to this small corner of the world.

Shortly after "the day Tex almost killed Stellan," which was how I alluded to it, Gril and Donner arrived back in Benedict with Jin in tow. She'd been hiding in the ice cave, but they'd found her. Gril had interrogated Jin into confessing to the murders. She'd wanted all the gold; Peter's, too. According to Gril, Jin ran out of excuses and just gave in to the questioning. She told Gril that she killed Nancy and Brubaker because they confronted her about how much gold had been recently mined. They both thought she was hiding some. She was. And, she killed Peter simply so she could take his mine for herself. They'd talked to Brick, too, who, despite the confession, was still sure that Jin was innocent. She was in Juneau now.

It was a tough pill for everyone to swallow, including me. I didn't want her to be a killer. But gold did strange things to people, and there sure was a lot of it out there, which was going to cause a whole new mess, or so Gril predicted. After Jin was delivered to the Juneau authorities, who flew over to pick her up from the airport, Brick hopped on the ferry and made his way there, too. He went directly to the newspaper and asked them to listen to him, to write a story.

They were all over it.

But it wasn't the story any of us might have expected.

Brick, the man who'd thought a Bigfoot costume was a good idea, knew how to divert and distract. Reporters would eat up the Blue Mine story and its gold, its history, even the fact that Jin's grandfather might have been a killer, too. But that's not what happened.

Somehow Brick spun it to be about the old mine that Peter Murray's family had purchased, how it was right next to one of the biggest salmon runs in the state. Brick claimed he'd heard that not only were state officials never going to let poor, now tragically deceased Peter Murray mine his family's rightful property, the state itself was going to come in and take all the gold.

It was a smoke-and-mirrors move. Now no one cared in the least about Blue Mine, its gold, or its horrific tragedies. Suddenly, everyone cared about what had been named "Peter's Mine" and the injustices coming its way. The public didn't even pay attention to the fact that it seemed that Jin was a ruthless killer.

Today, there were people marching and camping on the tundra, carrying signs saying that no mining should be allowed, along with a healthy amount of folks who just thought the Alaska state government should mind their own business and stay out of the mining business. There were probably about fifty people out at Peter's Mine and ten or so reporters with microphones and cameras.

None of the seeds that Brick had planted were verifiable, but he knew the buttons to push, and in three short days, the site had turned into a protest zone.

"It's pretty cold at night," I said.

"I don't think they care," Orin answered. "Some people sit around waiting for opportunities like this. It's perfect. Environmentalists, off-gridders, antigovernment types, so many people love this."

"Is there any chance the government was going to come in and take the gold?"

Orin laughed. "Probably not before Brick planted the idea with them."

"Oh, the irony."

Orin shook his head. "And Blue Mine is being ignored."

"I don't see how that will help Jin if she really is guilty."

Orin smirked. "I don't think Brick's efforts are truly about saving Jin. It's about the gold. He might not want her to be guilty, but I'm sure he wants everyone to leave him and the other villagers alone so they might get all the gold out of Blue Mine."

I thought about the man I'd met. He'd been what I would have called a nice guy—even if he had shot Tex—but he'd also been willing to try to attempt to scare people by wearing a Bigfoot costume. Yes, gold can be a pretty big motivator.

When Tex had learned the truth about who'd shot him, he'd simply rolled his eyes and blamed himself again for not being alert enough. No one had even discussed forcing Brick to face any legal action.

Orin continued, "They'll move along soon enough."

We were on a hike together, one of several I'd recently taken.

The only thing everyone had asked of me was that I not be alone, for a little while, at least. I'd had meals, hiked, and even worked in the shed with a chaperone ever since.

I'd sent Tex home to heal. I told him to spend a week with his daughters and then we'd regroup. We were going to be fine—no different than we were before all the craziness. It was a good place to be.

I'd hung out with Viola, Gril, Donner, Orin, even Stellan and my parents, who'd shown up not long after Gril and Donner.

They'd appeared with wide curious eyes, wondering if it was all over yet. Had we caught him? They sure hadn't found any sign of him anywhere. Gril had appraised them with eyes that made me think he might either arrest or shoot them, but he'd done neither. Instead, he seemed to accept their behavior and didn't even bother to tell them to shape up.

I did, though. I'd sat them down, fed them some of Viola's blueberry muffins, and told them that either they behaved or they left. This was my place, and they didn't get to mess it up for me. They were tired at the time, a little worn out from their woodsy adventure, the details of which they weren't sharing, so they nodded agreeably. I suspected I'd have to talk to them again when they got their second wind.

They'd both been a chaperone a time or two as well.

As much as I loved them all, I was overstimulated and wishing for some time alone in my shed to write, maybe with just Gus to talk to. I didn't know when that was going to happen.

The walk out to Peter's Mine was something Orin had suggested when he'd come to take over a shift from Viola at the shed. He had sensed my restlessness.

A walk is always good for the soul.

It had been, but I was glad we were headed back to the shed.

"Did Gril tell you that Jin is now claiming she's innocent?" Orin said over his shoulder to me.

"No. But I'm not surprised. Any other evidence yet?"

"I don't know what the Juneau folks have found."

"If the confession is thrown out, it could be a tough case to prove," I said.

"It's up to Juneau now, and that's for the best."

"I agree."

"Whatever the answer turns out to be, that mine needs some scrutiny. I'm all for people living the way they want, but that can go too far sometimes. Murder is not a good result. I don't know if anyone will get around to it, though. We'll see," Orin said.

"Agreed."

Storm clouds chased me and Orin back to the shed, rain pouring down only a few minutes after we'd made it safely inside. Viola had dropped me off and then spent a few hours watching me type, which was completely unproductive for me, but she'd found some enjoyment in a shot of whiskey from a bottle I kept in the drawer, a tradition I'd kept from the original *Petition* publisher, Bobby Reardon.

Orin made his way to the small window next to my desk and peered out toward the library. He grumbled something undiscernible and then pulled back. "We need to walk up there."

"In the rain?"

"I need to make sure some windows are closed. No one is in my office. I should have closed them before I left, but I didn't."

"I'll wait here," I said. "You'll be right back."

"No, Beth, not an option. If you don't come with me, I'll just have to let the damage be done."

"This is getting old, Orin, and it's only been three days. I need to have another meeting."

"That's fine, but for today, you and I are together for a few more hours."

I sighed. "All right. Let's gear up."

Because it rained so frequently, I had plenty of gear in a box by the door. Orin and I both put on rain ponchos and then added hats with brims to keep the rain out of our eyes.

I opened the door. It was really coming down. I sent Orin a weary look, but he didn't take it personally.

"Let's get this over with," he said.

If he'd driven to the shed, we wouldn't have to walk the quarter mile to the library, but it was just a quarter mile, after all. No one in their right mind would drive that. (I'd driven it a time or two—it can get cold out there.)

We trudged our way down the unpaved path that led to the library. It was muddy and only going to get muddier. The rain pelted and blinded us. We were stupid to be out in it, but it wasn't that far.

It happened so fast, and I couldn't see anything anyway, but I really didn't see it coming. I didn't see the person approach from the woods to my left. I didn't see if Orin noticed them, either. I didn't see the arms come around me and drag me away from Orin—the rain was coming down so hard that I didn't even see Orin as I was pulled into the woods. I registered that I lost the hat, though.

I screamed, but between the poncho and the rain, I barely heard myself. No one else could have heard me. I was pretty sure Orin didn't see where I went, either. He probably missed the whole thing, wondering where I'd gone after he'd made it inside the library.

I struggled, but the wiry arms that grabbed and held onto me were strong. I knew who they belonged to. I'd felt them around me before.

Travis Walker had finally made it to Benedict.

Twenty-nine

continued to be blinded by the storm, Travis's arms, my own panic. I felt like my heart was going to explode. I made noises—whatever I could get out of my mouth as the rain nearly drowned me. I was loud in my own ears, but the sound probably couldn't travel much farther than that.

I didn't know what had happened to Orin, but I didn't think he'd been hurt. In the seconds before he grabbed me, I was sure Travis hadn't taken the time to do anything to Orin—that was what my brain held onto. Orin was unharmed, right?

I'd made a promise to myself. I would never allow myself to be taken again. I would die first. That's what my goal was as we struggled through the muddy forest. I did all I could. I fought and kicked, scratched, would have plunged a knife into my own heart if I had one. I could have shot myself before allowing Travis to take me, anyone to take me. But I didn't have a gun. Despite my proclamation from a few days earlier, I hadn't spent one moment learning how to use a firearm. The sheathed knife around my waist had only gotten in my way, so I'd taken it off. Besides, I was never alone. I would be fine.

"Shut up, Beth," Travis said. He'd been saying it over and over as we'd made our way, but I finally heard the words.

It was him, there was no doubt. I knew that voice, that Missouri twang mixed with chronic anger. Travis Walker was mad about everything and everyone, and I was the one he took it all out on.

I wasn't going to shut up. When his words registered, a new wave of resolve pushed through me.

Travis chuckled. "Well, well, someone's gotten a little stronger."

Not stronger than him, though. I would never be stronger than him.

But you're smarter, Bethie, and you know it. Use it. You got this. Take him down.

My grandfather's voice rang through my mind. God, I missed that man. He was the best of all of us, the best of Milton, Missouri, maybe the whole Midwest. I hadn't really heard his voice since he'd died. His down-home wisdom had been a part of my life, and he'd come to me in dreams every now and then, but this was the first time I actually heard his voice—no, that wasn't it, this was the first time I really felt him.

The poncho might have protected me from the rain, but it also contributed to blinding and binding me. The hood came over my face, and the body gave Travis something to twist to keep my arms from being able to do what I wanted them to do.

Everything suddenly changed, though, and he threw me to the ground—though it wasn't muddy, and I was no longer being pelted by rain. With flailing arms, I attempted to swipe the hood away from my face. Once I was free of the poncho, in quick agile moves, my ankles and wrists were zip-tied together.

When I managed it, I could see where we were. A cave. One that couldn't have been far from either my shed or the library, but one I didn't know existed. Some light came from what must have been the opening somewhere around a rocky jut, but a battery powered lantern filled the space with a glow, both bright and yellow, stark yet sickly.

From the cold hard ground I looked up at Travis. He loomed like some stupid giant, his arms crossed in front of himself.

"Hey there," he said with that goddamn twang.

I didn't respond, but my throat made some sort of growling sound.
He chuckled. "Miss me?"

I looked at the ground at his feet and took a shaky breath. I knew
I needed my wits about me. I needed to get it together. Finally, I
found some words: "Why didn't you just kill me?"

He crouched down. "What fun would that be? I got you, Beth
Rivers, and not only that, can you even believe it, I can get your
loser parents, too. How does one man get so damn lucky?"

In fact, I thought that was a great question, but I didn't answer.

I didn't want to talk to him. I wanted to ignore everything he
said. It would have probably been smarter for me to sit here silently,
no matter what happened. I needed to think about how I was going
to get away. But I had questions. So many questions.

"Where are we?"

"What do you mean? We're right where you were about thirty
minutes ago, a small Podunk place in Alaska. Alaska! Good choice
of places to hide, by the way. Were it not for all the news coverage, I would never have known this is where you went. I would
never have guessed Alaska. Shame I had to ever be caught in the
first place, huh?" Travis sat and faced me. He crossed his legs as he
blocked the way toward what I was sure was the opening. Not that I
could get up quickly or easily anyway.

"We're in a cave?" I asked.

"How about that? There are a few around here. I've been hanging
out for a few days, spying on you, scoping out the caves, making
plans. You didn't notice me?"

I didn't respond, but I had no idea there were caves in this area
of the woods. The surrounding land wasn't mountainous, but there
were hills, and I knew the ground was rock hard in places. Of course,
there were caves nearby. This land held every possible wild thing.

He continued, "Well, it seems no one did. I even ate at that restau-
rant and shopped in the store. I needed new socks. You know, Beth,

never underestimate the value of good thick socks." He paused when I still didn't respond. "Well, I suppose if you were going to be out here much longer, socks would be more important, but those days are over. Oh well."

He leaned a little closer to me, trying to get me to look into his eyes. I kept my gaze on the ground to the side of him.

He grabbed my face and squeezed my cheeks together hard. "Look at me, bitch."

While I would have rather just died, pain is a motivator. I moved my eyes to his. He smiled and released his hold. I sniffed hard.

"That's better," he said. "You will look at me or I will hurt you. Got it?"

I gritted my teeth and kept my eyes on his. Tears choked my throat, but I didn't want to cry. I remembered the time in the van. I'd gone through a spectrum of reactions. I'd screamed and yelled, then cried, then fell silent, then allowed silent tears to fall. He hadn't been so adamant about me looking into his eyes, but we hadn't been facing each other in the same way.

I couldn't have stopped the tears that fell from my eyes now, but I sniffed again, hoping to at least choke the flow.

Travis smiled his familiar smile—a happy evil. Whatever I hadn't remembered from those three days in his van came back to me in flashes and floods as I took in his crooked teeth, the gray stubble on his chin. Moments of torture, fear, and pain.

I realized that he had a point. If he hadn't been caught in the first place, he'd still be on the run, probably never finding me in Benedict. Maybe my mother would have found him someday, and maybe she would have killed him. At that moment, it certainly seemed like the better outcome.

I really wished she'd accomplished it. I could no longer remember what it felt like to want her to keep her hands clean.

"Who helped you?" I couldn't stop the question.

"Helped me? Why would I need help?"

I shook my head. There was no way he could have gotten away without help.

"Oh, silly girl, I just paid off the cop. It's one of the easiest things these days." He sat back and unfolded his legs, only to bend his knees and set his arms on them. He shrugged. "I paid off the cop driving me to the penitentiary. He won't get away with it. They'll figure it out sooner or later. I told him he should take off, but I don't think he did. Poor guy."

I'd thought Travis had no money, but that had been a mistake. Just because someone lives like they don't have money doesn't mean they don't. I should have known better.

Stellan hadn't helped him; the letter he'd received had probably been a prank. My parents hadn't helped. The police officer who'd "been struck ill" as Travis made his way into the prison van had been the one to help Travis get away. I was distraught enough to wish that Mill would take care of that officer, too.

"How did you get here?"

Travis smiled and cocked his head. "Well, it took a little planning, I must be honest. But money does all kinds of things that couldn't be done otherwise."

Money again. I waited. Travis wanted to tell me all about it, but he also wanted me to beg for it. I didn't beg.

He lifted his eyebrows and then lowered them. "A private plane."

"A plane?"

"Sure, a seaplane in Juneau. I told the pilot I wanted to be dropped down into the middle of everything but close enough to Benedict that I could walk there. It was as easy as it gets. Oh, and I paid him enough not to file a flight plan. He might be in trouble, too, but he was pretty sure he could talk his way out of it. I wish him well."

A seaplane? Without a flight plan? How were there so many secret ways to get to this hidden place when the obvious known ways were so limited?

I should have just left, hidden someplace else.

Why hadn't I just left?

Because this was my home. And he would have found me eventually, anyway.

Travis continued. "I've just been hanging around town a little, too. I thought I'd see if I could run into you or your parents. See what might happen. Not one person even looked at me sideways."

It was because he looked like so many other Alaskan men, a little scruffy and pale from no sun, even if his clouds had been prison walls.

"Beth!" a voice called from outside the cave.

Though I was quick in opening my mouth to yell back, Travis was quicker. He sprung toward me and covered my mouth with his hand. I tried to bite his fingers, but he knew how to protect them and keep his grip tight.

I was pretty sure it was Orin's voice. My throat was able to make some noise, but nothing that could be heard outside the cave.

"I'll have to gag you like I did in the van," he said in my ear. "Too bad. I was enjoying our conversation."

"Beth!" Orin called again, but his voice was moving farther away.

I registered that it must have stopped raining, which would make any search for me easier. Orin might be by himself now, but he'd gather everyone else. I would be found. Someone was sure to know about these caves.

After another few moments, Travis said, "Now, look, Beth. If you remain quiet, I won't gag you. It's up to you, though. I'm sure you remember how much fun that was. Will you keep quiet?"

My only option was to be agreeable, no matter that I'd hope for another opportunity to yell out. I allowed one quick nod.

"Okay, then, I hope you mean it. I don't like people who break their promises. I mean, look at me, I'm keeping mine."

Slowly he lifted his hand from my mouth. I kept quiet. For now.

"Good," he said. "Not difficult at all, is it?"

I wanted to yell, but Orin might not hear me now and he'd surely passed out of hearing distance. I'd have to wait for another opportunity—until then, do what Travis said so he wouldn't gag me.

I hadn't spotted any weapons on him, but he had mentioned that there was more than one cave in the area. I wondered how outfitted he was, and how many caves he'd found.

Travis sat across from me again. "There. Easy. Good girl."

I gritted my teeth harder. "Why?"

"Why what?" he asked innocently.

He knew what I was asking. Again, I waited.

"Oh, why do this to you? What did you ever do to me to deserve this? Weeeelll, you didn't do anything except ignore me. Do you remember me in your life right before I brought the daisies?"

He'd been delivering a bouquet of daisies when he took me.

"Yes. Didn't we go over this? I did see you, but I thought it was all a weird coincidence."

"You write thrillers! You know there's no such thing."

I shook my head. "Not true. Maybe people don't like them in their mysteries, but they happen in real life all the time." I paused. "Haven't you ever been talking, and you say the exact same word that someone on the radio or television does? Or, what about when you sense the phone is going to ring and you know it's going to be someone specific? What do you call those? I call them coincidences."

"Shit happens, you know. It's better to be suspicious all the time, particularly when someone you don't know keeps showing up in your life."

"I can't argue with that." Particularly when it came to seeing Travis. I did wish I'd paid attention. "What did my parents do to you?"

Travis's eyebrows came together. "You don't know?"

"Report you to my grandfather?"

He hesitated a moment but then laughed, guffawed, actually. "They didn't tell you? I'll be darned." He rubbed his chin. "No, I don't suppose they ever would tell you." He frowned. "They took half my money, Beth. Even half was a lot."

"Money? This is all about money?" I felt my own chuckle rise up from my sick stomach. "Travis, you do know that's the one thing

I have a lot of. I could have covered the debt. None of this had to happen."

"You are wrong, Beth. It absolutely had to happen. There was no other way to communicate to your parents that what they did was wrong. It wasn't about being paid back, it was about me paying them back for betraying me." He squinted at me. "Plus, we've had some fun, haven't we?"

"So, if I were to offer you a million dollars, you wouldn't let me go?"

"A million dollars? Are you kidding? That doesn't even scratch the surface."

"How much did they take from you?"

"Twenty. Seven. Million. Dollars."

I swallowed hard. How was that possible? Where had that money gone?

Suddenly, something came mostly clear to me. The edges of it were fuzzy, but it was there. It was as if there was a shift in the universe. I thought I could feel real movement as my perspective transformed.

"My parents didn't have the money," I said, knowing this, not doubting it even a tiny bit.

"Of course they did."

I shook my head and laughed once. It was an awful phlegmy sound. My mind had been replaying memories, the time in the van, but now it went back farther, back to my times on the road with my mother. We'd broken into places, homes and businesses, but we hadn't just looked around those places for my wayward father—Mill had peered inside things like drawers and closets.

She'd never taken one thing. I remembered asking her what she was looking for, and she'd said that she was looking for a sign that my father had been there. I'd been too young to argue with her. I suddenly realized that she—we—hadn't been looking for him at all. We'd been looking for money. Or possibly a clue as to where it had gone. Twenty-seven million dollars wouldn't have just been in someone's desk drawer, but . . . there could have been a receipt of some sort, somewhere. A treasure map? I didn't know, of course, and I didn't think that Mill would confirm my suspicions.

Fast forward to three days ago, when my parents emerged from the woods, their eyes wide, their expressions grim. They hadn't reacted quite right, I'd thought, but I'd chalked up their glazed stoicism to some sort of argument they'd had.

But that probably hadn't been it at all. It wasn't that they'd fallen out of love or didn't like each other anymore. No, those emotions had gone by the wayside years—decades—ago. Mill had questions for Eddy. Eddy had questions for her.

Oh my God, they were both after the money and neither of them knew where it was.

I coughed and sniffed again with the goal of hiding the fact that a light bulb had just gone off in my head, one that would change a whole bunch of lives.

Thing was, I thought I knew exactly where that money was, even if my parents didn't. I was pretty sure I knew, but I'd never tell Travis. I might not tell anyone. However, for it to be found I was going to have to stay alive long enough to get away.

And I didn't *want* to die. I didn't even want Travis's money, but I didn't want him to have it. I needed to think. I needed to come up with something to keep him from killing me, which might mean I'd have to tell him what I knew. I'd play along until a plan came to me.

Thirty

I was shivering so hard, I thought my limbs might break off. I needed heat, but I knew he wasn't going to light a fire.

Once darkness hit, Travis cut the tie around my ankles, and we walked about half a mile to another cave. This was where he'd set up his real camp with all his supplies. There was evidence that he'd lit a fire right outside the cave, but he wouldn't do that tonight.

He'd secured me in place, zip-tying my ankles again and then tying a rope around my waist and then a boulder that had somehow conveniently found its way inside the cave. And then he'd gagged me again. He'd left me there in the dark for what must have been a couple of hours. I'd yelled and screamed around the gag, but no one found me. I wondered if my voice carried out of the tiny opening.

He'd claimed that he was heading out to hunt for my parents. I'd told him exactly where he'd find them, hoping he would take some risks as he tried to grab them. Either Gril or Viola would take him down fast.

But he returned empty-handed, and he hadn't wanted to talk about it. He hadn't wanted to talk about anything.

I'd started shivering by then, but now, a few hours later, as he snored away in the warmth of a winter sleeping bag, I was sure I was close to dying from exposure. I needed to do something to warm up.

Not only were they shaking from the cold, but my limbs were also numb from being tied and kept in the same horrible positions. I could scoot along on my bottom, but even that part stung painfully. I could only move as far as the rope's slack allowed anyway, which wasn't far, but I knew I needed to do something to get my circulation going.

I made my way closer to the boulder, wondering if there would be some warmth there, but my movements were awkward and silly. The closer I got, the more I realized I wasn't going toward any warmth. The only warmth in the cave was Travis.

I needed to keep moving. I'd just keep going, scoot the other direction, but as I turned, I tipped over, my face slamming into the boulder.

Pain stabbed through me, blinded me in the dimly lantern-lit space. I bit down a cry of pain and closed my eyes tightly as I tried to silently recover. I could feel warm blood rolling down my cheek and then watched it pool on the ground when I opened my eyes.

I'd cut myself, badly, if the amount of blood was any indication. Shit.

"Beth!" a voice called from outside.

"Here," I choked out around the gag, but not loud enough. I was gathering my voice again when Travis woke up.

In a flurry of movement, he was out of his sleeping bag, his hand covering the gag over my mouth. With his toe, he flipped off the lantern light. Blood was going everywhere, but I could only feel and smell it in the dark.

"Beth!" I heard Tex call. And then Gril and then Viola.

They called and called and then their voices got farther away until we couldn't hear anything else. When Travis pulled his hand away again, he flipped the light back on. Even if he'd kept it on, the cave was carved out at an angle that put us far from the opening. I doubted anyone would hear me even if I could yell.

"Jesus, what happened to you?" Travis said as he lifted the lantern and inspected my face.

"Cold. Moved. Fell into the rock," I forced out.

"Goddammit, you're bleeding everywhere!"

"Sssorry."

Travis sighed. "It would serve you right if I just let you bleed out, but I still need your parents here. All right, let me get you cleaned up."

Travis went about taking care of my face. He'd set a cooler on the far side of the cave. I'd thought he'd kept food or drinks inside it, but it was where he went to gather a first aid kit.

It wasn't a fancy premade kit, but a random assortment of supplies he'd put into a box. Band-Aids, antibacterial creams, anti-itch. Mill had been right, Travis wouldn't buy a new anything; he'd make his own, even if he did have money.

He took off the gag, and I yelled, "Here!"

In a flash, he had his hand over my mouth again. Instead of admonishing me again, he seemed to be listening. No one called back.

"They aren't going to hear you. We're too hidden. Do you want to keep bleeding, or do you want me to get it cleaned up?"

I tried to bite into his hand, but he maneuvered it away from my teeth again and managed the now bloody gag back into place. "Have it your way. You need stitches, though.

"Right," he said when I continued to make whatever noise I could around the gag. "You'll see, though, no one will hear you."

Travis sat back from me. "I learned how to take care of cuts like that in prison. Not the one I escaped from, but one I was in back when I was in my twenties. The guards didn't like taking us to the infirmary. We had to figure out lots of things on our own." He inspected his hands, wiping my blood on his pants. "Too bad you won't get that handiwork. Now, try to get some sleep. It's still the middle of the night." He frowned. "Don't bother yelling, Beth. They can't hear you, I'm sure, so why not save your energy?"

"For what?" I said around the gag.

Travis smiled evilly. "Oh, you'll see." He patted my shoulder. "Get some rest. I'm going to grab a few more hours myself."

I wasn't shivering anymore, but I wasn't warm either, just not freezing.

However, it was my brain that had come back to life. A new idea had come to me. I didn't know why it hadn't been clear before, but it was now. I could only chalk it up to the cold freezing the synapses in my brain. They were thawing out now, though.

Travis turned the lantern off again and, in the dark, crawled back into his sleeping bag. It was too dark to see anything, so dark that even when my eyes adjusted, they still couldn't really see much of anything.

It took long enough for Travis to start snoring again that I was starting to feel the cold again, though I tried to ignore it.

Finally, when his breath fell into a noisy rhythm, I got to work. I scooted even closer to the boulder. I was still bleeding but not as profusely. I could feel the pull of dried blood over my skin as well as wet drops still falling. I couldn't worry about that, though. I had a choice to make: which thing should I try to break first?

I chose the ties around my hands. Using the boulder, I levered myself up, working hard to keep from making noise. I leaned gently against the boulder and determined where a sharp spot jutted out from it. In an awkward leaning-over-sideways maneuver, I started sawing the tie against the boulder. I wasn't going to be able to hold the position for long. What I thought I'd lose in stamina, I hoped to replace with force and speed.

I wasn't quiet. There were noises inherent in what I was doing, but I kept my voice silent and hoped Travis would continue to snore. I remembered his odd ability to fall asleep deeply even amid me yelling at him in the van. It had struck me as a nice skill to have. I was extra glad for it tonight.

I did make a noise when the zip tie broke apart—a surprised gasp. For a long moment, I waited, still frozen in that awkward position as

Travis's snores stopped and then started again. Slowly, I let out the breath I hadn't known I was holding.

My hands were free!

But that didn't mean the rest of me was. I still needed to break the rope around my waist and the tie around my ankle. I didn't know where a knife was, and it was too dark to search, even as far as the rope might allow. I'd need to keep using the boulder's sharp edges.

I chose the rope next. Holding it at an easier angle than I'd needed for my wrists, I was able to saw through it quickly. The spot I'd found on the boulder was knife-sharp. My face might be the worse for it, but it was the thing that was going to get me out of there.

Once the rope broke apart, I became torn. I could either work on my ankles or just drag myself out of there now and risk waking Travis. He'd be able to catch me easily with my ankles still together.

I did have another option. The thought that I could now use the rope and put it around Travis's neck, pull it tight until he stopped breathing altogether. But he was so strong. He would fight, and though I thought I could best him, there was a chance he would win.

I couldn't risk it, I decided. I lifted my ankles to the rock and started sawing.

Though the angle wasn't as awkward, it wasn't as easy to move my legs as it had been my arms, and this was a little slower going than the others.

I had no idea what time it was, but light suddenly seeped into the cave from the distant opening. I knew the light would rouse Travis. It was as if the dark allowed him to automatically sleep, but the light automatically told him to wake up and get to work.

I was running out of time. I tried to move my legs faster, but the harder I tried the clunkier it all got.

I pushed even harder as even more light filled the space. Like a finger reaching toward Travis, it moved closer and closer to him as I watched. It was only a foot away from him when the tie snapped apart.

I gasped again but put my hand over my mouth quickly.

Travis stirred but didn't wake up.

Well, not until a moment later, when voices rang out from outside again.

"Beth! Beth! Beth!"

Travis darted out of the sleeping bag again, but by then, I'd already scrambled to my feet and was headed toward the perimeter of the cave to make my way around him and out of there.

And then, maybe because someone as evil as Travis shouldn't get all the good luck, his feet got tangled in the sleeping bag.

I was gifted with enough seconds to make my way out of that cave.

"Here! I'm here!" I screamed as I ran with abandon. I didn't look where I was going, or even that far in front of me. I just ran. "Here! I'm here."

The sun was up, the sky was currently clear, but I didn't see anyone. I'd heard people, hadn't I?

"Beth!" Travis yelled from somewhere behind me, giving chase.

No, he couldn't catch me. People were out here looking for me, weren't they? Where were the people attached to the voices I'd heard?

After all that, he couldn't catch me again.

I stopped in my tracks, my heart beating fast and furious, tears rolling down my cheeks, the one with the cut burning from the salt—I registered the sharp pain somewhere in the back of my mind. My head and the world were spinning. Time was both slowed and speeding by at a breathless pace. I knew enough to know that this is what out-of-control felt like. And I didn't like it.

"Enough," I said to myself. "Enough."

"Beth, wait!" He was on his way.

I looked for something that I could use as a weapon. I wished I'd brought the rope, but I hadn't. I wished I'd had time to look inside the cooler for a weapon, but I hadn't. I had only me and maybe a tree branch.

I looked around for one I could use, having to settle for a skinny weak thing that wouldn't do me much good but might delay things enough. There was a chance I could hurt him.

I stood my ground. I waited. It was past time for this to be over.

Thirty-one

He was there only a moment later, coming to a halt in front of me, surprise on his face. I didn't know if he was shocked I'd waited for him, or if he didn't like the branch I held high, or maybe it was the blood or the look of pure hatred on my own face, but for an instant I saw the real Travis Walker, the one not working to create a tough façade.

He might be evil, but there was something else there, too. He was unsure, insecure, maybe. A tough guy until someone bested him, like all bullies.

But he was still stronger than me.

The façade came back. "Put that down, Beth. You can't win and you know it."

"Come and get me," I said.

Travis smirked. I might not be a religious person, but I was certain that if there was a Devil, Travis Walker was one of his errand boys.

I was going to kill him. I lifted the branch.

A growl came from his throat, and he crouched a little as if he was going to pounce. I held the branch out in front of me with both hands. I hadn't been able to find a sharp point, so I was going to have to swing.

My arms were stronger than they'd ever been. There was a time when I couldn't have held the heft of much of anything out in front of me. But I could now. And I was sure I could swing. I would swing as if my life depended on it. It did.

But as he leapt toward me, something boomed so loud that I reflexively closed my eyes and ducked, dropping the branch on the way.

I opened my eyes. Clarity fought with confusion, but I stood up on shaky legs and looked around.

Travis was face down on the ground, blood coming from his neck or shoulders or something in the general vicinity. He wasn't moving.

I blinked my eyes away from his body and looked around. With a first scan, I didn't see anything or anyone, but with a second look over the woods around me, I saw it. It was far away, thirty yards, maybe.

With one hand, Bigfoot held up a shotgun, and with the other, it sent a small wave, before it turned and seemed to be swallowed by the dark trees.

"Brick?" I said.

Did that make sense? Had the costume been retrieved from the hollowed-out tree that Brick had stored it in that day before we set out and came upon Viola? If so, by whom?

It looked like the same one. Or at least similar enough. From that distance and with the trees, I wondered if it wasn't a costume at all. Of course it was. It was ridiculous to think otherwise. Maybe the shock of what I'd been through was making me hallucinate anyway. I shook my head and my eyes landed on Travis again. My stomach roiled but I wasn't sick.

"Beth!" I heard.

I turned quickly and looked toward the voice. "Here, Tex! Here," I called.

"Stay where you are. I'll find you!"

I turned in a circle, the light filling the sky. Clarity was winning. I looked at Travis again. There was no doubt he was dead. This wasn't going to end like some horror movie. He wasn't going to rise again.

He was gone.

It was done.

"Beth," Tex said.

I could see him now, hurrying toward me. "Tex!"

"She's here," he called over his shoulder but didn't stop moving in my direction.

I lifted a heavy leg to meet him part way, but my knees buckled. I didn't go down all the way, but I had no choice but to wait for him.

He grabbed me and lifted me, holding me tight. I put my arms around his neck and held on, too. He smelled like the Tex that I had, no doubt, come to love—earthy with a touch of his spicy soap.

"You're okay," he said. "Your face, the blood?"

"I'm okay," I said. "I'm okay."

I didn't want to let go, but we were soon joined by Gril, Donner, Orin, and my parents, my mother the last one to appear.

"Oh, Beth, I'm so sorry," Orin said. "What's all the blood?"

Tex let me go and I went to hug Orin. "I'm okay. It's okay. It was all going to happen at some point."

Orin nodded.

Mill toed Travis's side, like he hadn't been a human being only a short time ago. Maybe he hadn't. "You killed him. Nice job."

I looked at her. There was something to her cold eyes that I couldn't immediately read, something more guarded than I'd ever seen before. There was also something that looked like fur on her shoulder. I squinted at it. Her eyes went to where I was looking, and she swiped it away. Her eyes didn't return to mine but back to Travis's body.

"Mill, step away," Gril said. He crouched and put his fingers on Travis's neck, surely covering them with blood. "No pulse. He's gone. Donner, confirm."

Donner crouched. A moment later, he looked up. "I'm not getting a pulse, Gril. I think he's gone. We could hurry him back to Benedict if you want, though."

"Gun?" my dad asked me.

I shook my head. "It wasn't me."

Donner stood up. "What happened?"

I pointed. "That way. It was . . . oh, this is crazy. It was Bigfoot."

Gril turned to Orin. "Can you stay with . . . the body until I can get Juneau folks out here?"

"Sure, but . . . do we need to get authorities involved?"

"Yes, we do, Orin."

"All right, then. I'll stay with him."

Gril turned to Tex and my parents. "Get Beth back and have Dr. Powder give her a once-over."

"I'm fine—"

"No arguments," Gril said.

"We got it," Mill said. "No problem, but I'm with Orin. Do we need to tell anyone about this? Can't we just bury the body? None of us will tell."

"Do as I say. Donner and I need to go . . . see what we can find."

In the next minute, Gril and Donner were gone, heading in the direction I'd pointed. I looked at my mother, who sent me a brief knowing smirk before looking away from my eyes again. I'd pointed in the wrong direction, just by a little because of trajectories and such, but enough that the trail Gril and Donner were taking wasn't quite right.

"Let's get home." Tex looked at Orin. "You really okay staying with the body?"

"Absolutely." Orin gave me another hug.

"Viola and Benny okay?" I asked.

"Yes," Mill said. "Viola's got an eye on Stellan. Gril didn't trust him to help us. He wondered if Stellan helped Travis."

I shook my head. "He didn't."

Mill smiled. "I know. It's over, girlie. How about that?"

I wasn't gleeful, but maybe I was relieved. It was all too much at the moment. I pulled a small smile and hugged my mother.

"It's over," she whispered to me.

After hugging my mother, I went to my father, who didn't seem to know what to say but pulled me close, too.

"I'm glad you're here," I said to him.

Finally, he said, "Well, I'm not going anywhere."

It was still all too much. I had to disengage. I had to process. There was a dead man at our feet.

I looked at Tex, Mill, my dad, and Orin, and then back at Tex. "Let's go home."

We did. There's really no place like it.

Thirty-two

It only took a week or so for life to turn into something resembling normal.

Stellan left, still using the fake ID he'd taken from one of the Missouri criminals he'd arrested. We all agreed not to tell anyone he'd been there.

That's the thing about a community like Benedict, Alaska. Secrets *can* be kept, even if they are known by more than one person.

Yet again, my story was splashed all over the news, but only for a day or two. Tragedy moves quickly through today's news stream.

Juneau authorities were brought in to remove Travis's body, and I told them what I knew of the person who'd killed the man who'd kidnapped me. It was the truth, after all, and the Juneau authorities didn't seem overly excited about hunting for Bigfoot. Time and resources and all. Besides, Bigfoot? Really?

Mill and I would never talk about the piece of fur I thought I'd seen on her shoulder. And, neither the costume nor the gun that had been used to kill Travis has been found. It's turned into a real Alaskan mystery that might or might not die over time.

I wished I'd gotten to know Peter Murray. I was going to get to know as many people in and around Benedict as I could, if they would let me in.

Benedict was my home. I wasn't leaving. I was going to write my books from the *Petition* shed. I might move into my own home some-day, but for now I enjoyed living with Viola.

Tex and I were together, though we might never live together, and that worked for both of us.

He was with me as we took Gus out for his morning constitu-tional. As September approached, it was getting colder and darker, but I didn't care. No, that wasn't it. I did care—I loved everything about it. I'd lived one trip around the sun in Benedict. Now I knew what to expect, and that was part of the fun.

As we watched Gus, I said, "Tex, I've thought about something and I've decided not to do anything about it, even if I do have an answer."

"Okay? That's vague."

"Travis talked about paying people off, but he also talked about my parents taking his money."

"Ah. Well, it's always about money, isn't it?"

"That or power, I suppose. Anyway, this conversation is just be-tween you and me for now. How do you feel about keeping that secret?"

"That Travis talked about money?"

"No, the part where I think I know where it is, but I'm not going to do anything about it. I want to tell you where it is just in case something does happen to me."

"Oh, Beth, money is dangerous. I'd rather not know—"

"I think my mother was looking for some sign of it all those years ago. I don't think she was looking for my father at all."

"This sounds messy."

"Yes, it does. May I tell you?"

Tex took a long moment to think about it. "Only if you really need to."

"I do. I don't want my parents to know. I think it would only ruin them, but I can't be the only one. Just in case."

"In case of what?"

"I don't know, Tex. You can't see it coming. If I've learned anything, it's that."

He nodded. "All right, then."

We were far enough away from everyone that I could have spoken the hiding place out loud and no one would have heard, but I didn't do that. Instead, I cupped my hand around his ear and whispered the location.

He pulled back and chuckled once. "No kidding?"

"No kidding."

"Do you think they'll ever find it?"

"I don't. Is it cruel not to tell them?"

"About drug money that would probably ruin their lives just as they are getting back on track? No, I don't think so. I won't tell."

"Thank you, Tex."

Gus ran toward us, and I crouched to greet him.

"Hey, boy." I laughed.

He kissed my ears and whined happily. He would be fine, too. Suddenly, his attention turned toward the Benedict House. I followed his curiosity to see what was happening.

Gril was there, guiding a woman, someone I'd never seen before, inside.

"Oh, a guest?" I said to Tex as I stood. "How exciting."

"Should we see who she is and what she's been up to?"

I thought a moment. "Absolutely."

In this small place, hidden from most of the rest of the world, so far away from what I'd once known my life to be, and even though Travis was now gone, there were more adventures to be had, it seemed.

Gus, Tex, and I forged forward to meet the next one head-on.

About the Author

Jacqueline Hanna Photography

Paige Shelton had a nomadic childhood, as her father's job as a football coach took the family to seven different towns before she was even twelve years old. After college at Drake University in Des Moines, Iowa, she moved to Salt Lake City, where she thought she'd stay only a few years, but she fell in love with the mountains and a great guy who became her husband. They made Utah their home until 2015, when their family moved to Arizona.

In addition to the Alaska Wild series, she writes the Scottish Bookshop Mystery series, beginning with *The Cracked Spine*. Her other series include the Farmers' Market, Country Cooking School, and A Dangerous Type mysteries.